To Chelsea Best Wishes

TORN

James Owens

[signature]
John 1:1-5

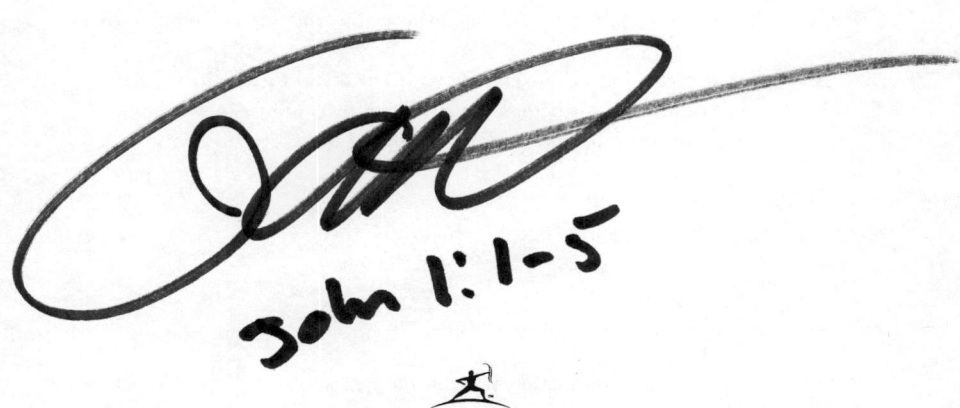

Copyright © 2018 James Owens.

All rights reserved. No part of this book may be used or reproduced by any means, graphic, electronic, or mechanical, including photocopying, recording, taping or by any information storage retrieval system without the written permission of the author except in the case of brief quotations embodied in critical articles and reviews.

This is a work of fiction. All of the characters, names, incidents, organizations, and dialogue in this novel are either the products of the author's imagination or are used fictitiously.

WestBow Press books may be ordered through booksellers or by contacting:

WestBow Press
A Division of Thomas Nelson & Zondervan
1663 Liberty Drive
Bloomington, IN 47403
www.westbowpress.com
1 (866) 928-1240

Because of the dynamic nature of the Internet, any web addresses or links contained in this book may have changed since publication and may no longer be valid. The views expressed in this work are solely those of the author and do not necessarily reflect the views of the publisher, and the publisher hereby disclaims any responsibility for them.

Any people depicted in stock imagery provided by Getty Images are models, and such images are being used for illustrative purposes only.
Certain stock imagery © Getty Images.

ISBN: 978-1-9736-2707-4 (sc)
ISBN: 978-1-9736-2706-7 (hc)
ISBN: 978-1-9736-2708-1 (e)

Library of Congress Control Number: 2018905159

Print information available on the last page.

WestBow Press rev. date: 05/22/2018

Acknowledgements

To my wife, thank you for the countless hours helping and collaborating with me on this book. Your ideas, suggestions, and proofreading helped this book come along. Your encouragement has helped me tremendously and now this book has come to fruition. I am forever thankful for you.

Pastor Richard Motzing. I appreciate all you have done and the time you took out of your schedule to read and give a review for this book. I am pleased you enjoyed it and how it touched your life. Your insight means more to me than you know. It is my hope that this book will touch many lives as it has touched yours.

Pastor Mike Modica. Thank you for taking time out of your very busy schedule to read the book and give a review. I am forever grateful to you. You are a great blessing in my life. I am glad the story captivated you and you were able to embrace the characters. The mere fact this book captivated your attention is humbling. May God continue to bless you, your family, and your Church.

Chapter 1

Connor Smith checks the time, 4:45 p.m. He doesn't hide the fact that he continues checking it every couple of minutes. Everyone in the room is wondering what could be more important to him. His business partner Frank moves closer and leans in toward him, "Are you alright?"

"I'm fine. I wish this meeting would end. I need to go home, church tonight. Theresa will kill me if I'm late again."

"Who cares!" Frank hissed, trying not to attract attention. "This is important, we want this contract; this could be the biggest ever. We need this one. Once we close the deal, we can leave. We go to the same church. I have a wife too. Think of what this deal could do for our families, our business, and our employees."

Connor ignores him, packs his briefcase, and sneaks out of the conference room. Some people see him leaving and shake their heads in disbelief. Leaving the building, he walks to his car and feels the extreme heat. Kansas City is having the worst summer in over a decade.

His car is sitting directly in the sun, no shade. Connor turns the air conditioner on full blast hoping to cool the inside as soon as possible. He pulls out and drives toward I-65. As he merges onto the interstate, he can see traffic is backed up for miles; the tiny amount of patience he has quickly evaporated. He grudgingly sits in his car sweating, waiting for traffic to move. After about thirty-minutes, traffic begins to crawl. He's now only five exits away from his turn off. He presses the horn and begins screaming out, "Hello! What's going on? C'mon, let's move it!" After a few minutes, traffic starts to move again slowly.

Approaching the source of the backup; he sees a horrible accident. One car is a heap of metal, and a body is on the ground covered by a blanket. And another vehicle is crushed from behind. Two people are sitting by an ambulance while EMTs attend to their wounds. All he can do is ask God to forgive him. He prays internally for the victims; his heart humbled, and all he can think about is his family.

They attend church faithfully every Wednesday and Sunday. He is usually home by 5:00 p.m. to help his wife make sure the kids are ready to leave on time. The twins Marcy, and Chris are the oldest. They are seventeen-years-old. Stephen is fourteen-years-old and is sometimes a little late getting ready himself. Stephen takes great pride in his appearance. Sammy is a wild four-year-old little girl who loves to run around the house; she presents a grueling task for her mother.

Theresa is trying to finish cooking dinner; wondering what's taking Connor so long. She sets the table and everyone, but Connor is ready to eat. He pulls into the driveway at 5:50 p.m. Connor walks into the house and put his things in his office. He walks into the dining room and explains why he is late.

They eat dinner as quickly as possible; they want to be on time for church. Stephen and Connor walk outside to the car. A Cadillac Escalade, the perfect-sized SUV for a family of six. An excellent way to show off their social status. Soon after, Marcy and Sammy get into the car. Theresa and Chris are the only two remaining in the house. She is getting restless waiting for him and yells out in frustration. "Christopher!"

"Yes, Mother," he answers in disgust.

"Hurry up. We are leaving for church."

"I will as soon as I find my Bible."

"I don't want to be late again," she tells him. She keeps checking the time on her Rolex that Connor gave her for her birthday.

"Okay, Mom," he replies; wishing she would back-off.

He pushes stuff off his desk and tosses around clothes that are scattered on the floor; searching for his Bible. "Where is it?"

"We need to go!"

"Give me a minute!"

"No, let's go!"

He slams his door and runs downstairs.

"Where is your Bible?"

"I couldn't find it. You were rushing me, so I gave up."

"Whatever, let's go," she closes and locks the door behind her. They walk over and get into the car.

"Ah, Son, glad you're ready to go."

"Yeah, okay ha-ha very funny," he replies. "I didn't mean to hold us up, but I guess we should hurry now, Dad, because you drive like Grandma and we will be late for sure."

Connor bows his head, "Lord, we ask You to keep us safe on the way to church. I pray that You will reveal Your word to us and help us understand Your will. In Jesus Name Amen."

"Why do we pray every time we go somewhere?" Chris asked.

"For God's protection, so nothing happens to us wherever we go," Connor replied.

"Well, then why don't we pray for others to be safe too, so they don't kill us?"

"Really!" Marcy shouts.

"Shut up Marcy!" Chris responds.

"That's enough. Chris is free to speak his mind like everyone else in this family."

"Dad, I can fight my own battles," Chris said.

"Well, Son, I'm sorry. Maybe if you guys behaved, I wouldn't butt in. Since you can't, I don't have a choice."

Chris smirks at his father's remarks. Connor pulls out of the driveway and drives to church. Sammy is restless, squirming around in her car seat. Marcy is reading her textbook, but Sammy keeps kicking her arm. Stephen starts poking Chris. As Chris becomes annoyed, he thinks, "If he doesn't stop, I'm going to punch him. Of course, Stephen doesn't and pursues his torment. Frustrated, Chris snaps.

"Stop!"

Stephen laughs and pokes him again; with more force this time; right his ribs.

"That's it," he punches Stephen in the arm.

"Dang, Chris!" Stephen shouts. "Why did you have to hit me so hard?"

"Whoa, you boys need to calm down."

"He hit me, Dad," Stephen belts out. Chris begins to argue. "So, what are you saying Dad? I do what you say even though he is poking me and won't stop?"

Connor lashes out at Stephen. "Leave your brother alone, stop it! I'm not going to say it a second time; is that understood?"

"Yes, Dad," Stephen replies.

Conner peeks in the rearview mirror at Chris. He is staring out the window, no longer interested in talking to anyone.

Upon arrival, Connor tells Marcy, Stephen, and Chris to have fun at youth group. Marcy replies, "Okay, Dad, we're not little kids anymore." Chris shrugs his shoulder as he walked away. Theresa takes Sammy to children's church and meets Connor in the sanctuary.

"Theresa, we need to pray for Chris."

"Why, babe."

"I think something is bothering him."

"He is young and confused. He needs guidance from God to deal with his issues, whatever they may be."

"I don't know. I agree Chris needs to learn and understand how to handle issues and feelings. It's driving me crazy. Something is bothering him."

"Whether something is bothering him or not, let him approach you, and show him that you are here to listen."

"Will you pray with me tonight after the service, Theresa?" She shrugs her shoulders as if to say, I don't know, as they walk into the sanctuary to find their seats. They sit next to Conner's business partner, Frank, and his wife, Karen.

The senior pastor, Pastor Shane, starts speaking, "This week, ladies and gentlemen, I will be preaching a short sermon." He pauses. "I hear a few cheers in the crowd." He begins to laugh. "That is okay; I understand. I have heard the cry of my people," he said, as the whole congregation laughs. Pastor Shane points to the worship leader, "Brother Taylor, lead us in a hymn of worship."

"Yes, Pastor, I shall," he replies with a Shakespearian tone. He turns toward the choir and lifts his arms like a well-seasoned maestro. Dan then faces the band and with a gleaming grin, moves his hands gracefully up and down to direct the song, "Our God Reigns."

Stephen sits in his typical spot, playing guitar in the youth group band as they hold their worship service. He started playing a few months ago and is getting better each week. He loves to play Christian rock music. All the girls love his sweet, charming Casanova personality. He is fourteen-years-old, his hair is dark brown with a spiked hairstyle, and his hazel eyes draw in the girls. Casually dressed is an understatement for him. He is preppy, wearing nothing but high-end clothing and expensive cologne. It appears he wants to mimic his father's appearance; instead of that of a typical teenager.

Chris sits in the back away from everyone. Pastor Mark approaches him and asks, "Is everything okay Chris?"

"I'm fine."

You don't seem okay, what's going on?"

"Well, people make fun of me. They say things that are mean. They make fun of my clothes, my hair, and make me feel like an outcast. They say I'm the oddball of my family."

"Oh, I see. Do you want to talk about this more after service?"

'No."

"Okay Chris. I am here if you ever need to talk or want to hang out."

Youth group service ends, and Chris immediately walks out. Shelly approaches Stephen. She is a shy, blond-haired, blue-eyed girl, and she has a crush on him. She's a jean's and t-shirt kind of girl; not one that would typically capture his attention. He prefers the, "rich" girls. Ones whose parents are friends with his, and who are prominent in the community. He is very shallow; upper-class tastes and looks down on others who don't measure up

"Stephen," I like your guitar. You are such a hot, uh. I mean good guitar player."

"What's your name again?" Feeling embarrassed since he doesn't know who she is. Shelly looks him right in his hazel eyes and tells him, "My name is Shelly! I can't believe you, Stephen Smith. How rude can one person be?" She runs away feeling humiliated. Stephen stands there stunned as she runs out the door. "What did I do?"

After packing the rest of his things, he walks out to meet his family in the foyer of the church. His father is talking to Frank. His mother is talking to Frank's wife Karen with Sammy by her side.

"Where is Chris? Marcy asks.

"I don't know," Stephen replies scanning the room looking for him. Suddenly Chris appears from the dark shadow under the stairs. Conner looks away from Frank and says, "Oh! There you are. How did church go, Chris?"

"Fine."

"Just fine?"

"Yes!"

"Don't give me an attitude."

Chris rolls his eyes and walks outside. Connor and Theresa say goodbye to their friends and walk outside. Conner decides to follow Chris who is walking around the parking lot. He tells everyone to go to the car.

"Chris," he yells. "Hey, Hey, Chris! Hello, I'm talking to you!"

"What, Dad? What do you want?"

"What's going on, Son?"

"I'm sick and tired of this church. People pick on me, make fun of the way I look. No one likes me here. They all like Stephen, but if people knew his true colors, they wouldn't think so highly of him."

"What is wrong with you, Chris? We're a good Christian family; there's no need for you to talk about your brother like that?"

"Sure, we claim Christians but my god, we are not perfect, so stop acting like it," Chris said.

"So, you think that we can't control what words come out of our mouths?"

"Whatever, I don't care. I'm tired of the whole thing. Everyone in this family has friends except for me I don't belong here, or anywhere for that matter."

"So, you feel insecure?"

"No, I wish people liked me as much as they like him, they think I am weird."

"Why do you think people don't like you? Why do people think you're weird?"

"Never mind, Ugh! Dad, can we please go?"

"Okay, come on. Let's go."

Chris cringes in his seat. The unpleasant drive home leaves his dad with uncertainty. Things are getting worse with him, and the negative energy is filtering out to his family. When they arrive home, Chris runs upstairs, slams the door and locks it. Everyone can hear him throwing things against the walls in his bedroom.

"Theresa should I—" Connor begins to say.

"No, leave him alone for now. He's obviously upset."

"What's wrong with him? He told me he doesn't fit in with anyone. There has to be more to it than that, right?"

"Don't worry about him right now. Give him space. I need you to take Stephen to school in the morning. I will take Sammy to daycare, and can you pick up dinner on your way home from work?"

He rolls his eyes, as he packs his things for work tomorrow and says, "Yes dear, I will take care of it," he grumbled. "I need to present the firm's design to the Kansas City Council; we are putting in a bid for a new Stadium."

"How soon will you begin construction? The firm still uses Miller Construction, right?"

"This is not a done deal. We still need to go over our designs and place a bid just like everyone else. To answer your other question, yes, we still use Miller Construction.

Theresa walks away to tuck Sammy into bed. Marcy wants to tell her mom that she is looking into three different Universities, but she notices her mom tucking Sammy into bed and walks away to her room.

Theresa is ready for bed when Connor comes walks into the bedroom. Scattering things around searching for a folder with necessary information. Theresa ignores him. Connor asks, "Did you see my red folder, Theresa?"

"No, Connor. It is not my place to keep track of your things! Goodnight!"

Early the next morning, Theresa wakes Sammy up while Connor is in the shower. "Sammy, wake up baby. Time to wake up, honey." Sammy whines, "no Momma, no."

"Yes, little girl, time to wake up," Sammy kicks and screams as Theresa picks her up.

Marcy is up and ready, she walks down for breakfast. As she passes in front of Sammy's room, he mom asks her to take Sammy downstairs with her. "Sure, Mom, no problem," she replies.

"Thank you, Marcy it helps me. I need your dad to hurry out of the shower, so I can start getting ready too."

Chris opens his door, peeks out. No one is in the hallway, so he sneaks downstairs. When he gets to the bottom of the stairs, Marcy spots him.

"Where are you going? Are you sneaking out, Chris?"

"No, I'm going outside to wait for Rocco."

"Chris, please! I'm your twin, and you cannot fool me."

"Ugh, I'm going to school, okay?"

"Aren't you going to eat breakfast?"

"I don't want any. I'm not hungry."

"Fine, your choice. Go hungry—grumpy boy."

Theresa is growing restless with Connor because he is taking too long. "Goodness, Connor! Why are you taking so long?"

"I'm about done." He replies.

"Well, I need to start getting ready too."

"Uh, yeah, and we have other bathroom's," he said, not hiding the irritation in his voice.

"Don't you dare give me an attitude."

"I'm not but give me a break! Can't a man get ready for an important day?" Connor replies. He gets out of the shower and dries off with a large, oversized towel. Freshly groomed, he places his Armani suit on the bed and puts his best dress shoes on the floor.

Stephen comes down to join Marcy and Sammy who are eating breakfast. He sits down and folds a napkin into his shirt. Sporting his new khaki pants with a light blue polo shirt. He spreads strawberry jelly over his toast, and he winks at Sammy. Connor comes downstairs with cheers from Marcy and Stephen.

"Ha-ha-ha, okay, very funny you two," he said as he grabs a bagel off the counter. He lets out a loud burp that makes Sammy laugh. "Shouldn't you be leaving for school, Marcy?"

"Yes," Marcy replies. She stares at her dad and gives him, The Look.

"Uh"! Hello! Excuse yourself," she said.

"Uh, yeah. You're right, excuse me."

"Daddy, can I have thirty dollars for gas?"

"Here you go, Marcy, but this is all you will have for the next four days."

"Okay," she said with a big grin. She kisses her dad's cheek and says, "I love you," before walking out the door to go to school.

"Sammy, stay here with Stephen."

"Dad, I don't know how to care for her," Stephen groans, "I don't want to either—that's what her parents are for."

"I need to go to my office and get a few things."

"Fine, but hurry."

Connor gets all of his things from his office and walks back to the kitchen, "Okay Stephen I'm ready, are you?"

"Yes."

"Theresa," Connor yells.

"Yes."

"Are you coming downstairs soon?"

"Yes, calm down, I'm coming now. Quit nagging me."

"I don't mean to be a nag, but I don't want to be late. It's an important day; the firm finally gets to present to the city."

"Yes, Connor, I know. I know all too well."

"Well, hello! The deal is huge for us."

"For your firm or us?"

"For all the above; I need to go," Connor slams the door behind him forgetting he left Sammy with Stephen.

He walks over to the car, but Stephen isn't there. He decides to get in the car and blow the horn, "C'mon, Stephen," he said, looking at his pricey Rolex. It is 7:25 a.m. Stephen runs out to the car. "Sorry, Dad, I was waiting for mom to be with Sammy and I had to tell her I need some new shirts if she goes to the mall."

"Oh, I forgot about Sammy! Sorry. But you couldn't wait to tell your mom about the clothes? Oh well. We need to go. I need to be at the office in like forty minutes."

"Dad, school starts in fifteen minutes there is no way you are getting me there on time!" "Don't worry, Stephen. You'll be on time, but if you're late, I will give you a note."

"Dad! The whole point is not to be late. My homeroom teacher, Mr. Anderson, is not so forgiving."

"Well, blame your mother."

"How is it Mom's fault?"

"Because she takes forever."

"C'mon, Dad."

They finally pull in front of the school at 7:45 a.m. The school is on the same property as their church, Freedom Christian Center. As Stephen gets out of the Escalade, he checks the time, "great; I'm late Dad, I need a tardy note."

"Why do you need one, Stephen? We are right on time."

"Because I won't make it to homeroom in time."

"Well, I gotta to go. Tell your teacher to call me if there's a problem."

"Fine!" Stephen replies as he slams the passenger door."

Chapter 2

Connor rushes to work after dropping Stephen off. His office is only about twenty-minutes from Stephen's school if the traffic isn't bad. He exits the busy interstate and turns right on Merry Lane. Two traffic lights down, he makes a left on Harold Drive. He pulls into the parking lot and parks. He walks into the building and Frank runs over to him

"Connor, man I'm glad you're here."

"What's up? Is everything okay?"

"Yeah."

"Well, what's going on?"

"Our meeting has been moved up two hours. We need to be there at 11:00 a.m. now instead of 1:00 p.m."

"You can't be serious!"

"I am, we must rush on the final details. I want to win this job."

"I understand, but wow! I mean, this is too fast."

"Yeah! I know, but we are playing with the big boys here." Frank said.

"Are we close as to what our bid will be?"

"Yes!"

"Well! What's the agreement?" Connor asked.

"The same one that you and I went over last week," he chuckles. "Remember?"

"If I remembered, I wouldn't be asking, now would I?"

"Connor! Seriously!"

"Listen, Frank, I don't remember the thing; So, unless you are hiding something from me, then for pity's sake let's do this."

"We will take care of business, don't worry about that, as long as our figures are right, and the cost is accurate, then we should be fine. The only other thing is I want you to present. I don't want to do it." Frank said.

"Are you kidding me?"

"C'mon, man," Frank pleads.

"Fine! I will! But I'm not happy about this. Presenting is your part in this business."

"Think of the nice check if you close the deal."

"They either accept the bid, or they don't. Either the city likes the proposal, or they don't.

Connor and Frank leave the office and drive out to City Hall. They don't say a single word to each other on the drive. They pull into the parking lot and jump out of the car. Sweat rolls down their face from the intense heat. They walk into the building quickly. After walking into the building, they wait for an elevator while wiping sweat from their face. They only lock eyes for a couple of seconds. Upon arriving on the 6th floor, they exit the elevator and walk down to room six-seventy-five. They both walk in, and Frank sits down on the lounge chair in the waiting room. He fans his face with a magazine from the table.

Connor walks up to the receptionist. "Hello, ma'am. My name is Connor Smith my colleague and I have an appointment at 11:00 a.m."

"Wait a moment, sir," the receptionist said. Connor feels jittery and nervous. His palms and face sweaty, he takes a handkerchief out of his pocket to wipe some sweat from his brow.

"Okay, Mr. Smith, the board is ready now."

"Oh, okay, thank you," He replies. The chairman of the City Council Mr. Chandler welcomed them in and says, "Now, what you gentlemen have for us."

"Thank you, sir. On behalf of myself and my colleague, Frank Douglas, it truly is an honor to be here and to represent our firm, Douglas & Smith Architecture LLC. Our firm's proposal for the Board's consideration. The new Stadium and Sports Complex the City wishes

Torn

to build is by far a monumental task for our firm to take on. However, we are ready to take up that partnership with the City that we love," Connor rambles.

"First things first, Mr....um, who are you?" the chairman asked.

"Forgive me, sir. I am Connor Smith," he replies.

"Okay. Well, Mr. Smith, is there a formal proposal with you that the Board may review? We would also need to present it to the Mayor."

"Yes, sir." Connor fumbles through his briefcase. Oh, now is not the time. Where is the folder?

"Mr. Smith, we're waiting."

"Yes, sir, I apologize. It appears I misplaced the folder in my briefcase."

"Well, we can't wait all day."

"Ah! Found it Thanks for your patience. Here is a copy for each of the members to review. You will find our sketches, and also an estimated construction cost, give or take."

"Are you associated with this, uh, Miller Construction Company?" Chairman Chandler asked.

"Yes, sir, we've contracted work with them on many projects over the years. Shopping Centers, Malls, and Home Subdivisions."

"I'm not interested in—allow me to rephrase; we are not interested in the size of a firm. What we are interested in is the cost. The cost to our City and its Taxpayers. That is all the board is concerned about Mr. Smith."

"Yes, sir! I hope you choose our firm for that exact reason."

"Well, I appreciate you, and your business partner being here today. The Board will entertain all bids. We will have a decision by the end of next week."

"Thank you, Ladies, and Gentlemen, Mr. Chairman."

They walk out of the boardroom and into the hall waiting for the elevator. Connor turns to Frank and says, "Talk to you tomorrow."

"What do you mean tomorrow?"

"I mean, I'm taking the rest of the day off. We can finish up the other projects this week," Connor said. "I know why you are looking at me like that too."

"Wow! Guess you know me, don't you?"
"Yep! Not like I haven't known you for forever."
"Bye," Frank waves, as Connor rushes to his car.
"Hey! Wait, you're my ride, how do I get back to the office?"
"Can you call a cab?"
"Fine! Thanks for nothing.

Connor drives over to the Country Club to play a round of golf; he is making calls to some buddies to meet him there. A day of golf with some friends helps him to relieve some of his stress. After he plays his eighteen holes; he thanks his friends for the game and heads home.

Theresa's day is a little more hectic, she drops Sammy off at daycare and begins running errands. She needs to collect college information for Marcy, find a summer camp for Stephen, and schedule her woman's ministry activities at the church. Her long day will not end anytime soon, even when she gets home she needs to take care of her family's needs.

Theresa is about to merge on I-65 from the Ellis Road on-ramp. She begins to accelerate and looks in her mirror as she turns on her left turn signal. When ready to merge over, Theresa hears a semi-truck blowing its loud air-horn. The big-rig isn't slowing down to let her over; so, she slams on her brakes in and pulls in behind the truck.

She is frustrated that she forgot to go to the mall for Stephen. She doesn't care about it at this point. She wants to go home. She drives down the interstate to exit forty-one. She pulls off and comes to the traffic light. When the traffic light turns green, she makes a right and drives down Kipling Street to pick Sammy up from daycare.

"I hope Connor remembers to bring dinner home. "She pulls in to Mary's daycare at 1:30 p.m. and leaves her car running, which Connor told her time and time again not to do. Theresa never pays much attention to his warnings. She walks out with Sammy and tries putting her in the car seat. Sammy squirms and whines. Theresa has learned to turn a deaf ear.

On his way home from golf, Connor calls Theresa to ask what he should bring for dinner.

"Hello," Theresa answers.

"Hi, babe."

"Oh hey, how is your day? How was your meeting?"

"Stressful, I do not want to talk about it."

"Okay, then what do you want?"

"For you to tell me what to bring home for dinner."

"How about I order something, so it's ready when you get home? You've had a busy day and should relax. Wait, are you off?"

"Yes, I left early today. Thank you for ordering dinner."

"You're welcome, honey. Drive safe and see you later," Theresa said hanging up the phone.

Conner pulls into the driveway and puts the car in park. He gathers his things together, loosens the tie from his neck, and drags himself to the front door. He walks into the house, places his keys on the table, and drops his briefcase on the floor; he kicks off his shoes by the sofa, throws himself down, and drifts away.

Chris's friend, Rocco, is one of his classmates. They met each other in the Spring semester. They had an instant connection and formed a strong friendship. Chris confided in him and explained why he hates church and doesn't fit in anywhere. He told him how he felt demoralized by Christians, people who were not supposed to act that way. Rocco assured Chris that he isn't like that and mentioned they were kindred spirits. From that point on, they became inseparable. Rocco drops Chris off at home around 5:15 p.m.

"Catch you tomorrow, Bro. Thanks for the ride,"

"No problem, Bro, remember class will be later tomorrow, I will be here at 9:00 a.m. to pick you up."

"Ok!"

"Later dude."

Chris walks into the house and places his keys on the table in the foyer. His father's briefcase is on the floor, but he doesn't care enough to put it away. He walks right past it, as his father is sleeping on the sofa, he says. "Hey dad, how did your day go?" He gets no response. He goes upstairs but forgets to take his shoes off and scuffs the new wooden floor in the hallway. He must have had a small pebble stuck on the bottom of one of his shoe's.

Marcy came home later than Chris. Her dad's briefcase is still on the floor, so she takes it to his office. Marcy walks into the living room and finds him asleep on the sofa. She picks his shoes up off the floor. Marcy walks to put her things away as well as her dad's shoes. She notices the scuff-marks on the new wood floor. After she puts her things away, she comes downstairs to tell her mom.

"Hi Mom," she says.

"Oh, hi Marcy. How did your day go?"

"It went fine. Hey, did you see the scuff marks on the floor in the hallway?"

"What!" Theresa yells as she makes her way to the hallway, her face turns red. "Who did this?" She yells. "You kids, I can't believe this!"

Marcy's eyes open wide. She doesn't know what to think about her mom's outburst.

"Mom, calm down."

Startled, Connor wakes up from all the yelling. He gets up off the sofa and walks to the kitchen; he doesn't see anyone there, so he strolls to the hallway yawing. He sees Marcy and Theresa standing there.

"What's going on in here?" he says stretching.

"Someone scuffed the floor, Connor."

"So that's what this ruckus is all about?"

"Yes! I'm quite upset, we just had the floor installed, and it's already getting ruined."

"Okay," he said, shrugging his shoulders like he didn't care. "We can buff it out, Wow!"

"Fine!"

"Theresa."

"Yes."

"Did you order dinner?"

"Of course, I did! Do you think I'm a bad wife and mother? Do you think I won't feed my family?"

"Theresa, it was just a question. I didn't say anything about you being bad at anything."

"Whatever! I don't care!"

Chapter 3

School ends at 3:00 p.m. and then Stephen attends band practice at 3:30 p.m. The music instructor, Mr. Carlson, puts everyone into his or her respective positions. Stephen plays lead guitar; his friend Erik plays bass. Brian Matthews, Pastor Shane's son, plays the drums. Kelly plays the keyboard; Amanda sings background vocals, and Drake is the lead singer.

The youth group band practices after school and Mr. Carlson volunteers his time to help the young men and women fine-tune their gifts. After settling in, Stephen plugs his cable into the amplifier. Erik plugs in as well. They strum their guitars, and Mr. Carlson isn't happy.

"Hey! You two knock it off, understand?"

"Yes sir," they say laughing under their breath.

Mr. Carlson brings order to the room. Their practice lasts longer than expected due to Stephen and Erik wasting time. Nonetheless, they finish late in the afternoon. Stephen waits for his mother, or father to pick him up. He looks at his watch and agonizes at the time. "4:45 p.m., where are they?" Pastor Mark is walking to go inside the church office entrance and notices Stephen standing on the sidewalk.

"Stephen, what's up buddy? Why are you standing out in the blistering heat?"

"What's up, my parents aren't here. I don't care about the heat right now."

"Wow! Well, would you like a ride home?"

"Are you leaving soon?"

"Yes, in about fifteen minutes."

"Okay! That works."

"Well, you should call your parents in case one of them is on their way or something. Maybe you should come inside and cool off."

"Okay, worthless to call though."

"Well, give it a try for me, okay pal?"

"Yeah! Okay, but only because you asked so nicely," Stephen laughs.

They walk away toward the double doors on the side of the building that leads to the church offices. Pastor Mark opens the door, and they step inside. Stephen stands in the waiting area. Pastor Mark walks by his secretary Mary, he pulls the day's mail, messages, and places them on his desk. He shuts down his computer, writes down a few notes, gathers his things, and turns off the lights.

"Goodnight, Mary."

"Goodnight, Pastor, is there anything you need me to do before I finish up?"

"Nope."

"Okay."

Pastor Mark walks back to Stephen and pulls out his car keys.

"Ready to go?" Pastor Mark asked.

"Yes. Been ready for the last thirty minutes."

"Well, let's go."

They walk over to Pastor Mark's car. Stephen stares at the old Durango as if it should be in a junkyard. He gets in the car, and he buckles his seatbelt. He hopes the car can make it to his house. Mark turns the key, and the engines let out a loud rumble. Stephen laughs as Pastor Mark lets out a big, "Oh yeah!" He enjoys the sound the engine makes. It embarrasses Stephen. "Hey! Did you call your parents, Stephen?"

"I tried like I told you I would! And it was worthless..."

"Well, let's go over some rules here. First, don't speak to me like that. I'm your Youth Pastor. I won't tolerate it. I'm not your mom or dad. You may talk to them that way, but you will not do it to me. Second, show gratefulness, I'm an adult, you're a kid..."

"I'm not a kid!"

"Listen, I'm trying to help you; I want to teach you that there are rules in this world to follow. You choose whether you follow them or not. And there are consequences for our actions and decisions."

"I'm tired of my parents always thinking about themselves. My sister has a car; freedom to come and go whenever she wants. Chris's friend drives him around. Me, I'm at the mercy of my parents who fight over everything. They even fight about small things like dinner. I don't expect for you to understand that."

"Wow! I'm sorry. I thought you were just a rude kid! Please forgive me for judging you without knowing your situation first."

"Don't sweat it. I deal with it."

"Well, if you ever need to talk, or if you want to hang out, let me know. The Youth Group does a lot of things. We go to concerts, and we feed the homeless on Saturday nights. We help the elderly with landscaping and home maintenance. Whatever you want to participate in."

"Thanks, I'll think about it."

"You do that."

The doorbell rings and Theresa walk's over to answer the door.

"Good evening."

"Hello, how much do I owe you?"

"$34.95."

"Here's $40, keep the change." Theresa closes the door in the delivery boys face. She walks to the kitchen with her arms full; no-one is willing to help her. She yells, "Dinner is here!" Everyone comes running to the kitchen. Amid the chaos, Marcy looks around; Stephen is missing. "Um, where is Stephen?"

"What," her parents reply.

"Stephen, your other son? He dresses like his father—don't ask me why. He's not here!"

"Babe, you were supposed to pick him up," Theresa says.

"Uh...no! I don't recall deciding that."

"Connor, our son, is outside the school waiting for me—I mean, waiting for you."

"Oh, boy! Here we go again; you're the perfect one who never makes a mistake."

"You guys! Knock it off! Your son is out there with no ride home. He must feel so embarrassed that his parents forgot about him. And not to mention how hot it is outside, "Marcy says.

"Well, he didn't call me."

"Oh! He called my cell twenty-minutes ago. Oh, I feel horrible."

Stephen is almost home, and he asks Pastor Mark if he can meet with him after school to talk. Pastor Mark is more than happy to accept the request. He even tells him that he will take him home if he needs a ride. He is delighted and takes him up on his offer. Stephen's cell phone rings. "Hello."

"Stephen, are you okay? Where are you?"

"I'm fine, Mom. I'm with Pastor Mark. He offered me a ride home."

"Oh, okay. How soon will you be here?"

"In like five seconds, we're almost in the driveway now."

"Whose he with, Mom?" Marcy asked.

"Pastor Mark, he gave him a ride home."

Marcy leaves the table in hast and runs upstairs; she wants to look her best. She checks herself in the mirror, making sure her hair is perfect. She swishes mouthwash and spits it out.

They pull up to the house, parking right next to his dad's Escalade.

"Sweet car."

"Yeah, my dad's."

The driveway runs up the side of the house. It holds up to seven cars. The garage is straight back with Connor's weekend car, a '67 Shelby GT500. The car never sees winter weather. And not this Summer either.

They get out of the car. Pastor Mark leaves his car running to keep the air cool inside. As he walks up to the beautiful home, he admires the red brick, the six white pillars, and the lavish French-style front door. Pastor Mark turns around, but Stephen isn't there. Marcy opens the door before he can even ring the doorbell.

"Hello."

"Hello, Marcy, how are you doing?"

"I'm fine, and I'm doing well."

"Great, glad to hear it. I gave your brother a ride home, but I seem to have lost him."

"Oh! He probably just went to the side door. We usually come in from there."

"Oh, okay. Well, I guess I will go now."

"Oh! Before you go, I'm sure my Mother will like to thank you."

"Okay…uh, where is she?"

"Mom," Pastor Mark is here!"

Theresa walks over to the front door, having already greeted Stephen. He seemed to want to sneak into the house, but she caught him. She apologized and kissed his forehead.

"Hello Pastor, thank you for bringing Stephen home. He did call me, but I didn't hear my phone. I lost track of time today."

"My pleasure, Mrs. Smith, anytime he wants or needs a ride home, I'm more than happy to accommodate."

"Well, thank you again, goodnight Pastor."

"Goodnight ma'am."

"Goodnight Pastor Mark," Marcy shouts.

"Goodnight, Marcy."

The family begins to settle in for dinner. Theresa is about to do the unthinkable by bringing up an idea for a family vacation; when out of nowhere Connor looks around the table and says, "hey, let's talk about a family vacation? We could all use some time off to reset our inner clocks." Connor suggests a trip to Israel, so the family can visit the Holy Land. Theresa is not sure about that idea because it will be expensive. She suggests something cheaper like Yosemite or Yellowstone National Park. She tells Connor they can rent an RV, but he shows no interest. So, as usual, the discussion is over with no results. Not even Marcy can interject with an idea when her parents talk.

Chris goes upstairs to find a book his friend Rocco gave him—a book about spirituality. He walks downstairs and quietly goes into the den. He wants to study the book and compare it with the Bible.

"What are you doing, Chris?"

"I'm researching different religions for school."

"What kind of religions?"

"Well, Mom, your religion. Christianity and new age stuff. You wouldn't understand."

Theresa's skin begins to crawl. She tries to talk some sense into him. "That stuff is nothing but deception, and it will lead you into darkness."

His face turns red as he grits his teeth at his mother's remarks. He decides to share his feelings.

"I don't care! I want to know where I fit in, in this world. No one at church likes me they look at me like I'm some weird guy; like how can I be a part of this family? They all make fun of me, and I'm tired of it. I talked to Dad about this last night. I'm making my own decision. I have a right to choose what's best for me, and God isn't for me. Christianity isn't what I want. With so many different religious views—one makes more sense to me and helps me understand my life without condemnation. I want to be free, and your form of religion does not make me free. Your religion expects a lot, whereas I can be me; I can focus on doing what I want to do."

Theresa's heart drops, she realizes the confliction. "Chris, I'm sorry. I wish I could say something to help. I don't know who or what is influencing you, but whoever is telling you these things is wrong. Yes, you need to decide things for yourself. God gives us free will, so only you can decide what you want to believe," she says with a broken heart. "This has nothing to do with your school studies either."

"Fine, Mom, whatever, I want people in my life like me," he said as he stomps out of the den and runs upstairs to his room. He must make some choices if he is going to walk this path.

"Hey, honey?" Connor calls.

"Yes," Theresa responds as she looks at the clock. "What do you need?"

"I need to finish things for work. I'm on a tight deadline. Can you put those files on the coffee table in alphabetical order?"

"Okay, honey, I will do it shortly," she replies. Theresa cleans the dining room table off and realizes Sammy needs to get ready for bed.

Her bedtime is 7:30 p.m. and it is 8:00 p.m. She needs a bath; her hair needs to be blow-dried, brushed and put on her pajamas.

"Marcy, can you please get Sammy ready for bed? I need to help your father," Theresa asked. Marcy is always willing to help with her little sister.

"Sure, Mom, no problem," Marcy comes out of her room and gets Sammy. "Come on, time to get ready for bed."

"No," Sammy whines.

"Oh, yes little girl Let's go."

"No."

Sammy is playing with her toys and doesn't want Marcy to bath her. "No, I don't want to. I want momma."

"Well, momma is busy, Sammy. She told me to bath you and put you to bed. I'm sure momma will kiss you and say goodnight."

"Okay, Marcy, but can you read me my little lamb story after bath time? Please?"

"Yes, I will. Once you're done with your bath and dressed for bed."

"Okay."

Theresa is working on Connor's files when she uncovers some disturbing magazines. Chris; he must have left them by accident.

"Connor, I need you to come here please."

Annoyed by the interruption, he replies, "What, Theresa? I told you I'm busy."

"Babe, please. I need to show you something."

Connor stops what he is doing and gets up. "Okay, I'm on my way."

When Connor enters the room, Theresa begins to explain what she discovered. "Connor, this is what troubles me. These are Chris's magazines on different religions. One on new age stuff and these others—what is Luciferism?"

"Beyond what I know, except that was Satan's Angelic name." A little shocked, Connor flips through the magazine. "Oh, wow, that's bad. I knew Chris was curious; he talked to me—well I talked to him,

I should say. He said he felt out of place; he doesn't have friends as Stephen does. He is insecure."

"It appears as though he wants to engage in this, Connor."

"He's being influenced by someone who is a part of this religion. We need to pray and then talk to him about this." Connor and Theresa prayed together and then call for Chris. "Chris," Connor yells without a response. So, he calls him again, this time with emphasis. "Hello, Christopher!"

"What...what do you guys want now?"

"Hey, we want to talk. There's no need to start up with an attitude, okay," Conner replies.

"I don't have one. I'm on my way down."

Chris closes his book and walks to the bottom of the stairs, he blurts out, "Okay, what do you guys want?"

"Well, your mother came across some magazines you left here, and she wants to ask you some questions."

Chris shrugs his shoulders and shakes his head with a no care attitude. "Well, what do you want?"

"To be honest, why you're looking into these religions? Especially this one on Luciferism,"

He can now come clean. He doesn't want to hide anymore and wants his family to Know where he stands. He walks to his parents and says, "Well, no big deal. I'm just looking at what it is all about. It is not like I'm going to kill someone or anything. I'm just comparing Christianity with other stuff, so yeah! I'm looking at some of them and Luciferism."

Trying to make sense of the situation, Connor asks, "Well, Chris, you're choosing a dark road to go down. Why aren't you researching Judaism to make a comparison? Why satanic ones?"

"Really? You will never understand me. You will never understand the satisfaction that this brings to me. I will be free to be me without condemnation from you, and your Christian ways. I don't need God or your religion. I will explore what I want and choose what I want. I can decide for myself! Christ runs upstairs and slams his door. The curiosity within him is intense, but his family will not approve of his decision.

Chapter 4

The Smith family aren't the Christian family they present themselves to be at church. A troubled family, on the edge of destruction, and hidden secrets. They are blind and selfish to their own needs and desires. Whether it be the desire for money, power, respect, attention, love, acceptance, or freedom.

Marcy keeps begging for her mother's attention. She is graduating high school next week and hasn't even applied to a single college. She wants her mother's help to choose the perfect college.

Stephen desires to be like his father; a successful businessman. They used to be best buddies, but Connor is too focused on work and has overlooked his family.

Theresa desires her husband's love and attention. She is distant from him—all the bickering, sarcastic comments, and lashing out at each other is tearing them apart. Their marriage is lacking passion, and the physical embraces from Connor that made Theresa feel secure is fading.

Sammy is four-years-old and the sole exception. She wants attention from her mom, dad, and her sister. She is innocent and stuck in the turmoil that is taking place around her. She is a cute little girl with sandy-blonde-hair, green eyes, and a smile to melt your heart.

Connor, well, he desires all the above. He wants money, and he loves to flaunt it, especially with his vehicles. He prides himself on his treasured '67 Shelby gt500 that he keeps in the garage. He only buys high-end-clothes; his image is critical to his self-esteem. He also craves his wife's respect, her love, and acceptance of the sacrifice with his work. Whatever he can think of, he wants it, but he never seems to spend time with anyone. His family used to be the center of his life, but somewhere along the way, he lost sight of that.

His childhood certainly hasn't helped him. His father, Bob, was also a workaholic and didn't pay him or his siblings any attention. He was a mean, abusive, and an alcoholic. His physical abuse was centered more on his wife, Rose. Rose always nagged her husband about being around more and doing things with the family, but Bob didn't care.

Connor doesn't reflect much on those days. All he remembers is he must be a provider, make a lot of money, and that show his family how much he loves them. Connor wants to be better than everyone in his life, outdo all of them. He thinks he's doing everything right, but no one shows him the appreciation or respect he deserves. He hates having celebrations. Birthdays, Holidays, all of them. He hated them as a child, and he hates them now. Whenever Theresa brings one up, he shrugs it off and says, "Great."

Marcy is getting ready to graduate from high school on Friday, May 24th, and soon the house will be buzzing with over one hundred guests, much to Connors dismay. Theresa is pressured to have a perfect party, sparing no expense. Things have been chaotic for her.

Connor, on the other hand, would rather take Marcy to dinner and give her a card with a little bit of money in it. Dinner would be better than having a party with friends, family, and whoever else decides to show up. He hates the idea of having to spend money on anyone else, except himself. He doesn't expect his brother Larry, or his sister Ashley to be there. They've not spoken a word in over six years. He hopes to avoid his father, but there is no way it will happen. He cherishes his mother; he will bend heaven, and earth for her. He talks to her as often as he can, and her visit is the only thing that making him happy; well, other than his daughter, his *Baby Girl*, is graduating from high school.

When Marcy comes home, she goes straight upstairs to her room. Connor is out golfing with Frank, Karen, and Pastor Shane. Stephen is outside in the backyard kicking his soccer ball around. Sammy is napping, and Theresa is in the den reading, putting *'US'* Back in our Marriage. Marcy walks downstairs and interrupts her mother.

"Mom!" She said with excitement.

"Yes, what do you want?"

"Don't mean to disturb you," she says with a big grin on her face.

"I'm trying to read, and have time to myself, Marcy. What do you want? Can it wait till later?"

"I guess! But I'm wondering about my graduation party."

"What about it?"

"Well! Uh, well, I guess..." Marcy freezes. " I'm hoping that the party could be on Friday night instead of Saturday. Can we do that?"

"You want your graduation party Friday night instead of Saturday? What on earth for?"

"I want to go out with a few of my friends Friday night after the party. Then I can sleep in on Saturday."

"No! Your party is Saturday. After the party is over, you, and your girlfriends can use the pool house."

"Ugh! Fine, I'll take what I can. By the way, you, and I still haven't looked at colleges. I would like to do this soon, so that I can start in the fall. Please make time, Mom. Applying to College means a lot to me."

"Okay, how about tomorrow night after church?"

"You want to do it after a Sunday night church service? Are you serious?" Marcy asked.

"Sure! Why not?"

"Well, because you're usually busy with Sammy, or putting your weekly calendar together. I want to make sure you will help me. If I can't count on you, I will have no choice but to do it myself."

"I promise, Marcy. I will help you, we will send out applications, and checks for the application fees," her mom replies with a smile.

Marcy walks out of the den with a glimmer of hope that her mom will keep her word. Marcy wants to attend *Shaler University* in Kent, MO. The school is only a forty-five-minute drive from her house. She hasn't decided whether to stay in a dorm or to commute each day. Either way, graduation is upon her. She is moving on to her next journey in life.

Chris moved ahead of Marcy; finishing high school a year early. Chris is an exceptional student and scored a *135* on his *IQ* test; which is in the range of superior intelligence. He is attending *Hampton University* on a full Academic Scholarship. Chris chose to major in Philosophy and minor in Sociology. Most of the time he doesn't show up to class but goes to the library instead. Chris has the favor of his professors because he always aces his exams, so he is not forced to attend class. His friend Rocco also attends the university but hasn't declared a major; he is taking liberal studies for the time being.

Chris is in his room reading when his cell phone rings. "Hello."

"Hey bro!"

"Hey, Rocco!"

"Hey! Are you busy?"

"Nah! Just chillin' over here, you know. Reading the book, you gave me about Luciferism though.

"Hey man, if you want, I have someone I would like you to meet. You said you wanted to explore new things, right? And that is sweet that you are reading the book. What do you think about it so far?"

"Yeah, pretty good man, I like it. When are we going to go?"

"Uh, duh. I can be there in like twenty minutes. I'm on the sixty-five."

"Oh, sweet! Okay. I'll be ready."

Marcy knocks on his door.

"What."

"Hey, it's me, Marcy."

"Uh, okay, so what do you want?"

"What are you doing in there?"

"I'm getting ready to leave. I'm going out for a little while tonight."

"Where to?"

"None of your business. Can't I go somewhere without you having to be so nosey?"

"I'm just pickin' at ya," she said giggling.

"Fine! Then you can leave now."

"Okay, okay," she laughs.

Chris looks out his window and sees Rocco has already pulled up in front of the house. He walks out of his room. No one is around, so he opens the front door, and his mother spots him.

"Where are you going?"

He clinches the door handle, squints his eyes, and grits his teeth. He looks over at his mom and says, "I'm going out with Rocco; he is already here. We are going to the mall. Maybe we will go to a movie while we are there or something."

"Rocco? Oh, he goes to school with you, right?"

"Yes, Mom, I will be home before midnight, if that's okay?"

"Wow. You're asking me?"

"Yes, ma'am."

"Well, I'm impressed, Chris. I hope you have fun," she replies, calling him Chris instead of the usual Christopher when she's mad at him.

Chris has pulled off the lie and walked out to Rocco's 1987 Chevy Camaro. He looks back to wave goodbye and gets into the car. "You ready for this?"

"Yes, let's do this." Rocco and Chris head over to the south side of Kent. Chris is wondering who he is about to meet?

Theresa begins her list of duties, scheduling a graduation party for Marcy, helping her apply to some colleges, and getting summer camp ideas together for Stephen. Stephen had gone to only one of his church's youth group summer camps. He wasn't very fond of it. Theresa is looking into other summer camps to see if Stephen will want to go to one.

Just as she is about to start her calendar, she hears a loud "Momma!" Ugh! She knows Sammy is awake.

"Marcy, are you up there?"

"Yes, what's up? Oh! Are we going to look at schools now?"

"No. Sammy is awake, can you bring her downstairs, and put her in the playroom please?"

"Fine!" She believed her mother made some time for her.

Theresa is going crazy now that Sammy is awake. She is trying to do her schedule, and it will be dinnertime soon, but Sammy keeps coming in and out of her playroom. "Sammy, hey listen to Momma. Play with your toys, okay? Stay in your playroom."

"No! I want to be here with you, Momma."

"Little girl, oh my goodness, you are too big to hold all the time. I am busy."

"So not hold me, Momma," Sammy smiles with her cute little face.

"Fine baby! Come it up here and help Momma plan her week, okay?"

"Is Dadda comin' home soon, Mamma?'

"I'm sure he is on his way here now, baby."

Connor leaves the country club, thanking everyone for the game. He gets into his '67 Shelby and backs out of the parking space. After looking in all directions. He calls Theresa to tell her he is on his way home and ask if she needs him to pick up anything. After getting her voicemail, he hangs up. *"Why can't she answer her phone!"*

Meanwhile, Marcy is in her room reading all about *Shaler University*. Could she be offered a scholarship? Probably not, but she is applying for one anyway. After all, Chris had an award. Of course, he's almost a genius.

Bob and Rose fly in on Thursday. They love visiting their Grandchildren. They don't visit them as often as they would like; mostly only for special occasions. Theresa is hoping everything will go smooth, because of the tension between Conner, and his dad. Theresa's parents, Eddie and Mildred, will be driving over from Topeka, Kansas. They had lived in Kent, Missouri where they raised their family. They moved to Topeka to be closer to Theresa's oldest brother Kevin. A drunk driver took the life of her youngest brother, Ricky. Ricky was only twenty-six-years-old when he died.

Chapter 5

Rocco and Chris arrive at a house on Merrick Street. The front of the house is dark gray with black window shutters. Rocco will introduce Chris to a man who can enlighten him, maybe even change his life! He knocks on the door three times. Chris is nervous.

"Hello! Welcome, please come in," said a man wearing all black. Rocco follows Chris inside the house, the walls are ash gray and lit only by candlelight. A fresh smell of incense fills the house.

There is a slight, soft whisper from people who are praying. Chris looks around; he gives his friend an eerie look. "Come this way, gentleman." The old wood floors creak with each step. They take a seat in a living room that has beautiful old Victorian furniture.

"Please, wait here. I will inform his Excellency you are here." Chris's heart starts pounding in his chest.

"Hello, Christopher Smith," a strange, wicked sounding voice said. "My name is Zaga. I'm the priest who runs this establishment," he said.

"Hello, sir! I prefer Chris if you don't mind."

"Yes, of course, Chris. I've heard so much about you—wealthy family, church-going people. However, you're not happy with the Christian life. I think you question the existence of God or any god," Zaga said. "Chris, let me tell you a little about myself. I'm a generous man; I care for people, and their well-being. I teach what I know is real. We are real, Chris. We are free to enjoy ourselves with the presence of mind, body, and spirit. You are those things, Chris. I'm my own god if you want to think of things that way; I choose to serve the needs of those around me who cannot do so for themselves.

I'm the headmaster; I am the power on the throne here. I listen to your concerns. I give guidance and provide a life without persecution. I was once associated with *Satanism*. I decided not to serve him, but I do believe in the power of myself, my mind. I can be who I want to be, and that is my faith, that is what Luciferism teaches. Be your own god. Rocco tells me you are struggling to accept your religion, or should I say, the Christian faith."

"Yes, sir," Chris replies. "It's tough believing we need to work so hard to please God. I say, *"Who is God?"* Why should I be submissive to someone, or something I cannot see, I want freedom, to seek what makes me happy; this is not acceptable in the religion I grew up in."
"Young man, I think you, and I should meet more often—to see if what I have to teach you is what you can accept and enjoy. Something that will give you true peace."

"Yes! I want that."

"Then it is done. Rocco, can I count on you to bring Chris weekly?

"Yes, your Excellency," Says Rocco, as he kisses the ring on Zaga's right hand.

"Okay, then. We will meet three times a week for one to two hours each time."

Zaga will be able to turn Chris from the Christian church in no time. Zaga is a profoundly spiritual man, and believes in the powers of darkness, but not Satanic worship. He uses cunning dialogue to sway eager young minds. His philosophy is to gain control by showing the strengths of self-righteousness, and acceptance without judgment of others—The way of Luciferism.

Chris feels torn inside; he is happy that he found a group he can soon become a part of but is unsure at the same time. He will need to remove himself from everyone who serves God, including his family. Chris doesn't want anything from that faith. He only wants to be happy.

Rocco and Chris leave Zaga's home. Chris is in deep thought and is home before he realizes it. "Okay, buddy! I will see you Monday morning."

"Alright, Rocco. Be safe brother."

Chris walks into his house and goes upstairs. It's 10:00 p.m.

Everyone is asleep; probably because they need to be up by 8:00 a.m. to get ready for church. Chris is hoping to avoid it. Morning came quickly, and he wakes up from the noise of his family. Peeking out of the bedroom door; no one is in the hallway, so he walks to the bathroom.

"Ah! Hello brother," Stephen shouts. The house filled with the intensity in his voice.

"Man, why do you do stuff like that? Where did you come from anyway?"

"I was hiding, duh. How do you think I surprised you?"

"So, you were waiting for me?"

"Eh! I figured for a time that you might come out."

"Okay, you can go away now."

"Are you going to church?"

"No! I don't feel like going today."

"Did you tell mom and dad?"

"Mom, Dad I'm telling you I'm not going to church!" Chris yells, "Now you can't rat me out." He didn't hear anything back, so he realizes when Marcy came upstairs that they were already gone. "Why aren't you coming to church Chris?"

"I don't want to, okay?"

"Hey! You don't answer to me, buddy," she says as she walks away. "Stephen, let's go!"

"Coming."

Chris sits around the house reading. Reading anything to help explain why he feels the way he does, and why he feels torn inside. He's able to make his own choices, but he is dealing with conviction. The beliefs his family raised him in is weighing on his mind. His mind is always racing, but his ultimate goal is to wipe his memory of Christianity.

Best to go with the flow until he turns eighteen. It is only two weeks away, and then he will not have to follow the family's Church rule. Conner and Theresa decided not to bother him about not going to church. No one wants to make any waves anyway since the family is coming for Marcy's high school graduation.

Marcy's graduation week is here. Connor is taking time off work starting on Thursday because the family will begin to arrive. It's not for this reason he is taking time off, no! He is taking time off to play golf and to use the time to relax before the unwanted relatives arrive. His mother is the only exception. Marcy's last day of school is Wednesday.

Theresa has all the orders complete for Marcy's party. Hill Street Bistro will cater the party, Jewel's Bakery will make the cake along with cupcakes, and other delicious goodies. All she needs to worry about now is the family coming in. She decides to put her parents in the guest room downstairs, and Connor's parents upstairs in the guest master bedroom. She did this, so she wouldn't hear Bob whining about where he sleeps as if he were six-years-old. Her parents don't care where they stay. They are easy to accommodate, and they never fuss much.

"Mom, when will Nana and Papa Ross come in?"

"Late Thursday afternoon. Why do you ask?"

"Just wondering, no real reason," she replies.

"Well, Marcy, Grandma and Grandpa Smith will be here early Thursday afternoon. Their flight lands in Kansas City at 1:00 p.m."

"Oh, okay Mom, thanks."

Marcy isn't waiting on her mother any longer, filling out the application for enrollment to *Shaler University,* and mailing it along with the $50 application fee. Anticipation and the hope of an acceptance letter to come in the mail.

Stephen puts a packing list together for the church youth summer camp. Theresa insisted that he goes since he turned down all the other ideas she had. Pastor Mark will be taking sixty-seven young people along with twelve adult chaperones to Lake Champion. Lake Champion's cabins are beautiful with excellent accommodations for both male, and female attendees, all kinds of water sports, and land activities. There is also a large amphitheater where the worship services will be held each night at 8:00 p.m.

Chapter 6

This week will be horrific for Connor; his parents are flying in today plus his firm is still waiting to receive word from the city regarding the new stadium. The firm has been working with their construction contractor on another project designing and building new homes. The plan is for a new subdivision on the south side of Kent; that's been in the works and leaves Connor working longer than usual. If they can finish this housing project on time and under budget, it might impress the city to ensure the same thing.

The contract on this job will pay Douglas & Smith some big bucks.

Frank is the only one that deals with Miller Construction Co. And over a ten-year partnership, worker's compensation claims are very high. Some cases involved wrongful death. Frank handles that side of the house. He works with Miller Construction, its insurance company, and their lawyers to settle out of court cheap. Having the architecture firm, and a construction company on their side, they make money on both ends, and Frank gets more. He gets quarterly checks since he invested in the company.

Frank always blamed the accidents on drugs, and alcohol abuse, as well as lack of sleep. Not the fault of the employer. Connor, having no idea about the settlements. Conner and Frank leave the office and play a round of golf. When times are hard, they've always found sanity on the golf course. Conner is going to be face to face with his Bob soon, and he needs to destress before he goes home. As they are playing the last hole on the golf course Conner's phone rings, "Hello?" He answers.

"Hey, babe, it's me. Please tell me you didn't forget about your parents coming in today."

"No, of course not. Flight 3304 from Houston, TX, right?"

"Yes! Your mother called and said they landed early at 12:45 p.m. instead of 1:00 p.m. and they can't find you."

"Why didn't she call me?" he asked.

"Not sure, but they are waiting for you. Can you walk and find them?"

"I, Um, I hired a limo service to pick them up."

"You did what? Connor, you're serious, aren't you?"

"Yes, I am! I don't want to put up with Bob. The limo service will bring them. I will be home soon."

"Bob? He's your father," she said in disbelief.

"Whatever! When have I ever called him my dad? Call my mom, tell her to go to the gate; a man will have a tablet with their names on it. Tell her he will bring them to the house."

"Fine! I'm not happy with you!"

"Fine to you too, you didn't grow up with the man. "Things can't seem to be any worse—bob and his in-laws are staying with them for four days. Escaping the house as much as possible is the goal. The only time he cares to be there is for his *"Baby girl."* Seeing her graduate, going off to college, and becoming a woman; still hasn't sunk into his mind yet.

Connor's parents make it to the limo service. The driver loads their luggage and pulls out from the airport heading to the house. Bob's wife, Rose, tells him to behave himself while visiting. Rose wants to enjoy her time with her son and his family. Bob could care less. He wants the time to pass. He wants to see his granddaughter graduate and then start packing for the trip home.

Theresa is staring out the window when her phone rings. "Hello," Theresa answers.

"We're here!" Rose said with excitement. A long black Lincoln pulls up to the house. Bob and his small, fragile wife get out of the car. Rose may be little, and weak in her old age, but she is still a bold granny. Theresa runs down the driveway to welcome them. Stephen looks out of his bedroom window. Nana and Papa Smith are here. He runs downstairs, and bolts out of the front door, all-the-while Sammy is left inside in her playroom.

"Nana," Stephen shouts.

"Stevie," Nana replies. "How are you, champ? Are you keeping up with that guitar thing?"

"I'm good, and yeah, I'm still jamming."

"Hey there, Stevie," Papa Smith said.

"Hi Papa," Stephen replies. "Here Nana, I can take your bags for you."

The four of them walk into the house, and Rose looks around for Sammy. "Where is Sammy?" Rose asked.

"Oh, she's in her playroom, come with me," she walks into the playroom and says, "Hi Sammy." Her face lights up as she yells, "Nana!" Sammy shouts.

Stephen is aware there is a problem between his father, and papa, but doesn't dare ask why. He hopes that when his dad gets home, there will be peace.

Marcy comes home from her friend's house to find her grandparents already arrived. She is happy, and filled with excitement, but had wished her other grandparents would have arrived first. Her relationship with her Grandparents Eddie and Mildred are better than with Bob and Rose. She walks into the house and her Grandma Rose and gives her a big hug. Her grandpa is in the living room almost asleep when Marcy approaches him. "Hello Papa," she says to him, her eyes open wide. "Hey, there's my Granddaughter?" They hug each and kiss each other on the cheek.

Theresa and Rose are in the kitchen making coffee. Stephen sits in the family room watching T.V. and wonders where Chris is. He hasn't seen him and isn't sure if he went to school today. " *Oh well! Who cares!*" The bigger issue is when his father comes home. Connor and Bob under the same roof—It's bound to be epic. His heart begins to pound in his chest as his dad pulls into the driveway. He turns the T.V. off and runs upstairs to his room. He wants to listen to the fireworks, not witness them. The rest of the family hears him pull in as well; Rose stares at Bob with that, *"You better behave yourself,"* "look. Bob rolls his eyes and turns his head.

Connor gathers his briefcase, suit coat, and a box of files. He pushes the button on the key fob to lower the tailgate on the Escalade. Connor walks to the side door that leads to the kitchen. He wants to walk in the house without having to see his Bob. Connor opens the door and then kicks the door with his foot to close it. He walks past his wife and his mother, and down the hallway toward his office. "Well, that was weird," Theresa said.

"He didn't even stop to say, hi, or give me a hug," Rose replied.

"Well, maybe he's having a bad day."

"I'm here though, shouldn't that make a difference?"

"Well, when Connor is in a mood, he isolates himself."

"Yep, just like his father."

"Don't tell him that!"

"Oh, I would never," Rose replies.

As Connor approaches his office door, the dreaded voice speaks. "Well, hello Connor. I'm glad you made it home." Connor bites his lip and drops a box and briefcase on the floor. He walks into the living room where his dad is sitting and unleashes, "Yeah! Well, it's my house, I come and go as I please, Bob..."

"Yep! Same ole' same ole,' isn't it?"

Connors face turns red and clinches his fists. "Drop it, let's not start this right now. Enjoy your time with your grandkids and leave me alone."

"Fine by me, but you had better enjoy the time yourself; your daughter is graduating from high school. She is becoming a woman, look at her over there. She is moving on in her next phase in life. You..."

"Oh! Please, don't even say what you are about to say. I can handle my home. Don't you dare sit there and think you can lecture me on anything? I don't care what you have to say; you're a bitter, old man."

"Well, now you wait just a minute, boy!"

Theresa and Rose are in the kitchen and can hear their voices getting louder; they walk into the living room to stop them from getting out of control.

"I'm no boy—you old, bitter, hateful person. I can't even call you a man!" Connor shouts.

"How sad for you. You're still holding on to the past, and yet you have the guts to call me bitter."

"Robert! I told you to behave; now look what you have done, it needs to stop!" Rose shouts at them, "Enough, if you can't solve your problems, just stay away from each other! Look what you're doing to Marcy?"

Marcy's hands cover her face. She hoped they would get along, at least for her. The family is here for her moment to be the center of attention.

"Fine!" Connor replied. Theresa and Rose try to comfort Marcy, but she runs to her room. Stephen is laughing, but when Marcy slams her door, he stops.

Theresa calls Connor back to the living room.

"What do you want?"

"Thanks for nothing! Did it ever occur to you guys that Marcy would like there to be peace? Maybe you two stubborn men can tolerate each other for her sake!" Theresa says." Rose looks at Bob, and Connor, and shakes her head in disbelief. *They will not put themselves aside for one second,* "Pitiful, " she mumbles. Connor and Bob give each other one last stare. Bob walks to the family room and sits down on the reclining lazy-boy. Connor walks upstairs and knocks on Marcy's door, but there is no response. He leaves her alone and walks to his room to lay down.

Sammy roams around the house forgotten. Her playroom door somehow opened without anyone noticing. During the commotion, she walked outside to the backyard. Sammy is young. She's running around laughing, having fun. While running, she slips and falls into the pool. Marcy heard the scream and ran to her window overlooking the backyard. Sammy is flailing her arms and kicking her legs to stay above water.

"Mom, Mom! Hurry, Sammy fell in the pool!" Marcy screams running downstairs. Marcy rushes through the kitchen to an open the back door. "Sammy," she screams as she dives in. Everyone heard Marcy scream and they run to the backyard, Bob yells," Stephen, stay here with me."

Connor reaches the pool and grabs Sammy from Marcy. He begins CPR right away.

"Is she breathing, Connor? Connor, is she breathing?" Theresa screams in agony. Bob and Stephen observe from inside the house.

"No! Call 9-1-1 now," Connor screams as tears run down his face. "C'mon baby...C'mon, breathe," he said. He continues with Marcy at his side telling Sammy to breathe. Emergency responders arrive within five minutes; the fire station is just down the street. They tell Connor to let her go so they can take over. Connor refuses to stop trying, crying, and begging for Sammy to breathe. Theresa has to pull Connor away from her so that the paramedics can do their work. Finally, Sammy coughed up water and starts crying. "She'll be okay, sir. She is shaken up, and obviously frightened, but she will be okay. How did this happen?"

"The door was open," Theresa said.

"You may want to think about child locks on your door."

"Yes, sir, I will get that taken care of, thank you for getting here so fast," Connor said.

"Your welcome but thank yourself sir; you saved your daughter's life. Knowing CPR kept her alive."

"Thank you again, and you're right, but my daughter Marcy is the one who got to her first. My daughter Marcy is the hero here," Connor said with tears in his eyes. Sammy put her arms around her father's neck very tight, almost choking him. Marcy sits on the deck crying, as her father takes Sammy into the house.

"Is she, okay?" Bob asks as Conner walks into the house.

"Get out of my way."

"This is all your fault! Both of you caused this," Stephen yells as he runs upstairs.

Theresa and Rose try to console Marcy. She can't stop trembling. They tell her how brave she is, how she saved Sammy. They pray asking God to bring peace to her.

Chapter 7

Chris is supposed to be in class, but instead he, and Rocco meet with Zaga. They meet with him three times a week. Monday, Wednesday, and Thursday. They discuss minimal topics. He shows Chris that Lucifer is the *True light*, a deity that teaches men to accept their own will. Zaga won't go in depth with Chris because he is eager and impatient. His desire to learn is impressive; however, he doesn't want Chris to engage in the faith too fast.

He wants him to gain a full understanding of what it is and how it is applied. Lucifer is not Satan, and Satan is not Lucifer. Chris, on the other hand, wants to grow, but his eagerness is getting in the way. Zaga worries about this; he's seen it before, though not in his faith. He had an encounter once with a young pastor who was eager. He pushed his religion on the homeless during community outreach.

Chris plans to move out of his parent's house. He can no longer stand being around. He plans to drop out of college and move in with Zaga. Chris wants to be Zaga's apprentice. Whatever he can learn, whatever he can do to grow in knowledge, he will do it. His mind is like a sponge. Nothing gets in his way. His friend Rocco thinks he is seeking some higher power to empower him.

Zaga believes Chris can be an excellent student; if he will put his ego aside. He can be a good student, he needs to absorb the information, and meditate on it. Zaga gave him homework at the last visit. Chris was to write a statement that explains why he wants Luciferism instead of traditional Christianity. What he hopes to achieve with Zaga as his teacher, and leader, where he is going, and if he understands everything.

Rocco is waiting in his car while Chris and Zaga say goodbye. They conclude each session by giving a handshake, a kiss on each cheek, and a blessing given by Zaga. Chris walks away and gets into Rocco's car, buckles his seatbelt, and they drive away. They are heading to Chris's house. He remembers his grandparents are coming in today.

Approaching the house, they notice emergency vehicles in front of it, two fire trucks, and an ambulance. He thinks that something happened to one of his grandparents, whichever ones had arrived. Rocco stops the car, Chris darts out, and runs inside the house. He looks no one is around; he sets his attention to the kitchen where he hears voices. His is grandpa is crying. He walks past him and goes outside.

Marcy is crying with their mom and grandma. He walks to the gate, and stares down the driveway, as emergency responders are loading up to leave. He turns and lets out a horrendous shout, "Can someone tell me what's going on here?" Marcy tells him, "Sammy almost drowned."

"What! How? Who was watching her?"

"Apparently no one. We can't point fingers here. It was a tragedy, thank God, it didn't end badly," Rose said as she walks over to hug him and kiss. She had hoped to greet him under different circumstances.

Chris kisses his grandma back. He's still angry about Sammy's accident. He knows someone neglected her and they are the reason she almost died.

Marcy gains her composure although her head hangs low. Rose hugs her, tells her she loves her, and that everything is fine. Marcy politely walks away, up to her room.

Sammy lays quiet on her father's chest, as they sit on the sofa in his office. Her death grip around his neck is gone. Connor prays silently, "God, thank you for not taking my little girl," as tears continue to roll down his face.

Theresa and Rose spend time together in the kitchen baking; hoping it will help them move past the tragic event. It's been a rough day, but still not over. Theresa stares at the clock in the kitchen, 4:00 p.m. She thinks, *"Mom and dad should be here soon."* Rose makes another batch of Connor and Stephens favorite peanut butter cookies. Rose asks Theresa, "Are you okay, Dear?"

"Yes, I'm fine, just watching the time. My parents should be here soon."

"Oh, how nice. I like your folks."

"Well, thank you for that Rose."

"Well, when you're family, you're family, right?"

"Yep, we sure are."

"Well, I will finish the baking, so you call them and find out where they are."

"Are you sure, Rose?"

"Yep, you betcha honey. I'll be fine."

"Okay, thank you."

Theresa walks to the family room and sits on the love seat in front of the beautiful bay windows. She calls her mom to find out where they are. The phone rings. *"Oh, come on, pick up,"*

"Hello, Daughter," her mom answers.

"Hi Mom, how did you guess it was me?"

"Caller I.D., hello. I'm guessing your call is to find out our whereabouts?" she said kindly. Her mom is a confident woman, and as sharp as a knife.

"Yes, Mom, where you are," Theresa replies.

"Well, if your father wouldn't drive so slow, we can be at your house by 5:00, but it may be closer to 5:30, hopefully."

"Mildred, we're only ten minutes away."

"Oh my, Eddie. She can hear you. Goodness, you don't have to blow my eardrums out."

"Okay, guys, no fussing. see you soon, I will let you go," Theresa hangs up without waiting for a goodbye.

Marcy is up in her room; still traumatized by the event. Her little sister could've died. Shaking her head, trying to understand how her baby sister made it out of the house without a single person noticing. Conflicted between her father and grandpa as the cause of the problem. She tries to clear her mind because she needs to finish things up for graduation. Pictures to take, a dress to buy, shoes to match her dress, and new makeup to look her best.

Marcy is sad that high school went by so fast. The uncertainty of being accepted to the University, and having to choose a major, leaves her frazzled. It will be the second most significant moment in her young life—she imagines her future being a college graduate.

With the sound of a car horn and cheers of joy from a happy daughter, Theresa runs out to greet her parents. She waits for the car. Her father gets out of the car, and she leaps into his arms with joy, "Dad," She shouts.

"Oh, my baby girl," he said teary-eyed.

"Well, hello sweetheart," her mother managed to say. Mildred and Theresa aren't exactly close to each other, especially since Theresa's brother died. Her mom took it very hard, and she has never recovered from the loss.

"Hi Mom," Theresa said. "I'm sorry, I wasn't trying to ignore you. I'm happy to see Dad. I have always been a daddy's girl."

"Yes, Theresa!" her mother replies, "at least your father still has you."

"What do you mean?" Theresa asks, but her mom gives no response.

They walk inside the house are greeted by the family. Theresa pulls her mother aside.

"What did you mean outside, Mom?"

"Nothing, Terry."

Theresa steps back in shock. "Mom, you haven't called me Terry in years. What's going on? Please tell me."

"You're a daddy's girl, that's fine. I'm okay with that. I struggle because Ricky was my baby boy. He was a momma's boy, and he's not here anymore. Kevin doesn't say, *hello* half the time. I feel like I'm alone. Of course, I have your father, but I lost the joy I had with Ricky," she said placing her hand over her face.

"Momma I'm sorry, I didn't know you're still struggling with this; I loved my baby brother so much. God took him home, Momma, but he didn't leave us alone. Myself, Kevin, and Dad will do anything for you, Momma."

"Stop! Please stop. I don't want to talk about it anymore. I have to live knowing my baby is gone and is never coming back. I'm here for my granddaughter."

"I'm sorry, momma. I hope God will help you so that you can be happy again."

"Yep! Okay," Mildred replied.

Connor looks around the living room at everyone doing their own thing. He ponders the thought of taking everyone out to dinner, *"Nah,"* he thinks to himself, *"What a train wreck it could turn out to be."* His thoughts continue as he watches Eddie sitting in the lazy-boy rocking chair holding Sammy. "Theresa, should we order some pizza for dinner?" Conner asks.

"Yes, that will be fine. The kitchen's a mess anyway."

"Okay, I will order it then," Conner said as he goes to his office to place the order.

Marcy gets up to talk with her grandma's and mother. She hopes they will be able to go dress shopping at the mall. Chris and Stephen are ignoring everyone by staying in their rooms. They are too angry to be around anyone.

The doorbell rings, so Conner gets up to answer it. "Pizza's here! Everyone in the living room gets up and sits at the dining room table, but there are two empty spots.

"Where are Stephen and Chris?" Marcy asks.

"They must still be in their rooms. They haven't come down all day. Conner, can you please tell them to come eat?" Theresa asked.

"Yes." He walks over to the stairs and yells for the boys to come down for dinner. Chris and Stephen hear him screaming and decide to walk down the stairs and sit at the table.

After dinner, Mildred says, "Okay, ladies we're going to find Marcy a dress for graduation." They drive over to Highland Park Mall. Marcy appreciates her Grandma Mildred's determination to make sure she gets what she needs for graduation. Marcy has been neglected by her mom lately. Theresa has been pushing Marcy off and focusing on other things. Now Marcy can relax and feel like she is a priority.

The day is finally here. Marcy is excited—she will be graduating at 2:00 p.m. at the *William J. Foster Auditorium*. They arrive, and a massive line of people waiting to enter the auditorium. The doors will be opening up soon, so the family gets in line. Marcy must go to a different door, specific for the graduating class, so she kisses her mom on the cheeks and tells everyone "good-bye."

"I hope we can get good seats," Bob said while holding his wife's hand.

"I took care of it already," Connor said.

"How so?"

"Because I'm me, that's how. My firm designed this place. I secured the seats months ago."

"Very well," Bob replies. He's not about to start an argument with his son today. Today is Marcy's day.

The graduation ceremony starts, and each presenter speaks at their appointed time; it seemed to last forever. The time has now come for each graduate to be called and walk across the stage to receive their diploma. Marcy's turn came. And the family starts screaming and cheering her on as she walks across the stage. She stops midway and raises her high school diploma high in the air. Marcy is proud of herself for all the hard work she put into high school. She is now ready for college. After the final remarks from the principal to close out the ceremony, the auditorium empties out. Marcy meets up with her family. Her family presents her with roses they purchased from a vendor.

There are tears in her eyes as she kisses each one of her family members on their cheeks and tells them how much she loves them. The women are ready to take some pictures; however, Marcy gets a few photos taken before a group of her friends crowd her. "Marcy!" they all scream, causing her family to plug their ears. "Congratulations, Marcy," said Amy, Carly, Michelle, Kirk, Shawn, Shawna, Peter, and Keisha.

"I can't wait for your party, girl," Kirk said.

"Hey! That goes for me too," Shawn uttered loudly.

"Okay, everyone, remember the party is tomorrow, not today," Connor said.

"We will be there, Mr. Smith," Peter said.

Word of the party spread around school for the last week. And plenty of people were invited. And people who weren't will still show up.

Everyone piles in the vehicles and heads to Maggiano's Italian Restaurant for dinner. They arrive, and a line of people are waiting. Conner enters the door ahead of the family and walks up to the hostess.

"Welcome to Maggiano's. How many people in your party, Sir?"

"There are ten of us," Conner answered.

"Okay, sir. It will be an hour wait. Is that ok?"

"Certainly not! Let me speak to Greg."

"Just one moment, sir. Let me go get him for you." The hostess leaves and goes to the manager's office. She tells Greg a customer wants to see him. Meanwhile, Theresa whispers to Conner. "Why do you need to make a big scene? We can wait."

"Well, we are not waiting today, Theresa," she walks away and rolls her eyes. Greg and the hostess walk to the front podium.

"Hello, Conner. What can I do for you today?" Greg asked.

"Hey, Greg. Why do I have to wait an hour for my family to get a table?"

"Oh, I see. I can take care of that for you." Greg turned to the hostess and told her to put the family in the private party room. Some of the guests waiting for a table shake their heads in disgust. "Please follow me." She leads them to the private room; the family sits down and starts looking over the expensive menu. Eddie glances over at Conner and asks, "How did you pull this off?"

"Well, my firm designed the restaurant, so I have a little pull."

Bob turns to Conner after looking at the prices and says. "This is too expensive. Why did we to come here?"

"If you don't like the prices, then don't to eat. Besides, I am paying, so what should you care?"

"Ok, you two. Everyone, please order whatever you want. Today is Marcy's day so let's enjoy it," Theresa said. The family orders and eats their meal, enjoying the time spent with Marcy. Tomorrow will be a busy day trying to set up for the party.

Saturday morning, the women wake up early to make breakfast. Theresa is praying that today will be a perfect day for Marcy. The last thing anyone wants is more conflict to ruin the party. Once the food is ready, Theresa goes to wake everyone up, so they can eat. After breakfast, everyone will need to pitch in to help decorate the backyard for the party.

The backyard is enormous, and Theresa wants every inch of it decorated. A grand balloon arch for Marcy to walk through. The tables will need to be set up and centerpieces put on them. The swimming pool will have candle roses floating on top of the water giving off a beautiful light display once evening comes. A memory book will display pictures of Marcy growing up. So many things to accomplish that it will require everyone's help.

Time has gone by much faster than Theresa would like. People will be showing up soon, and the finishing touches need her attention. Theresa begins to panic. She wants everything to look perfect, after all, they are the Smith family. And their reputation has high expectations among the guests. Theresa starts yelling, "Let's hurry up! People are going to start showing up. We need to finish everything. Now!"

"Don't worry, Theresa. Your mom and I can finish things up."

"Are you sure, Rose?"

"Yes, we will be fine, go."

Theresa goes upstairs to get ready. She checks to see if Marcy needs any help with her hair or makeup. "Marcy, do you need any help?"

"No, mom. I'm fine. I'm just finishing up now," Marcy replies back.

"Ok. I am going to greet the guests as they start arriving. We will announce you right at 2:15 p.m. so make sure you are by the door and ready to come out."

"Ok, Mom."

Once Theresa is done getting ready she meets the rest of the family in the back so that she can start greeting guests. The day turned out to be a beautiful day. The sun is shining bright. Only eighty-five degrees with a slight breeze, which is cool considering the heat wave they've been having.

The guests start to arrive. They are ushered to the backyard and are told to mingle amongst themselves until everyone comes. Theresa waits until 2:05 p.m. to make the announcement.

"Good afternoon, everyone. Thank you for coming out today to help us celebrate Marcy's high school graduation. There is plenty of food and drinks for everyone. Please don't forget to get your picture taken with Marcy over at the photo booth. Now, the time we have been waiting for. I present to you, our graduate, Marcy."

Marcy makes her entrance in a beautiful sea blue dress with dazzling jewels and her hair glistening in the sunlight, which immediately catches Pastor Mark's attention. *"Whoa,"* He says to himself. "She is so beautiful." He stops himself, although he didn't want to. She is too young, and he couldn't bring himself to think about the possibility of dating her.

Everyone claps as and cheers on the newly graduated Marcy Smith. All her friends are in their shorts and t-shirts feeling a bit underdressed. Marcy's lives in an upper-class life and they had no reservations about showing it off. Amy and Shawn were used to it; they came around

Torn

more than her other friends. Peter felt way out of place. He whispered to Carly, "They are using real plates, glasses, and silverware." He had never seen anything like it. His family used Dixie plates, cups and plastic ware.

"I know! It's cool, huh," Carly replies back to him. She was attracted to such beautiful things; Marcy never said her family was wealthy although Carly often wondered if they were.

"I don't think cool begins to describe it, Carly. I'm afraid to break anything, I can't imagine the cost of replacing them," he told her laughing.

"I want to thank each of you for being here. Having all of you here is such a special moment for me—to have all my family and friends here. Moving on to the next phase of my life is very exciting. I love each of you, now let's get this party started." Marcy shouts.

Chris decides to leave the party. There are too many people; people he didn't care to be around. Instead, he snuck up to his room and decided to read more about other religions. Bob went into the house to use the restroom and then ventured upstairs to see if his grandson is there. He knocks on Chris's door. "Hey, Christopher, are you in there?" Chris opens his door. "Hello, papa, what do you want?"

"I was wondering why you were not enjoying your sister's party."

"I don't want to. I don't mean to be rude, Papa, but I want to be alone and read, okay?"

"Oh okay, no problem, buddy. Say, uh what are you reading?"

"Nothing, just school stuff. Kind of how it is."

"I thought college was out already?"

"I still have finals."

"Okay," Bob said as he peeked in and saw the Lucifer book. "I hope you are doing okay, buddy. Remember, though; you can always trust in God; don't ever forget that," he said softly. " *What is going on here?* "Bob wonders, but he will not bring it up. Conner resents him and will take anything he says the wrong way. Bob re-dedicated his life to God and

James Owens

is waiting for the right moment to approach his son for forgiveness. He believes he responsible for whatever evil force is attacking his family. All Bob can think about is the sins of the father traveling down through the generations. He knelt in the living room to pray.

Chapter 8

Two months later, Chris and Marcy turn eighteen-years-old. They decide not to put on a birthday party, mostly because Marcy just had a big graduation party, and Chris no longer wants to associate with his family. Chris also pulled away from his family's church. He wants to follow Zaga and begin his self-enlightenment journey with "Luciferism."

Zaga is a deeply spiritual man and believes in the powers of darkness. Zaga's philosophy is to gain control over each person slowly by showing the forces of darkness and accepting each person without any judgment. Chris asked to become a member. Now he tries to explain to his friends the freedom he gained. Chris appears to be happy. The battle within him, however; is knowing right from wrong.

The effect on his family is not easy to handle. They can sense the evil force that is controlling him. His parents pray for him every day, and although it seems as if nothing is changing; their prayers haven't been in vain. They believe God will, in His time, reach Chris. Marcy is in a tailspin of emotions. She asked her mom and dad for advice on what she should do. Marcy is devoted to God and loves her brother but doesn't want the enemy to destroy her family. Her parents merely tell her all she can do is pray for her brother.

"What will happen when Stephen comes home from youth camp? He doesn't know anything about Chris turning away from the church."

"Stephen is a strong young man. Maybe youth camp made him spiritually stronger. I'm sure he will devote some time to pray and seek God on behalf of Chris."

James Owens

Chris is engaged in the "Luciferism" lifestyle. He wears a necklace with the pentagram and a ring on his right hand with the head of a goat and a small 666 under it. The numbers are barely visible. Both were a gift from Zaga. He told his parents he is a child of Lucifer and that he feels free. His parents say to him that it isn't real freedom; it is deception, and it will eventually destroy him if he continues on his current path. The devil, and the sin of self-righteousness, now hold their son.

When his family first confronted him about his new venture into this Luciferism theology, Chris insisted and tried to convince them it's not about satanic worship. It's only about power in oneself and self-acceptance. His parents don't believe it because his appearance, the way he talks, and attitude changed. He is wearing all black, trying to pull off a gothic look. He only listens to hardcore metal, feeding on it day and night. He's been slandering Christians daily. He even burned a Bible at a meeting with Zaga and his new friends and bragged about it to his family. He entirely renounced Jesus openly to everyone.

The presence of evil is becoming more and more prominent in his life. Since Chris started engaging in darkness, Conner and Theresa have been fighting the enemy with prayer. They could sense a brutal spiritual battle on the horizon.

Connor put in a request for his pastor to come and pray over the house. There is a robust satanic influence invading his home. Pastor Shane is more than happy to answer the request and sets an appointment to come by in a few days. Theresa and Connor decide to move Sammy into their room and move Stephen into her bedroom. They don't want Stephen close to Chris; they are unsure of what kind of influence Chris could have on him. Chris publicly renounced Jesus and states he hates Christians, but he is their son, and they will never stop loving him, or praying for him.

Theresa is still concerned about Chris being in the house. The evil, the disrespect, and the lack of any feeling for them frighten her. She asks her husband, "Should we ask him to move out?" Theresa blurts out. She is only thinking of protecting them.

"I don't think that's the right thing to do right now. Chris needs to see God in us, and we need to know what's going on with him. He is quiet for now, not bothering us, except with his lack of respect and bad attitude.

Weeks go by, and Chris engages more in-depth, into Luciferism. He is now seeking the possibility of becoming a priest. He surprised many members of the group because he is demonstrating some unforeseen powers that make him an influential person. These powers come from the devil himself, but why? What can Satan use Chris for will he give him certain powers to attract others? All that is certain is that Chris is in control so much, even Zaga is beginning to submit to him. Zaga is like the student instead of Chris's teacher.

Zaga taught Chris everything about reaching into the dark spiritual world. Zaga can't remember a person so focused, so intensely motivated to learn, and seek, as if his very life depends on it. It appears to Zaga that Chris is finding things more and more interesting the deeper he dives into the darkness. Chris envisioned speaking with demons, which he calls the self-glorified spirits of darkness.

He asks for things that no man should ask for and soaks in the evil that dwells around him. His engagement with the spirit world captured his mind, body, and spirit. He invites them to use their powers through him. He is fully engaged and rapidly progressing into leadership. Chris is thinking about moving out of his parent's house in a few weeks, and his parents are questioning him about it.

"I must leave. We cannot get along. I serve a different god than you. If I don't leave, there will be nothing but fighting. My faith says I must abandon you and go so you will not be a hindrance to my calling. Do not attempt to stop me or get in my way. Do not call upon your God for me. I'm in the care of the god who chose me, and I chose him me. He is the rightful god, and he shall reign in amazing glory. I will help him attain his rightful place and be a prince in his kingdom. Sealed with his presence; I possess powers to bring others to him

Marcy hears the commotion. Chris leaves to go upstairs, and Marcy stands in the hallway to talk to him, she looks concerned. "What is going on here, Chris?"

"I want, need to leave, Marcy. My new faith is what suits me best. I don't need Christianity. I'm trying to tell you what I decided to believe."

Marcy is shaking her head in disbelief.

"I have chosen to serve Lucifer; I found freedom and self-esteem that I have never felt before. I am accepted and respected by my fellow followers," he said, pleading his case.

"Don't! Chris, please, don't say that to me," Marcy said as she began sobbing and gasping for air. Her heart is racing as adrenaline pumps throughout her body in response to her brother. She can't understand why. *"Why is he doing this?"* she says to herself.

"I must express my faith, my new-found faith."

"Chris! You accepted his lies. He's nothing but a liar, Chris. He is pure evil; he will destroy you! Please don't do this to us. I love you; you are my twin."

"No! Marcy, he is everything God fears. He is Lucifer, son of the morning. His very name means light bearer. He was dealt a bad hand and cast out of Heaven just because he said, "I will" five times. And your God cast him out because he was going to be just like God."

"Listen, brother," Marcy said as she pulled her emotions together. "Yes, he said, "I will" five times to God; he said he would be like the Most-High God. You are being lied to, Chris because of the sin in Lucifer's heart. He got banished out of Heaven."

"Whatever, Marcy! I should have known that you would stand against me, that you won't accept me. Yeah, you are my twin sister, but we are individuals," he said with a cold heart as he walks away from her.

"Listen, brother! Your god said, *"I will"* five times—right?"

"Yes," Chris said hatefully. "He told him five times "I will" and he shall, Marcy; he shall rule," Chris uttered proudly.

"Well, brother, he may have said "I will" but my God said, "I AM!" she replies sternly. "He is the *Great I Am*; he owns the day. I love you, brother, but this is all wrong on your part." Chris walks and locks himself in his room.

Pastor Shane came to the house. Connor answers the door and tells pastor Shane what has just taken place. "We are going to be careful with this," Pastor Shane told him. "The enemy seeks people who are weak-spirited, and lack of faith. We need to seek God and ask Him what we should do; for now, we will pray over this house. You can expect some interference while Chris is here. The enemy entered your home, Connor, and we must now engage him with the right plan of action. We must come against him and his stronghold from your home and your family." Pastor Shane continued, "A battle is coming, and we need to be ready. We're not in a battle against Chris, but a battle against the forces of darkness in which Chris is the target. Both sides want him, but he chose the enemies side, and now we must fight for his freedom; he will need to see and want. We can't force it upon him. God gives us a free will to choose—whether it be for good or evil. We will need to keep praying and be strong for Chris. The powers of darkness are no joke and certainly not a game, but Almighty God is on our side, and when the time comes, there will be a fight. We will be victorious."

"Thank you so much for coming over, Pastor. We appreciate you. We will do what you suggested, and we will become stronger. We will battle for our son."

After Pastor Shane leaves, they sit down in the living room and talk about all that is happening to their family.

"Well, Connor, I think the pastor is right, but when is the time is right for us to do battle?"

"Theresa, we are in a battle. Praying for him is a battle, but we are not at the point where Pastor Shane said we will be going. I'm not sure what lies before us, but we need to be ready."

"Connor, we need to renew our hearts and lives to God."

"I know and now is the time. I am sorry. I will move forward from this point on."

Chapter 9

A month has passed since Pastor Shane's visit. And two weeks since Chris moved out. With a new school year around the corner, Stephen will be in tenth grade and Sammy will be in kindergarten. Marcy didn't get accepted into *Shaler University*, so she had to apply to Kent Community College. The community college is close to her house, so, she will live at home. She is majoring in Psychology and minoring in Family Studies.

Once Chris moved out, life became sad, and the family is doing all they can do to keep busy. They continue to pray for Chris; it helps to ease the heavy burden. They are unable to speak to him. Chris doesn't want communication with his family; he expelled them from his life.

Connor and Theresa rely on their friends, family, and fellow church members for support. They will experience a hard journey of faith and having the support of everyone helps alleviate some of the pain. Sammy is not as affected by what happened. She is so young and innocent and only interested in having fun like a typical five-year-old. Stephen, on the other hand, is having a more difficult time.

He loves going on youth retreats and other events; it reminds him of the times he would spend with Chris—going to the movies or on nature hikes. Now he spends his time alone listening to his favorite bands. There are no more youth retreats left for the year, just Wednesday night youth group. Chris was more than his big brother. He was his buddy and best friend. Stephen would like to learn more from his father, but he is always busy with work, and he doesn't spend much time with him. His sister spends as much time as she can with him, but her social life and preparing for college keeps her pretty busy. When they do have a chance to be together, they love to watch movies and go ice skating.

Sammy keeps asking her mom to take her to the park, so Theresa makes some time to take her. At the park, Sammy runs around and plays on the jungle gym. Her favorite thing to do is going down the slides. Before they leave, Theresa sees a member of her church named Kelly and walks over to her.

"Hello Kelly," Theresa said.

"Hi Theresa, how are you doing? How's the family?" Kelly asked.

"Well, I admit, things are hard for us. I wish things were different. Chris hasn't spoken to us since he moved out. Stephen is going through a lot. He is so alone since Chris is gone, and Connor's working so much lately. I don't think we can take much more, Kelly."

"Well, Theresa, all of you are in our prayers. If you and Connor need someone to help with Stephen and Sammy, just ask. You and your husband need a break and spend time together as well. Remember, there is a church family who loves you all, including Chris. We are all praying for God to move in your lives. We love you and are here to help in any way we can."

"Thank you, Kelly."

Theresa is grateful for all that Kelly said to her. She is overwhelmed with emotion, and tears ran down her face as she put Sammy in the car.

"Why are you sad, Momma?"

"I am not sad, sweetie. I am full of joy and peace, and thankful for the friends God placed in our lives."

"Does that mean that God will bring my brother home, Momma?"

"I hope so, baby. That is what we are all hoping for."

Theresa and Sammy arrive home, and Connor's car is sitting in the driveway. Unusual because it is only 3:00 p.m. Connor is never home this early.

"Connor," Theresa yells. "Hello! Connor, where are you?"

"I'm in the den."

"Why are you home so early, honey? Is everything ok?"

"Yes, Theresa, everything is fine. I took the afternoon off to spend time with you guys. I haven't had much time with anyone, and I have lost one son; I will not lose another child."

"Connor, Chris is not your fault. You did a fantastic job as a father. You love him and taught him right from wrong. You did not fail, and God did not fail him. He chose a path that he believes will make him who he wants to be. He's blind; he closed his eyes to the truth anymore."

"Theresa, please! I know what the issues are, I don't need you telling me time and time again; I can't deal with it. I'm hurting from the loss. I'm angry at myself for not being a stronger spiritual leader for our family. I became so obsessed with work and success—I didn't see my family falling apart. What else can I do? My son won't talk to me; we mean nothing to him anymore. How did it come to this? I am heartbroken. I have reached my limit. I'm torn apart inside Theresa, and I don't want to lose another son."

Connor walks away and goes upstairs. He knocks on Stephen's door. Stephen gets up and opens the door.

"Dad, what's up?"

"Son, I love you so much. I'm sorry for not making time to be with you," Connor said, as he cried on his knees in front of Stephen.

"It is okay, Dad. I'm not mad at you," Stephen kneels down to hug his father and comfort him. "I know you are working hard for us," Stephen hugged his father tight. "You are my hero, Dad. Someday I want to be just like you. You make me so proud because you care for us and provide for us. You're a wonderful dad, and I love you and Mom so much," Stephen said, as he cried on his father's shoulder.

"Well, Stephen, let's buy tickets for the concert coming to town the church talks about every week? It's in a few weeks, right? We can make a night of it together; how does that sound?"

"That would be so awesome, Dad! Yes, let's do it," he leaps with joy

Marcy arrives home before dinner. Theresa brings her up to speed on the day's events. Marcy doesn't want to talk about what her family is going through; she is not ready to open up and share her feelings at all. She hasn't told a single soul how sad she feels, how Chris's absence is affecting her. After all, he is her twin. They share a unique connection.

Marcy locks herself in her room; she looks at pictures of Chris. Pictures of them together when they were little, pictures of them throughout the years. He loved her so much that he would give his life for her, but now there is no relationship with him. She is cut-off and lost. The only thing she has now are memories. She asks God to help heal her broken heart; Marcy tries desperately to understand why he is doing this; why he doesn't care about his family anymore. Every night she prays for him as tears run down her face. She falls asleep like this most nights.

It seems that Chris's goal of achieving power over his family is working without him even realizing it. The enemy is using him to destroy the joy that was once so strong in their lives. His hatred toward his family and Christians is getting stronger each day. He no longer fears anyone or anything. He is a puppet to the powers of darkness.

Saturday morning Pastor Shane stops by to visit them. He's been concerned for them and plans to help them stay strong and help show them how to rebuild their lives as much as he can. Being a Pastor is rough; you must lead a congregation, over-see church operations, and of course, counseling members who are in need. Above all those duties, he must also lead his own family, take care of their needs, be a father and husband instead of, their pastor. "He takes a deep breath, as he exhales he knocks on the door.

"Hello, good morning, Pastor," Connor says.

"Hello, Conner. I decided to come by and see how things are going and how you're holding up."

Connor stepped aside to let him into the house and then closes the door. Pastor Shane walks down the hallway to the living room, where he sits down on a chair across from Connor who is sitting on the sofa.

"Can I get you anything Pastor? Coffee, doughnut, or a muffin?"

"No thank you, Connor. Thanks for asking. Can you tell me, how are things going?"

"Well, Pastor, I admit, this is more of a challenge than we thought. Theresa and I have emotional breakdowns. We cry out to God and ask him to heal our broken hearts. We each have our moments, like as if someone died, Pastor."

"Well, I can certainly understand that. I felt there is a heavy burden on your family. The church elder board and I pray for your family each morning. I know about loss, Connor. My sister, who I cherished deeply, passed away after losing her battle with cancer. I am sorry for you and your family. It hurts deep, but, Connor, let me tell you that none of this is your fault. You didn't do anything to cause this. Remember, he isn't thinking with a clear mind, but these thoughts and actions are true to him. He thinks his life has a greater meaning now."

"Again, all we can do is pray for him, and, of course, we need to keep praying for your family during this difficult time. Stay focused on God; seek his face, Connor, and be the pillar of faith that your family needs you to be. I am forty-eight-years-old. I have children ranging from thirteen to nineteen, but you must be strong and stand your ground. Do not give the enemy any more ground than he has already taken. Prepare for battle, Connor. We had this talk before, and you must prepare yourself for the fight. Chris's life and his spiritual life depends on it. Remember, you have many people praying for your family and Chris." He said to him as he stands up preparing to leave. He had other business he needs to attend.

"Thank you, Pastor," Connor said, seeing him to the door.

"You are welcome; God bless you and your family."

After Pastor Shane leaves, Connor feels a little better. He's trying to understand what he needs to do to prepare for this fight. Connor doesn't know what to think. Will he be fighting against Satan or a battle against his flesh and blood, his son? Will he be able to choose if someone must live or die? Connor needs to pray and prepare to battle Satan. Satan is taking over his family, using Chris as his weapon. He can't see the significant impact coming, but God can. Connor and Theresa need to seek Him. He will be their refuge, their strength. He will lead the charge against the powers of darkness. Christ is the Lord of their home, and the presence of the Holy Spirit will rise and defend them against the evil one.

Weeks continue to go by, and the family engages in Bible study every day. Spending more time in prayer together; learning more, and more about God and seeking Him daily. They are growing closer, and Marcy is doing better with her grief. Connor is more of a leader for his family. Taking the time to be a husband and father. Not only providing financial support but also spiritual support. He helps teach Sammy, Stephen, and Marcy to understand God and His love for them. He tells them the story of the old rugged cross. How Jesus, the Son of God, gave His life to forgive them of their sins. Not like they need to hear it again, but it only takes one time to truly understand in your heart what it means to be, *"Born Again."*

His children have been receptive and have grown spiritually. They are going in a great direction, and they are more involved in church. Stephen is keeping up playing guitar for his youth group band. Marcy is involved in the singles ministry now and helps feed the homeless on Friday nights. Connor is assisting in a ministry called, *Lost, but not forgotten* at the church on Saturday mornings, which helps parents cope with children who strayed away from God.

Theresa is leading a women's group that helps women learn how to nurture their children. This group also meets on Saturday mornings. She's been very successful in leading new mothers at the church. Theresa and Connor devote time on Saturday afternoons to take Sammy to the park. They enjoy time to bond at the park together, and sometimes Marcy meets them there. Altogether, things are looking up for the Smith family, even though rough roads are ahead of them.

Chapter 10

Chris moved in with a group of people who share the same views, and beliefs as him. The house is big; it has a spacious living room and family room. There are eight bedrooms in the house. The hallways are dim, lit only by candlelight. The old wood floors creak when you walk on them. The walls are ash gray. Zaga made an everlasting impression on Chris. Chris is leaning on a supernatural power that goes beyond his comprehension. Chris recruited several people into the group, much to Zaga's delight. They consider Chris to be more of a leader than Zaga. Although Zaga is not jealous, he doesn't like it.

"Chris, come here; I need to talk to you."

"Yes, Zaga."

"You are learning quick. I am worried you're taking things too far. You are being looked at as the leader here. However, you are still a student. These new people think of you as if you are a *god*. You are no *god*; you're a man."

"Well, Zaga! I understand what you are saying, but there is no reason to be jealous of me. Don't get me wrong, I—"

"Shh, Chris, please stop, you need to listen to me. I am still the leader of these people; a group which represents being of one mind, body, and soul. I am certainly not jealous of you."

"Zaga, I don't care what you claim to be or what you think this whole thing is about; there is a presence in me; a calling on my life..."

"Shut up! Boy, you need to listen to me. We do not go into demonic or satanic things, and I did not start this mission to be a cult, understand?"

"Zaga, you have no power over me, and you need to watch your step," Chris said.

"What are you trying to say, Chris? Where do you come off?"

"I am saying that you can claim to be the group's leader. You are nothing, no leader over me. My lord is Satan; I choose to accept him and seek his leadership."

"Chris, what in the world are you talking about? This is not about worshipping evil. We want a free spirit to enjoy life—no rules—be at peace with who we are. It's about self-enlightenment, not satanic worship."

"Zaga, you know what we are about, or I wouldn't be here. Do not argue with me! DO NOT TRY ME AGAIN," Chris's voice spoke in a demonic voice. Chris looked Zaga in the eyes and walked away. Chris knows he needs to find out which people will be on his side, so he turns to Jessie to ask where she and the others stand. He knocks on Jessie's door.

"Jessie, are you here?"

"Yes, Chris, I am here, hold on a second."

"I need to talk to you," he said with a soft voice.

"What do you need, Chris?"

"You are the only person I can trust. Since I joined, you are a smart girl, and I need someone I can trust with things I need to share."

"Well, of course, Chris; you can trust me. I admire you so much. You're a strong spiritual man; an influence on us all, though Zaga may not understand it, we do."

"Well, I thought everyone looked up to Zaga and only saw me as a recruiter or high-ranking member to give them guidance into a new world."

"Chris, your powers, and your spirit, I admit, are more than Zaga's. I sense he fears you. He is not sure what he needs to do, but he will not surrender to you. This place is his life's work. He will not give that up! He raised me since I was a child. I never knew my mother all I had was him. I will always be close to him."

"Why not? He should give it up. I am becoming..."

"What are you becoming, Chris?"

"I'm growing in power. I'm strong inside. I sense the powers of darkness within me. I will be the one who makes all the decisions, plans out our goals, and plans our missions. Are you with me, Jessie?"

"Yes, Chris, of course, I am. But what mission is this? Do you want to be a mentor? What vision is it you are talking about?"

"Find out who else is with us. Give me names. I will make my point known soon. For now, I'm going to meditate on things."

Chris walks back to his room and locks his door to be alone; he does not want to be disturbed. He thinks carefully about the events that have happened. *"Should I push forward or chill."* These Questions consume his mind. After an hour of meditating, he feels it is best to chill for a while. He walks down the hall to Zaga's room and lightly knocks on the door.

"Zaga, hello, it's Chris; I need to talk to you," he said with a soft voice.

"What do you want, Chris?"

"Can I come in, so we talk?"

"Yes, come in," Zaga said. What's up Chris."

"Well, Zaga, first I want to apologize for losing my temper with you earlier. I owe you more than that. You took me under your wing. And I am sorry."

"Well, Chris, I appreciate it. You are acting selfishly at times. You still need to mature and learn things. What you do and who you choose to call god is your decision. I do believe in Satan, but I do not worship him. I believe in God, but I do not worship him either. Why do you want to worship Satan?"

"Why, Zaga? I let spirits live inside me. I invited them in, and they showed me the true god. I am now at their service. I invited them to give me power. I will shake the Christian world. I want to show my family and their church what real power is."

"That's a dangerous road, Chris. Evil is coming from you when you speak to me. The demon uses you to fulfill his own will. I'm aware of possession. I never could invite them in. I'm afraid of what they would do with me and through me. I am not willing to do it, Chris."

"Well, Zaga, I am, and I think I am there already. I hate Christians.

They are such fake people, they are judgmental, and "holier than thou" kooks. This group needs a leader who dares to stand and fight. Are you prepared to do it or not?"

"Are you giving me an ultimatum, Chris? You want a war with people; your mission is not our mission—it's not what we're about."

"In a way, yes, I want to move this group in the right direction Zaga. But if you choose not to, then I will..."

"Chris, the direction of this group is and always will be to aid those who need refuge. This is what I've done for many people, including you. I went out to feed and give clothes to the homeless. I even offered them shelter. Pastors of the Christian faith also fed and gave clothes to the homeless, but they never offered them shelter. My mission for many years. So, if you are asking me to step down, my answer is *no*, I will not surrender."

"Zaga, try to understand what I'm saying. If you are not with the vision given to me, then I'm not asking you, I'm telling you, you will no longer be in charge. Out of respect for mentoring me and others, you will be kept on, you can continue teaching, but it stops there."

"Who do you think you are coming in here and telling me you are demoting. I run this place! I clothe, feed, and house everyone here out of love. How are you going to afford to do that without me?"

"I have been called to start a revolution, an uprising against all who stand against me. That includes you if you're in my way. Who am I, you ask—who are you, Zaga?"

"You have no idea who I am Chris, I tried to help you, but you refuse to open your eyes."

Chris storms out of the room. He walks into the living room to address Jessie and anyone else that is on his side. He is thrilled to see such an impressive turnout.

"Jessie, hey, did you get the list we spoke about? Are these the people who will follow me?"

"Yes, Chris, I told them what you want, and they are willing to stand with you. I's weird though because Zaga took us in and helped us all with our struggles. I have been with him since I was little, I love him."

"Yeah, well, things have changed, and he needs to understand we are growing and evolving in our spirituality. I am tired of feeling held back by him. He needs to join us. Where is Tanner?"

"Tanner is afraid. She's not sure what Zaga will do if she goes against him."

"Well, I will talk to her and make sure she understands Zaga cannot do anything to her for joining us. The time will come when everything will be lined up and in order. Things are coming, Jessie, and I want to start preparing us for those things," Chris walks upstairs and goes down the hallway to Tanner's room and knocks on her door.

"Tanner! Hey, it is Chris."

"Oh hey, Chris, come in." She's wondering why Chris is coming to her.

"Hey, I want to talk to you about the things going on. Do you understand what I am talking about?"

"Yes."

"Well, you are a little worried about things because of what Zaga may think or do."

"Well no, Chris, I am not afraid of that."

"Then why did you say you wouldn't join us to stand against our enemies?"

"I don't think that we should make Zaga believes we don't care about him. And I'm not sure what you exactly mean by, *"Enemies?"*

"I talked with him, Tanner. He doesn't want what we do. He is afraid of change and the powers I'm gaining. And our enemies are the self-righteous Christians; the enemies of darkness."

"Well, I think for now you need to drop it, Chris. I need to figure things out for myself. I don't need you deciding for me. I'm not going to abandon Zaga. He is like a father to me."

"Fine, Tanner, whatever! I will talk to you later," Chris said as he walks out and slams her door shut.

"*I don't think so,*" she said to herself.

Chris leaves Tanner's room and decides to talk with Jessie and the other members downstairs. They start talking about who should be their leader. The group agrees that Chris will be their leader. Chris assures the group that he will lead them to greatness.

After the meeting is over, Chris follows Jessie to her room. As they walk down the hall, he thinks about what he is going to tell her. They walk into her room, sit down on her bed and begin talking.

"Well, Jessie, I think things will become very interesting over the next few weeks. But all things aside, I have tickets to a concert if you will like to go with me."

"Of course, I am flattered you asked me."

"Well, we have a chemistry, Jessie, and would like for us to explore our emotions. That may come across as odd, but I am serious. You have a beautiful spirit, and I get weak in the knees when I'm around you."

"Well, yeah! I mean sure. I just never said anything because I was, well, let's say, I wasn't sure you'd be interested in me."

"Well, Jessie, I am, and maybe this will become something awesome. I am excited; this concert is supposed to be awesome."

"Who is the band?"

"*The Breed* and I have heard them before; they are amazing. *"A potential name for my group too."* He says to himself. "So, it's a date then?"

"Oh, for sure. I can't wait to go."

"Cool. Catch you later.

"Okay."

Chris leaves Jessie's bedroom and walks to his. While sitting in his bedroom, he meditates on the plans he wants to come together. Keeping his plans, a secret. He doesn't want to tell anyone just yet. For now, he will continue to meditate on them and work things out in his mind.

Chris finishes his quiet-time and decides to go the store. While shopping, he notices Pastor Shane, so he walks in the other direction. Pastor Shane saw Chris right away. He suspected Chris is trying to avoid him, so he purposefully goes up the other aisle to meet him.

"Hello, Chris," Pastor Shane said.

Chris heard his name but entirely ignored the voice. He turned around and walked in the other direction. Pastor Shane stood there a little shocked. He could sense an evil presence around Chris.

When Chris is finished checking out, he looks back at Pastor Shane again. The two of them look at each other and Chris gives him an evil stare. *"Next time you will regret that you even knew me. This God lover will experience my true presence when the time is right; until then, he better avoid me. In time, he will be afraid. His kind of presence will not prevail against me—he will learn soon. I'm not one to be messed with."*

Chris walks down the sidewalk and disappears from his former pastor and family friend. He begins to wonder why Pastor Shane was even there, *"Why is he in this part of town on a Saturday night?"*

Chapter 11

Connor and his family have been enjoying both spiritual growth in God and personal growth with each other. The family overall created a new dynamic that is making them stronger. They attended church with an eagerness to learn God's word.

After church, Pastor Shane asks to speak with Connor. They walk to Pastor Shane's office and sit down on Italian leather chairs.

"Connor, I saw Chris in a store the other night."

"You did, Pastor?" he asked eagerly. "Did he say anything? Did he tell you where he is staying?"

"Yes, I saw him. No, he did not speak to me, though he did give me an evil stare."

"He didn't say anything?" Connor asked with tears blurring his vision.

"No, Connor, he was distant and quiet. He didn't respond to my greeting at all. To be honest, Connor, I'm worried about him."

"Thank you for sharing the information with me, Pastor. I will tell Theresa about it."

"Well, I'm not finished."

"Oh okay, what else is there?"

"I sensed an enormous presence of evil around him. It seems that Chris has gone farther into the darkness, and by that, I mean; I believe Chris may be demonically possessed; making him extremely dangerous to himself and others. He will obey the demons. It's sad to say, but this is what he wants."

"Oh my! Pastor, uh—well, I can't find the words," he says as his head falls into his shaking hands.

"It's okay, Connor; This is hard to hear, but I needed to warn you about it," he said with a heavy heart.

"Well, thank you, Pastor; I am completely shocked. I didn't think Chris was going to fall prey to that. I thought it was a phase and it would be over. He would come back home; now it is obvious this is real."

"Okay, Connor, if you need anything, call me, okay?"

"Sure will, Pastor, and please keep us all in your prayers."

"I sure will, Connor."

Conner leaves the office and walks back to the front of the church where Theresa is waiting for him.

"What was that all about, Connor?"

"Well, Pastor Shane told me he had a little run-in with Chris at the store the other night."

"He did, oh my! How did it go?" she asked.

"Well, he said he tried to reach out to him, but Chris just ignored him."

"Really? I didn't think Chris would do something like that. I thought he would say, "hello" back or something."

"Well, Theresa, he said the only thing Chris did was give him an evil look."

"What! I can't believe he did that to Pastor Shane."

"Well, Theresa, he did, and Pastor Shane said he sensed an evil spirit in Chris."

"Whoa! What? Does it mean—no, I don't want to believe it! No, please tell me this isn't true," she said with tears building up, shaking her head in disbelief.

"Yes! Theresa, he believes Chris invited demons into him. To give him strength and power."

"Oh no! Please no! Not my baby boy! Lord, please watch over him!" Theresa shouts.

"Theresa, we need to pray for him. This battle is for his life, his soul."

Torn

"But, Connor," Theresa cries, "I can't fathom the thought of the enemy living in my son; I can't—I just can't."

"Theresa, we are in this together, okay? I am hurt too, but we need to be strong and allow God to shine through us."

As they return home, Connor sees a white envelope on Marcy's car. He walks over to pick it up. *"Why is there an envelope on Marcy's windshield?"*

"Connor, who is it from?" Theresa asks.

"Yeah, Dad, who is it from?" Marcy asks.

"It doesn't say who it is from." He tells them.

"Well, open it," Theresa tells him.

He opens the envelope as they enter through the side door that leads into the kitchen.

"Okay, here we go.

> Dear Smith family, I am writing to inform you that you may be in danger. I am friends with your son Chris. I obtained your address from his address book. Please forgive me for the invasion, but Chris became obsessed with his love of Luciferism. I fear that as he grows stronger and more powerful, you may be in danger. He took over our group from a man named Zaga. I'm only in the group out of fear. I'm not sure what would happen to me if I were to leave.
>
> I will remain anonymous—but please be warned, I wish I didn't give you Zaga's name, but maybe it will give you a clue, please be on guard. Guard your home and your family. He can no longer be trusted; he is becoming something supernatural. Something I've never seen before. I'm not a follower of Luciferism, and I will tell you that you either stand with Chris, or you're against him. I am not sure what he is capable of, but he does strike many into fear. Again, I am sorry for invading your privacy. Please destroy this letter, as I do

not want it getting back to him. Investigate if you wish, but do not act. Thank you."

"Wow! How crazy is this, Theresa?"
"Uh! I am speechless, but I do wish we knew who this person is."
"Yes, Theresa, but unfortunately we don't."
Sammy begins whining because she is tired. Theresa puts her down to take a nap.
"Hey, Marcy?"
"Yes, Mom?"
"Hey, can you come here, please?"
"What's up?"
"Can you pick Stephen up for me? He's at band practice. Please, we just got home. He told Pastor Mark that he isn't well. Pastor Mark called and asked us to pick him up. I just checked my voicemail."
"Yes, I will."
"Thank you, Marcy, I appreciate it so much."
When she arrives at the church, Stephen is standing, waiting outside on the sidewalk.
"Hey, I'm here buddy; are you ok? Why are you standing outside?"
"I'm not feeling well at all, sis. I'm dizzy and nauseous. Mom called me and said you were on your way, so I came outside."
"Oh boy! Not good," Marcy is worried about him vomiting in her car. "Well, let's go. Mom can check you out at home."
On the way home, Marcy, and Stephen are talking about the band and how things are going. He tells her he is doing well, and that Pastor Mark is teaching him a lot.
"Wow. I'm so proud of you!"
"Thank you, sis. I just wished Chris were here to see how good I'm getting."
"Well, it is his loss, but I understand. I miss him too. Remember to keep him in your prayers, okay?"
"Yeah, I will. Oh, ouch! Marcy, my stomach hurts bad."
"We're almost home, Stephen, hang in there," Marcy pulls into the driveway and calls out for her mother. "Hello, Mom! We're home."

Torn

"Oh, thank goodness! How are you, Son?"

"I'm dizzy and sick to my stomach; my stomach hurts bad, Mom," he says in agony.

"Well, go lay down and try to rest. I will call the doctor to see when I can make an appointment for you, okay, honey?"

"Okay, Mom, but please don't call me honey."

"Okay."

Stephen walks from the kitchen through the hallway when he lets out a loud scream of pain. He dropped to the floor and folded himself into a fetal position and begins vomiting. Marcy and Theresa run to his aid.

Conner is in his office doing some Bible study when he is interrupted by loud screams and crying. He opens his office door and looks down the hallway.

"What's going on?" he asked.

"Dad, Stephen fell. He has a sharp pain in his stomach. He's on the floor throwing up."

Connor gets up and goes down the hall to see what is happening. He gets down on one knee and grabs his hand.

"Stephen! What's wrong, Son?" he asks. But Stephen is unable to answer him.

"That's it! Marcy, call 9-1-1 now," Marcy makes the call and tells the operator that her brother is on the floor in agonizing pain and vomiting.

"Please hurry!" Marcy said, worried about Stephen.

"They are on our way, Dear," the operator responded. Marcy hangs up the phone. The ambulance pulls up to the house about ten- minutes later. The paramedics rush into the house. They ask Connor and Theresa to move aside so they can tend to Stephen. The EMT's immediately put Stephen on a stretcher.

"We have to take your son to the hospital ASAP!"

"What's wrong with him?" Theresa cries out.

"His appendix, Ma'am. We need to take him to the hospital before it ruptures."

"Are you sure his appendix is the problem?"

"Well, I'm not a doctor, but I've seen this enough to say I believe it is."

"Okay." She grabs her purse, and Marcy follows close behind her. "Connor, take Sammy and meet me in the car."

"Okay."

Connor calls Pastor Shane on his cell phone to make him aware of what is happening. He leaves him a voicemail. When they arrive at the hospital, they exit the car and run into the emergency room.

Theresa asks the person sitting at the front desk. "Where is my son?"

"Who's your son, ma'am?"

"My son is Stephen, Stephen Smith! He was brought in by ambulance."

"Let me check, ma'am. Please take a seat."

Theresa is not in the sitting mood. She paces up and down the waiting room, desperately waiting for an answer. Marcy tries to calm her mother down while Connor holds Sammy. After a few minutes, a nurse comes out of the double doors and asks to speak to Stephens's parents.

"Mr. and Mrs. Smith?"

"Yes." They both answered at the same time.

"Please follow me; I will take you to your son's room. Here you are; he is groggy, he was given morphine for pain."

"Can you tell us what is wrong with our son?"

"Sir, the Doctor will be in in a few minutes."

"Okay! Thank you," Conner is not happy with the lack of information he is receiving.

The doctor opens the door and walks in. "Hello there, I am Dr. Allen. I must say your son is lucky. The EMT's made the right decision to bring your son here. Stephen has appendicitis. He is going to need surgery we need to do it soon. Do we have your permission?"

"Yes! Of course, Doctor."

"Very well, I will call the surgeon. There is paperwork you will need to fill out."

Twenty-minutes later, the surgeon arrives, and the nursing staff comes in to take Stephen to the operating room. Theresa kisses him on his forehead as they wheel him off. Connor and Marcy leave and walk to the chapel.

"What are you going to read dad?"

"I'm reading the book of John. I am going over the first five verses."

"I'm going to fight this spiritual battle for my son's life, his eternal life; and I will not rest until we win. I will lay down my life for all of you."

"Wow, Dad. God is telling you that we need to put Him first. He is the word of God and the light of the world, but not all will receive Him. Maybe Chris will never accept Jesus as his savior, but I can hold on to hope and pray for Chris. We cannot change anyone—It is Jesus who changes people if they let Him."

"Marcy, God is truly speaking to our hearts. He will reveal His will to us. Not only with Chris, but also for other people we will encounter. Marcy, I think we should have more moments like this to spend together reading God's word."

"Yes! Dad, we need to do this more often."

"Let's pray; Father God, thank you for the blessings you have given to our family. Thank you for your Son Jesus and the gift of eternal life. We pray you will reach Chris, call him to you. Be with us Father. We are blessed to have such wonderful kids and no matter what they fall into, Lord, they are still our children. They are your children, Father. We are all yours. Use us and teach us to fulfill your will, God. We ask these things in Jesus name Amen."

Chapter 12

Marcy and her father walk back to the surgery center waiting room. Pastor Shane had arrived thirty-minutes ago with Pastor Mark. When they enter the waiting room, Pastor Mark's head turns to Marcy. She looks at Mark with a small, but meaningful smile, and a gleam in her eye. They are now sensing a connection to each other. Marcy thumbs through a magazine to distract herself from staring at him so much.

The surgeon walks into the room, takes a sigh of relief, "Mr. and Mrs. Smith, I am Dr. Roberts, your son's surgeon. The surgery went well; we successfully removed his appendix. He is in recovery. You will be able to visit him in an hour or so. Stephen will be able to go home today. I will prescribe some pain medication for him. Do you have any questions for me?"

"Not at this time, thank you, Doctor," Connor said. They all wait patiently for the time to pass when a nurse walks into the waiting room, "You can see your son now. He is still a little groggy, so be patient with him." Everyone gets up and follows the nurse to Stephen's room.

"Mom, Dad," Stephen said.

"We're here, Son, you're okay," his mother says with a soft, tender voice.

"What happened to me?"

"You had emergency surgery for your appendix. You had appendicitis," Connor told him.

"What's an appendix?"

"I'll explain it later, okay? Look who's here."

"Hey champ, how ya doin'?" Pastor Mark asks.

"Like I went one round in a championship fight and lost. Stephen says, trying to laugh.

"Well, you still have a sense of humor, buddy," Pastor Mark told him. After everyone finished talking, Pastor Shane led them in a word of prayer, declaring healing over Stephen's body. In a few hours, he will be home and back to his usual self in no time.

Chris became closer to Jessie since he found out she is attracted to him. The day draws near for the concert. Jessie and Chris talk to others in the group about how he wants things. Daren, who is a member, expressed his concerns. Chris always listens to the member's point of view, paying most attention the male members.

The leading members of the group are Jessie, Tanner, Daren, Rocco, and Thomas. Thomas came from a childhood of drugs and poverty. His mother was a drug dealer and was killed over a bad drug deal when he was only twelve-years-old. After his mom died, Thomas went to live with his grandmother. She is a Godly woman, but he was not into church, much like Chris. The difference between the two is that he had no siblings, no parents, and his connection with Zaga was strong—after all, it was Zaga who took him in at eighteen when he left his grandmother's house and had nowhere else to go. Daren came from a wealthy, un-religious family. He got involved in Luciferism quite a long time ago.

Zaga is forty-five-years-old. He is a peaceful man who cares about the people he helps. Many calls him a cult leader, and don't like his method of teaching. These are the ones who will eventually be on Chris's side when everything goes down. Zaga helped many people gain confidence. However, it is now apparent to him his control is hanging by a thread.

Zaga calls a meeting with Daren, Thomas, Jessie, and Chris. The meeting is about leadership, goals, and organization of spiritual needs. Everyone gathers in the living room. Zaga starts by saying,

"Okay, people, we are here to talk about some changes and make resolutions for our benefit. Chris mentioned to me that he is ready to lead and take care of you. What I would like to know is how everyone feels, and what you say about this. Daren, you first."

"I guess, to put it in perspective, I believe that Chris is a strong and influential person. He has a calling on his life and received divine favor. I'm not sure if he should lead us, but I say it would be a good idea to give him a chance. He can show us if he is ready."

"Okay, and how about you Jessie?"

"To be honest Zaga. I love and respect you so much. You've done wonderful things for me. You will always have a special place in my heart for that, but I believe Chris needs to show us he is ready to do it."

"Thank you, Jessie. So, Thomas. I won't ask you because I believe you are on his side."

"Well, Zaga, thanks for speaking for me, but yeah, I do," Thomas replied.

"Well, I guess we don't need to vote on anything. Chris, I will resign my position. I only want the best for everyone. I give you leadership and control of the group. Do what you must to lead them, be wise—you're responsible for these people and their lives. I'm going to make sure that we announce this to everyone. After that. I will be leaving the house. I will be moving to a new place with an old friend. I have done enough now it is your turn to do this."

"Zaga, thank you for this peaceful transition. I hope the best for you in whatever you do. I have desired to lead this group. I was called here to do that."

The announcement went out to the group, many were shaken by it, including Tanner. She cried for the better part of the day.

The time has finally come; a night out with Jessie. They are going to a concert to see a band only Chris has heard. Jessie is excited, and she can barely contain it. She puts on her best outfit, styles her hair, puts her makeup on, and her nails. Chris sits in the living room, anxious.

He is about to call for her, but she walks down the stairs. Chris freezes, mesmerized. He loses his breath. *"How beautiful."*

"Are you ready?"

"Wow! Uh, yeah. You look beautiful, I mean, wow! I am excited to spend this time together," Chris replies looking her up and down. Her dark hair is curled, and bounces softly, the sweet smell of perfume, the black leather pants, and a black blouse with shiny glitter. She is all he can think of at the moment; taken aback, she reaches for his hand.

"Are you okay?"

"Yeah, uh, yeah, I'm ready," he says as Jessie smiles and giggles. They walk outside and get into Jessie's car. Driving to the concert, Jessie shares her feelings with Chris.

"Chris, can I tell you something?"

"Sure, what's up?"

"I'm happy you asked me to come with you. I want to be with you, do you understand what I'm saying?"

"Wow, so weird because I was going to ask you to be my girlfriend at the concert. I invited you with the intention. I like you a lot. So, we are together. Jessie, you are my girl."

"Sweet, I'm so glad, now let's enjoy the concert."

They arrive at the venue, Chris finds a parking lot and pays the lot attendant ten bucks and parks the car. Chris and Jessie hold hands, they walk energetically to the arena's entrance.

After the concert, Chris and Jessie drive back to the house and kiss each other goodnight. The next morning, Tanner asks Jessie how the concert was.

"The band was amazing. It was so loud, I couldn't hear too much, but I still enjoyed it. There was a mosh pit, of course, but it was well controlled."

"So cool, Jessie."

"Yeah, and the best part, Tanner, is that we are dating now."

"What! Are you serious?"

"Yes! Why are you yelling at me, Tanner?"

"He is the leader of our group; don't you think it is wrong for you to be with him?"

"No! I don't, and actually, I thought you would be happy for me."

"HAPPY, Jessie, how can I be happy about this?"

"I don't, I mean, you're acting jealous."

"I'm not jealous, especially not of you," Tanner shouts and then tried to calm down.

"I'm just saying because you are a real pain about this." Jessie continues.

"Well sorry!"

"Fine, but we need to keep this between us, unless Chris tells anyone. I need to keep it a secret." Jessie explained.

"I will keep it a secret, Jessie. It's your business, not mine. It is your life; do whatever you want!"

Jessie and Tanner go their separate ways, both feeling frustrated and confused. The confrontation is the beginning of the struggles they will go through with each other. Their relationship is healthy, but will it begin to weaken? Only time will tell.

Chris, Daren, and Thomas have been discussing things. They hate saying they are a group. They want a name. Something that gives them an identity. Daren isn't sure what they should call themselves. Thomas suggests calling themselves, *The Devoted*. Chris laughs at the name, and Thomas asks him why he is laughing. Chris smiles, and says, "Thomas, that name sounds like an adult Sunday school group. *The Devoted*, ha-ha-ha! I understand the meaning of being devoted, but it sounds silly."

"Well then fine! I guess I will not suggest anything anymore. What will we call ourselves Mr. Leader?"

"Hey, no need for the attitude, Thomas. You better remember to whom you are talking. I won't take that attitude, so consider this your first and only warning," he said with a stern voice of authority.

"Warning? Who or what do you think you are, that you can talk down to everyone?

"You don't want to find out."

"Fine! Chris, whatever, you are in charge."

"I think we should call ourselves, " *The Breed*," Chris suggested.

"*The Breed*," said Daren, not fully understanding the name.

"Yeah! *The Breed*" insisted Chris.

"What are we the breed of?"

"We are, The Breed—It sounds catchy," Chris said trying to be convincing.

"Uh! I don't think it does," Daren said.

"We will be a superior force; our Lord will lead us into victory, to combat Christianity. I will show Christians they are not better than us. We serve a better god. I am a son to Lucifer, and you are all under my command; under my authority by order of my master."

"What, Chris, are you for real?"

"Yes. And you better be on board since you chose to be here."

"I don't have a problem with what you're doing. What are we going to be doing?

"We will discuss that at a later time, Thomas. Please go and make the announcement that we are now known as The Breed."

Thomas walks through the hallway of the house trying to summon everyone to gather together

"Attention, I need everyone to come to the living room for an important announcement—this is mandatory," Thomas said.

Chris looks at Thomas and tells him to make the announcement. Thomas stands up in front of the group. "First off, Chris will be assigning section leaders soon you will be told if we chose. Secondly, we came up with a name for ourselves. We are called *The Breed*. When, or if asked what you belong to, you will say, "I belong to The Breed." If they question what it means, say It's my family, That's all. You're all dismissed."

"Well, Chris, how was that?"

"That was fine, Thomas. I am proud of you."

Chris is unchanged in his desire to be a strong leader. Chris believes in the power of darkness, and the authority he received from Lucifer. He's still blind that Lucifer is Satan, and he is a puppet controlled by Satan and his demons. Satan deceived him.

The Breed is Chris's creation, his family. He gains full reign and control as he listens to the voices inside to guide him. He's in a state of mind that is going to lead down a path that is dangerous. Power is his only desire. Filled with what he thinks will lead him to ultimate greatness.

There are those who, in their hearts, do not want to follow Chris down this path. One person is Tanner. She is not going to follow, and although she fears him. She backed down from Chris only to show him support until she finds the right time to leave. From what she knows about Chris; her best move is to run away where he can't find her. She believes if he does, something terrible will happen to her. Maybe she can try reaching out to someone for help. The battle in her mind is a matter of life and death.

Chris calls Daren to his office to discuss the opportunity of going out into the community to find homeless people to recruit. Chris wants to expand the group, so he can set up channels to build up an army. Daren tells Chris "I don't have a problem doing that, but I'm concerned about bringing people in we that we have no idea about."

"You let me worry about that, Daren,"

"Okay, boss, I trust your decisions."

"Good, then find an area downtown to search in. Explain what we offer, and if they seem interested, set up a time for me to interview some of them. Then we will narrow down who we will invite in. Can you send in Tanner, please?"

"Sure thing," Daren walks down the hall to Tanner's room.

"Tanner, Chris wants to see you."

"Okay, where is he?"

"He's in his office."

"Okay, I will be on my way," Tanner stops what she is doing, and walks to Chris's office.

"Hello, Chris."

"Hello, Tanner, thank you for coming. I want to use you for a particular mission."

"Mission?'

"Yes, a mission. I want you to go out and meet some teens in the area. Find out if any stand against Christianity, and those who don't believe in anything. You can act any way you wish. Is this something you can do for me?"

"I think I can pull that off. Just one question."

"Okay, what's your question?"

"What if I meet people that want to ask me a lot of questions. Why am I asking people questions?"

"Well, if that happens, simply say you want help people, nothing more."

"Ok, Chris, I will do it," Tanner said. She feels torn inside; heartbroken Zaga is gone—no one has her back now.

Chapter 13

Connor begins his days in prayer. He is working hard at changing his life. "Lord, I thank you for my family. You have blessed us in so many ways, and I'm grateful for you; I praise your holy name Lord. Please fill my spirit, and my heart with your love. I ask this in Jesus name Amen."

"Connor, you need to hurry, you will be late for work,"

"I'm on my way down, Dear."

"Is everything okay?"

"Yes, Theresa, everything is fine. I was praying. We are starting the new project on the other side of the city today."

"Oh! What is the firm doing?"

"We won the contract to design the new stadium for the city, but don't spread the word. I'm not sure if I will be home for dinner, but I promise I will call to inform you."

"Awesome, God is so good; Congratulations," Theresa said.

"Thanks, babe, I love you."

Theresa walks upstairs to check on Stephen. He's been home for two days since having surgery.

"Hey, Stephen, how are you doing today, Honey?"

"Mom, please, the whole honey thing."

"Oh, sorry I forgot."

"Okay. I'm better, a little sore and dehydrated."

"I will go make you some soup; maybe that will help." She walks downstairs to the kitchen to make him food and sees Marcy.

"Oh! Marcy, I thought you left for school."

Torn

"Nope, I am taking today off. There are things I need to get done, and I don't have time to sit in class today. How is Stephen?"

"He's fine. He said he is dehydrated. I am going to make him some chicken soup and give him some Gatorade. Are you sure you should miss class?"

"Yes! I'm sure Mom. I'm doing fine, so missing a day won't hurt me. I have a lot to do."

"Okay, well I hope your day goes well…be safe."

"I will."

Marcy gets into her car and drives off. She is on her way to the church. She wants to talk to Pastor Shane. Marcy made the appointment without her parents knowing about it. Marcy pulls into the church parking lot, and parks as close as she can to the office entrance. Once Inside, she tells Tamika Williams, the church receptionist, that she has an appointment with Pastor Shane.

"Let me tell his secretary you are here, please have a seat," Tamika said. A few minutes passed before Cindy Rhodes, Pastor Shane's secretary appears.

"Hello Marcy, glad to see you, sweetheart."

"Hi Cindy," Marcy replied, hugging Cindy. "How is your family doing?"

"They are doing well. My husband, Dale, is working hard these days, and Scott spends time volunteering downtown with other church members on Friday and Saturday's. They witness to people and help pass out food."

"I'm sure Dale wishes he was home. He still drives over the road, right? Marcy asks.

"Yes! He sure does,"

"Well, it's a tough job."

"Yes, it is."

Cindy knocks on Pastor Shane's door, "Pastor."

"Yes, Cindy."

"Marcy Smith is here."

"Oh, please show her in."

"Hello, Pastor Shane!" Marcy said as Cindy left the office.

James Owens

"Hi, Marcy. So, what brings you in on a school day," He said laughing.

"Right! I'm here because I want to talk to you about a letter that was left at our house by an unknown person."

"What do you mean, Marcy?"

"Well, when we came home from church one day, there was a note on my car."

"What did the note say?"

"It said that our family might be in danger."

"In danger?"

"Yes, and it was left by someone associated with my brother."

"I'm quite surprised that it is you tell me this and not your parents."

"Well, Pastor, my mom is busy with my brother, and sister. My dad is busy with work."

"Okay, well I understand. So back to the letter then."

"Okay, well the letter is disturbing to me. I mean for someone to say we might be in danger, does that mean my brother will hurt his own family?"

"Well, Marcy, we should not assume what he may, or may not do. However, I will tell you I had an encounter with Chris, and to be honest, it wasn't him."

"What do you mean?"

"What I mean is, I felt a strong evil presence. I think the enemy is controlling him. It would not be Chris hurting people, but the evil within him."

"So, let me ask you this then, Pastor. Do you think he is demon possessed?"

"Yes, Marcy, I do. I believe he is under complete control of the enemy, and it is the enemy's mission to hurt the church, the family, and the people of God. However, we have protection under the blood of Jesus. God protects us; he gives us guardian angels. Satan has no authority over us. We have authority over him, in Jesus name."

"Okay, so there isn't any real danger, but scare tactics to make us think that?"

"Yes, that is what I think, Marcy. We need to continue to seek God and allow him to intercede on our behalf."

"Well, Pastor, I wish I knew who left the letter on my car. I think a girl left it because it showed a lot of emotion. It doesn't seem like something a man would write, no offense."

"Well, we cannot say for sure, Marcy, but it very well could be. You should pray about this, seek God, and ask him to reveal this mystery to you. This person may fear for their life also. This person went out of their way to do this; remember that."

"I never thought of that, Pastor. You're right, this person may be risking their own lives to keep my family informed, and safe."

"Possibility."

"Well, I guess we wait and see, Pastor."

"That's all we can do. Thank you for coming by and confiding in me."

"Of course, Pastor, it's a pleasure to speak with you. See you in church on Sunday."

Marcy leaves Pastor Shane's office, she walks down the hallway with her head down, and bumps into Pastor Mark. He is talking to Mary Collins, his new secretary. Mary is twenty-two years old and attractive.

"Oops!" She laughs frantically. I should watch where I'm walking."

"Happens to me all the time, Marcy." He laughs with her. "What a way to run into each other, right?"

"Mary, I will talk to you later, make sure you finish the plans I showed you."

"Okay, Pastor."

"How are you doing, Marcy?"

"I'm well, how about you?"

"I'm doing fine. Hey, how is Stephen?"

"Oh, he is better."

"I'm glad he is better. I wish he were here in youth group. But I'm sure he will be back soon."

"Oh yes! He will enjoy being back; he loves being around you."

"I like being around him too. I look forward to seeing him; maybe I can stop by for a visit?"

"I'm sure he would love that! Well, Pastor Mark, I need to be going, busy day ahead of me."

"Okay Marcy, Have a blessed day."

Marcy gets in her car to go home. While driving, she starts praying. "Lord, please reveal to me who this mysterious person is. I believe, Lord, that this person needs help, and I pray that you lead them into your light. Amen."

Marcy decides to take a long way home. She searches her heart for answers from God. After driving around for about an hour, she pulls into the driveway. Arriving back home, her mom meets her outside.

"Marcy, where have you been?"

"I have been out doing things, Mom. I told you I had things to do. Please don't treat me like a child."

"I'm sorry you see it that way, Marcy, but I need you to tell me these things, okay? I lost one child already."

Mom, seriously! Chris quit on this family, stop with the guilt trip. He made his own decision; you didn't decide for him. I don't want to hear you say he is not a part of this family. He is our family, and he will come back someday."

Theresa took her right hand and smacked Marcy across the left side of her face. "Don't you dare stand there, and lecture me, girl!" Marcy's head turns from the swift blow. She drops her backpack as tears begin to run down her face. She runs upstairs and slams her bedroom door. Marcy sits on her bed crying, hurt that her mother slapped her face.

Theresa's cell phone rings.

"Hello."

'Hey, babe! I told you I'd call.'

"Hi, dear. What time do you think you will be home?"

"Well, I may be late, babe. We are just finishing off some details, so a couple of hours."

"Wow, Connor, that is like 7:00 p.m."

"Theresa, this job is important, okay? Is everything good at home?"

"Yes. Marcy and I had a spat, but everything is fine."

"Do you want to talk about it tonight?"

"No."

"Okay, I will be home in a couple of hours."

"Okay, I love you."

"I love you too."

Connor wonders what happened between his wife, and daughter. His day is now over, and he is anxious to get home. He pulls into the driveway, turns the car off, and as he gets out of his car, he is greeted immediately with a hug from Theresa.

"Oh, honey, I love you so much," She said, kissing him.

"I love you too, babe. Are you sure you're okay?"

"Yes, I'm happy you're home. I haven't been showing it lately, but I do care about us. I care about our family, especially Christopher."

"Wow, Theresa, I haven't heard you say his whole name in, well, in quite a while."

"Well, I am turning over a new leaf, and I'm going to look at things as God looks at them."

"Sounds like a plan," Connor said. They walk inside and sit down for dinner.

The next morning, everyone is getting ready for their day Marcy, and her mother speaks briefly. "I'm sorry, Marcy; I was wrong. I am so ashamed of what I did," Theresa said, realizing how much she hurt Marcy.

"I love you, Mom. I forgive you," She said while hugging her mother. The two held each other tight for a few minutes.

"Would you like to go to a women's prayer group at church? They meet at 3:30 p.m."

"I can't make it, Mom. My last class gets out at 3:45 p.m."

"Okay."

Everyone leaves to go about their day, Theresa checks in on Stephen, and Sammy before she starts to clean the house. Stephen is sleeping, probably from the pain medication. She goes downstairs, checks on Sammy in her playroom, and then puts on her favorite radio station. Her favorite song comes on, and she begins to sing. The presence of the Lord is all around her.

"Lord, fill me with your spirit. You are my God, and I praise you. Thank you for giving your son Jesus so that all people can receive salvation. You are the mighty God." I pray for your guidance in my life. I want to be a woman of God, a good mother, wife, and friend. Lord, I pray for my Son Christopher. I place him in your hands. Speak your word into his heart and show him you are still there. Lord, whoever put this note on Marcy's car, I lift them up to you. I pray that whoever it was, they will listen to your voice, and embrace your love. I ask these things in Jesus mighty name Amen."

Theresa's spirit lifted. She cleans the entire downstairs of the house. She gets Sammy from her playroom, takes her by the hand, and they dance all around the living room. Sammy is having fun with her mother. Theresa looks at the clock and realizes time has flown. She orders pizza for dinner. Stephen wakes up and can walk, so he makes his way downstairs to the kitchen. "Son, you're up! Oh! God is an awesome God!" She starts waving her hands up in the air praising God.

"Hi, Mom, you're not going crazy, are you?"

"Yes, Son. I'm going crazy for JESUS!" She shouts.

"Hey, guys, what's going on?" Marcy asks.

"I'm Praising God."

"What's for dinner?" She asks her mom; ignoring her mother's emotional episode.

"Oh! I ordered pizza."

"Yes! Pizza!" Stephen shouts. "I hope I can eat it ha-ha."

"I'm sure you can," Marcy said.

Theresa turns her attention to Sammy. "So, little girl, what do you think about going to the park tomorrow?"

"Yes! Momma, I wanna go."

"Oh, little excited, aren't we?"

"Yes momma, I'm happy excited."

Conner opens the door, home from work. He is the last to arrive home, and Sammy is excited. He is hoping he will get a few moments to settle down, but before he can even put his briefcase down. Sammy runs past everyone and leaps into her daddy's arms.

"Dadda!"

Torn

"Hey." He said kissing her on her cheek.

"I love you, daddy. You are the best-est daddy."

"I love you too; you're getting so big," Connor said.

"Yeah Daddy, I'm gonna be you next big girl," she says giggling.

"You bet you are! You are daddy's baby girl." He said as he puts her down.

When Marcy heard her father say that to Sammy, she cringed inside. That was her thing. Marc is daddy's baby girl. Sammy is taking her place, she thought. Connor puts his things down and walks into the kitchen. Marcy and Stephen are already eating the freshly delivered pizza.

"Hey, Marcy, how is college going? What is the college group at church doing these days?"

"Well, Dad, school is going fine. At Church, we are going over some things about relationships and how to maintain the ones and start new ones. Keep our faith, and morals in place to make moral decisions."

"Wow, that seems awesome."

"Thanks."

"What about you, Stephen? How are you?"

"Fine, I guess."

"Do you miss youth group?"

"I like being around Pastor Mark."

"Well, I'm sure he feels the same way. You two are close and have a bond since Chris left." As soon as he mentioned Chris, Stephen put his pizza down and ran upstairs without any regard for pain. Connor was at a loss for words; he didn't understand why Stephen ran off.

"Had to bring that up, didn't you, dad?" Marcy asked.

"What! What did I do wrong?"

"It still hurts him. You need to leave it alone. Let Stephen heal," Marcy said.

"How am I supposed—"

"There is nothing you can do to make it better, just be supportive, and don't talk about Chris unless Stephen comes to you about it," Theresa said while Marcy goes upstairs to check on her brother.

Chapter 14

Tanner accepted an assignment given to her by Chris. This assignment is to recruit people. What she will do is look for teenage runaways, and people who are rejected by their families Those rejected by society.

She worries what will happen, especially now. Chris wants to bring more people into the group. She doesn't comprehend this and is unsure of his intentions when it comes to any new members. Tanner only took this assignment hoping to find a way out, away from Chris, and disappear. She is afraid of Chris, and afraid if she shares her feelings with someone they would tell him.

Jessie wants information about Chris's intentions. She walks into Chris's office to talk to him. Out of the corner of Chris's eye, he sees her coming. Chris is always one step ahead of anyone coming to him. He turns in his chair and smiles at her.

"Hey, Jessie, how are you?" he asks as he pulls her in close to kiss her.

"What a kiss, I'm good, Chris, thanks for asking. Her face bright red from blushing. She then asks him, "I was wondering how things are going, and finding out what decisions you made or will make."

"Well, to be honest with you, it's none of your business what I am thinking or deciding."

"Hey, I'm your girlfriend. How can you talk to me that way?"

"I will talk to you any way I deem necessary. Don't question me or attempt to think you can pry information from me."

Torn

"I'm sorry, I didn't mean to upset you. I thought—"

"That's your first mistake. Don't think you can't understand me."

"Fine! Goodbye! *Wow, what is his problem today?*"

Confused about her interaction with Chris, she walks to her room. She can't believe the way he is acting, and her feelings are hurt. She lays on her bed and cries until she falls asleep.

Daren decides to go out on the streets and see what kind of potential people he can find to bring to Chris. While he is walking down the street, he spots Rocco at a stop sign. He yells out to him, and Rocco shouts out, "What up, bro?" Daren shouts back, "Not much, haven't seen you in a long time. Where ya been?"

"School, man, hittin' the books. Hey, I have to go. Tell Chris I said hi."

"Okay, I sure will. Peace bro." Daren walks down the sidewalk, and a girl dressed like, well, like she is homeless.

"Hello there."

"Hello."

"What is your name?"

"Chelsea. What's your name?"

"Daren, glad to meet you."

"Nice to meet you too."

"Chelsea, do you have friends out here?"

"Nah, not really."

"Say, have you ever considered joining a group? One that could support you the same way it has with many others?"

"I ain't no gang girl, bro. I'm not into selling myself neither."

"Whoa! Hold on. I'm not talking about it like that, okay?"

"What do you mean then? Don't give me lies I want the truth."

"I mean joining a group of people like myself, where you're not judged, or condemned for being who you are. Being cared for, loved, fed, and sheltered Chelsea."

"So, what's this group all about?"

"We look after each other, and we don't let people rule our lives. We have a leader named Chris; he is very passionate about helping people." He said, trying to intrigue her mind.

"So, this guy Chris, he is in charge of you guys? Weird if you ask me."

"Well, yeah, but not to the point of telling us what we can wear, or how to act. Chris guides us into spiritual freedoms, and he teaches us how to stand against our enemies."

"Well, that sounds cool, but why me?"

"Well, you look like you can use some friends. I would like for you to meet Chris, and let him tell you more, okay?"

"Yeah, cool, when we gonna do it?" She asked. "I mean if you are telling me the truth. Why should I go off with you to meet some other guy?"

"I understand. I felt the same way at once."

"Alright, I'm down."

"Okay, here is the address. You can meet us there tomorrow at noon."

"I'll be there, and you better be. I don't like being played."

"Yep." He winks as he walks away.

Daren continued with his recruitment efforts, but the day dragged on. Not too many people he came across were interested in what he has to offer. Daren managed to talk to a few people about meeting with Chris. The others shrugged him off and didn't care about what he had to say. At one point, one guy told him to step off, or get busted up. Daren called it a day, he returns to the house and tells Chris how his efforts went.

"How did things go Daren?"

"So, things went well today."

"What do you mean by, well?"

"Oh, hey real-quick, guess who I saw today?"

"Who?"

"Rocco. I couldn't believe it. I haven't seen him in like two months. He told me to tell you hello."

"Well what-do-ya-know, I wish I would've seen him; I miss that boy."

"Well, I talked to a lot of people, and man I will tell you there are a lot of people sore in their hearts. People didn't want to hear me and told me to leave, or they would beat me up. I was able to reach a girl named Chelsea, and a few others named Tobey, Max, Mark, and Jenny."

"Oh! Okay, well, you had a productive day, Daren. What did these people say?"

"Well, most of them were interested as soon as I told them about us. I told Chelsea to meet me at the secondary address around noon, so that she can meet you, and then I will bring the others as well."

"Ah! Sweet, sounds good. Do the girls seem vulnerable enough to join us? We need more girls here. I will sweet talk them if I need to," Chris said laughing.

"Yeah, it seems like the girls might join us." He said. "They want security and off the streets."

"Ah," Christ said.

Daren left Chris's office, and Chris gets up to go into the hallway. He wants to talk to Jessie about their argument. He wants to resolve any issues that can keep them apart. Chris has a desire to keep her close to him, and away from the other guys. Chris has a problem with jealousy.

"Jessie!" Chris calls, "Hello, Jessie, where are you?"

"I'm in my room, what do you want?"

"I want to talk; can you meet me down in the living room, please?"

"Fine, I will be there in a few minutes."

"Okay, I will be waiting."

Jessie prepares to go downstairs. She wonders what Chris wants to talk about; she walks downstairs and goes into the living room.

"Okay, Chris, what do you want?"

"I want to apologize for snapping at you today. I shouldn't have done that. I want you to start treating you better."

"Chris, you hurt me. I thought we were a team since we are together."

"Well, we are together. We are a team. I am in charge, and responsible for everyone."

"Okay, now since you brought it up, I have a question. Why do we need more people?"

"We need them. We need a greater force than the small group we currently are. We need to be a force to be seen and recognized. I am building a following, and I want people to see we have as many people as Christian Church's do."

"Well, I can understand that I think, and thank you for answering my question," Jessie said.

"You're welcome, but for future reference, don't question me."

"Yeah, Chris, I got it. I will not do it again." Jessie said.

Tanner returns to the house. She's been out trying to recruit people but wasn't so lucky in her search. Tanner walks upstairs; Jessie is crying. She knocks on her door.

"Hello, Jessie?"

"Yes, who is it?"

"It's me, Tanner. Is it okay if I come in?"

"Yes."

"Are you okay?"

"Yeah, I'm fine, I have some issues with Chris. I don't like the way he is treating me. One minute he is considerate, and then the next he is rude. He only cares about himself. I apologize, and then all he does is to belittle me again."

"Ah, relationship issues…I mean, it will happen. you guys will fight and argue."

"Yes Tanner, but he won't listen to me."

Tanner begins to laugh. "Well, that is like almost every guy out there."

Jessie starts laughing with her, "Yeah, I guess you're right."

"Laughter is medicine for the soul, and girl we need to laugh at this stuff going on."

"Yeah, you're not kidding. Sometimes I'm stressed out like things are one-sided, and I can't do anything right."

"I know what you mean. Chris changes so much day-to-day; how in the world can you predict him.?"

"Yeah, but I like him, and I won't leave him; I want to be the only girl he wants."

"Well, that's your choice. I'm not sure if this is what I want the rest of my life to be. I would like to live, and meet a man, and have a family someday."

"Great, Tanner, but you are not going anywhere unless Chris decides you can. I'm not suggesting you disappear either because he will find you."

"I'm not planning on it. I want the chance at a real life, which is why I came here when you, and Zaga offered to take me in. I wanted to get on my feet, but I don't even have a job or anything. There is nowhere to go. I am here, period! Chris has intentions, but he must understand we have our own lives too."

"Well, let's talk about this some other time, okay? I don't think it is wise to talk at this moment."

"Okay, I will catch up with you later," Tanner said. She walks into her bedroom and realizes that she let her guard down and told Jessie how she feels about being there. She is now worried Jessie will rat her out. She needs to trust that Jessie will keep it to herself.

Thomas bumps into Tanner in the hallway. She can't stand him. Tanner thinks he likes her, and it makes her skin crawl at the very thought of him touching her. To keep the peace, she shows common courtesy. Tanner learned to be fake, and tolerant from her childhood. She locks eyes with Thomas and begins the unwanted conversation.

"Hi, Thomas, how are you?"

"Why don't you tell me?"

"I don't understand. What do you mean?"

"I overheard you, and Jessie talking, okay? You're not happy here."

"That conversation was between us, as friends sharing some feelings to vent. And you had no right to listen in on our conversation," Tanner screams as she tries to walk away.

"Where do you think you are going?" Thomas grabs her arm.

"Take your hands off me, Thomas! I mean it, let me go!"

"Fine! But I can't promise that I won't tell Chris."

"Do what you want, I don't care. I will tell Chris you were physical with me, and he won't like that."

"Whatever, you little brat. You are no one here. Chris could care less if someone hurt you."

"Whatever."

"Watch yourself, girl, I am warning you."

Cornered, she doesn't see a way out, so she screams, "Chris, Chris, please, where are you?" Chris runs upstairs, as Thomas runs away from her as fast as he can.

"What, Tanner, what's wrong?

"Thomas was listening to a conversation between Jessie and me, and we were only venting some feelings. Then he saw me in the hallway, and he grabbed my arm real tight."

"So, he grabbed you?"

"Yes, Chris, he did."

"Thomas!" Chris yells. "Thomas, come here."

Thomas came out of his room when Chris call for him.

"What, Chris, what's the uproar?"

"Tanner said you violated her, and Jessie's privacy, and that you restrained her from leaving, is this true?"

"Well, first off, I didn't violate anything or anybody. I was walking by, and Tanner said she isn't sure she wants to be here."

"No, not true, Chris, he is a liar! I never said that!"

"What did you say then?"

"I said I wanted a life where I can be married, and have a family is all."

"Okay, but we are your family.

"Yes, Chris, but why did he treat me that way?"

"Thomas, you will apologize to her, now!"

"Okay, fine. Tanner, sorry for grabbing your arm."

"Thomas, if you touch another female here, I promise you will regret it. Understand me?"

"Yes, I understand you."

She goes to her bedroom upset and cries.

Chris walks into Jessie's bedroom. He wants her side of the story. He opens her door and slams it shut behind him.

"Whoa!" She said. Startled at his abrupt entrance.

"I'm not here for romantic talk, Jessie!"

"Uh...okay, what is going on?" She asked, fearing something terrible just happened.

"I want you to tell me about the talk you, and Tanner had. And don't you dare lie to me."

"Well, she came to me because I was crying and upset about how you were treating me."

"Okay, and what did she talk to you about?"

"She said that she wanted to have the type of life where she could have a family."

"Is that all?"

"Well, no, she also said she wasn't sure if she will be here her whole life."

"So, she intends to leave us?"

"Well, maybe, but not us as in you, and me, but the group."

"I don't care how she meant it. We are all a family here. She needs to understand that we are here for each other. The house is not a prison to live in fear. We are offering you freedom to be whatever you want to be. I don't need trouble. We are a group of people open to serving one god, and that god is Lucifer. We rule with his will, and we accept new people based on the same principle. He is in charge, and he uses me to guide us where we need to go. Tanner needs to embrace who we, are and how we work."

"If she decides not to. Then what?"

"Then she will regret her decision to leave us."

"You are saying she can't leave if she wants to."

"No! If she leaves, I will punish her for leaving her blood, her god, and me, period!"

"She needs your permission from you or our god for her to live the life she wants to live?"

"EXACTLY, JESSIE, MY WAY—PERIOD!" He shouts at the top of his lungs.

"OKAY, FINE! I can yell too," she said. She leaves and walks down to Tanner's room. She wants to tell Tanner that Chris knows about her wanting to go.

"Hey, Tanner. Hello, are you in there?"

"Who is it?"

"It's me, Jessie."

"Yeah, come in."

"Hey, I want to tell you Chris knows."

"So what, who cares anymore?" She replied. "I guess you ratted me to your boyfriend?"

"No, I didn't, and you should care because he will not let you go. Tanner, you need his permission to leave, and that will not happen, so you must come to terms being here. Here refers to Satan as his god; he calls him Lucifer—It is best to obey him, okay?

"I will do what he wants, okay! I will not cause any more issues. You can tell him that I will do whatever he wants me to do. I will hit the streets again to find recruits to join us in his mission. I will try to bring in more girls."

"What do you mean more girls?"

"He told me he wants me to bring more girls."

"Well, he must have a reason, so do your best."

"I will do my best to please him, I'm tired, Jessie. I'm going to go to bed.

"Okay, you rest. You need it."

Chris isn't happy about the situation with Tanner. He has no intention of letting her go, so he decides to talk to Daren about it.

"Hey, Daren!"

"Yeah, Chris! What's up?"

"Hey, I need a favor from you."

"Okay."

"I need you to find someone to keep an eye on Tanner."
"Why?"
"I need to know where she is; she is supposed to be recruiting for me."
"Okay, no problem. I will take care of it."
"I need to make sure she doesn't pull any stunts."

As Chris leaves Daren's room, he sees Thomas is down the hallway, so Chris runs down to catch up to him.

"Thomas, hold up a sec."
"Hey, what's up, boss?" He said. "Why are you so out-of-breath?"
"Uh, I just ran over here. Anyways, Thomas, thank you for going along with the whole apology thing."
"Huh? What do you mean?"
"I mean I don't care if you apologize or not. Tanner needs to be kept in check.
"Okay, Chris, no problem."
"I have some shopping that needs to be done."
"I don't want you to go out alone."
"Take another member, and get what's on this list, nothing more, and nothing less. We have some preparations to make, so make it quick."
"Okay, be back soon," Thomas said. He looks over the list. Shotgun shells, ropes, duct-tape, ten gift cards of a hundred dollars each, and mountain dew, *"Weird."* He asked Daren to go with him, and he agreed to go.

Marcy and Stephen talked about Chris. Stephen felt, so much better pouring his heart out to Marcy. Theresa kept Stephen home from school. Marcy is about to start her homework; she has a lot to read for her Psychology class. Her mom interrupts her. She asks, "Marcy, will you go to the store to pick up a few things for dinner?" Marcy let's out a sigh and agrees to go. Her mom gives her fifty bucks. She leaves the house and heads out. When Marcy arrives at the store, she looks at her mother's list of needs. She needs to buy ground beef that is eighty-five percent lean, Italian breadcrumbs, eggs, ketchup, and a twenty-four pack of Pepsi. Her mom is most likely making meatloaf for dinner. She groans and takes a shopping cart. She walks the necessary aisles to get everything.

As she walks to the soda aisle, she bends down and picks up the Pepsi. She walks to the front of the store to check out, and a man is staring at her in the checkout line. Feeling awkward, she hopes to get out of the store and go home without any problems. The cashier gives her the total. "Thirty-eight dollars, and seventy-four cents, ma'am," The clerk says. She scrambles to find the money her mother gave her. The bag boy comes over to bag her groceries and recognizes her.

"Hey, Marcy! How are you?"

"Oh! Hi, Micah, how are you doing?"

"I'm doing good, thanks for asking. Say, I heard about your brother."

"Who? Stephen?"

"No, Chris! I heard he up and moved out a couple of months back."

"Yeah! He did. How did you…"

"Well, if church walls could talk, right? I overheard some people talking about it around the church. It isn't mine, or anyone else's business to gossip about it, but word got around."

"Thank you, Micah."

"Thanks, and hey, don't worry about the Smith family curse talk going around either!"

She walks out of the store furious. "*What family curse,*" She thought. Who is spreading rumors around about her family? She loads the bags into her car and pulls out of the parking lot. She notices the man that was behind her in the store in her rearview mirror. She thinks to herself, "*He is creepy.*" She wants to go home, finish her schoolwork, and forget about the whole thing; except for what Micah told her.

Chapter 15

Saturday afternoon. Daren gets ready to head out hoping the people he is trying to recruit into the breed will show up. For his sake, he hopes so. He leaves with Tanner and drives to the site within twenty minutes. Daren's recruits arrive at the address; they are right on time. They met the recruits and drove them to a local abandoned warehouse with broken windows, and rusted doors.

"Okay, people, when you meet Chris, you will show your utmost respect, and listen to what he has to say. Chelsea, you're first with Tanner."

"Okay, Chelsea, let's go,"

They all enter the building. They came to the center and stopped. Tanner and Chelsea walk into another area in the building where they are to meet Chris. Tanner looks around. She hears a noise from behind her. She turns and sees and a large industrial door open. To her surprise, Chris is in an old Camaro with Rocco. Rocco and Chris exit the car and walk toward the girls.

"Hello, Chris," Says Tanner with Chelsea by her side.

"Hello, you remember Rocco, don't you?"

"Yes, I do. How have you been Rocco?"

"I've been fine, thank you for asking. So, who is this lovely lady?"

"This is Chelsea. She may be worthy to be a member."

"Chelsea, I'm delighted to meet you," Rocco said as he kissed her hand, a perfect gentleman, and charming as well.

"Thank you, and the pleasure is mine."

"My name is Chris."

"Chris, nice to meet you."

"So, tell me, Chelsea, why do you want to be in the breed?"

"I was told you take people in without judgment, you shelter people, and feed them, give them freedom of religion. You genuinely care for people."

"This is true, Chelsea. We are family here; would you like to be a part of this family?"

"Yes, Chris, I would like that."

"Are you aware of who we serve?"

"I don't care. I want to belong somewhere. My life hasn't been easy, and I want a new start."

"Well, Chelsea, today you are truly blessed because you are a perfect fit for our family. Welcome home sister," Chris said, hugging her. Rocco's eye is on the girl. Something about her that stands out to him. He thought they had met before, but he dismisses the thought.

"Tanner, take our new sister home please, and show her around the house. Introduce her to the family. Give her clean clothes and prepare her a hot meal to eat. Show her a room she will be sharing with another female member."

"Okay, Chris. Let's go, Chelsea, follow me. Oh wait, Chris, we need to wait until you finish with the interviews. We came with Daren."

"Okay, no problem."

Chris interviews the other recruits while Rocco keeps an eye out for intruders. Chris decides to accept everyone if they are an asset he can use. Daren and Tanner drive back to the house and introduce them to everyone. Everyone is friendly, and are getting along well, except for one, Scott. Something isn't right with him. Chris and Rocco think he shouldn't be here. Chris made a lousy choice in accepting him. In reality, Chris believes he might be a spy sent to the house. He isn't taking any chances.

The others, Mark, Tobey, Jenny, and Max, are in the age range from sixteen to twenty years old. The breed is getting bigger, and the mission will soon be underway. The recruits will serve a purpose, and Chris can't wait to see how far into the darkness they will follow him. Once he unleashes his rage on the church of God; it will be something they had never seen before. What will happen next, Chris keeps that under lock, and key. Lucifer is about to bring destruction down on God's children.

Sunday morning. Everyone is rushing to be ready for church. Sammy is pitching a fit as Marcy is trying to do her hair. Breakfast will be cereal so that the family won't be late for church. They arrive, and the sanctuary is filling fast. Connor tries to find enough seats for his family, minus Sammy who is in children's church. He looks down each row; Frank is waving his hand. Frank whistles to him and points out seats he saved for them. Connor and his family make their way over and place their Bibles down. He lets out a sigh of relief and says, "Thanks, Frank. Man, I thought we were out of luck."

"No problem. I figured you'd be late since I beat you here."

"Yeah! Funny, let's enjoy the service, huh?"

"Wow! Connor, the message was amazing this morning. I mean, the pastor finished strong. I felt such conviction during the service. We are staying in our comfort zone, and God is calling us out. We should be out ministering in our spare time to reach the lost for Jesus. God is moving in me. I have a passion for reaching people. I'm not sure who I'm supposed to reach, but I have a fire burning inside. We can help people, and we need to start."

"God will lead and take us through it. I hope we can help those in need, and you're right; we need to step out of our comfort zone and do more. God gave Pastor Shane a strong message, he preached it right, and the people heard it."

"Hey, Dad," Marcy said.

"Yeah, Marcy, what?"

"I don't think Pastor Shane wants a message to simply be *heard*, and I believe he wants the message to take God's word to give life where death abounds. Actions speak louder than words, and I think that is what he was trying to say. I don't mean Pastor Shane either. I mean God.

We are to come out of our comfort zone like Mom said and penetrate areas where the devil has a stronghold."

"Good point. I think you heard what you needed to. We need to seek God what does He have in store for us. Maybe we are to be a church body, reaching out to our community, or maybe on a personal level. I'm not sure yet."

"Connor, I think God is calling us to reach out, and the church as well. All I know is a real spiritual battle is going on, and many people don't even realize they're in it. What do we do when we run into someone possessed?" She asked, "Demons are real. Many people have lost sight of it."

"Well, Marcy says. "We beat those spirits up in Jesus name, and we stand firm in His presence. Allow the power of God to cast it out. Then we tell them what Jesus has done, and how they can receive the gift of salvation." They continued their talk about Pastor Shane's message all the way home.

Connor has been working on a massive architectural project. He is still drawing up some new ideas. This could launch his firm and give him some significant recognition.

Marcy is working hard in college, but her social life isn't healthy. She is more focused on her schoolwork. Marcy is ignoring her friends at church. She is hiding the fact she has a crush on Pastor Mark. She's not sure if it is the right time, but she wants to tell him. Marcy dreams of having his last name, Fields. Maybe she will write him a letter to express her feelings.

Stephen is healing up quite well. He is still working hard playing his guitar. He enjoys youth group more now that he and Pastor Mark are so close. They will be attending a youth conference in a month in Kansas City. Pastor Mark told him that his band will be playing a song during the worship service. Stephen is excited about it, so he is practicing—a lot. It will be a big-time moment for him. He can showcase his talent. He wants to represent his church, his youth group, and his family.

Pastor Mark said to Stephen, "This will be your time to give all you have to God. We are not here to please man. If we can touch one person's life, we touch the heart of God."

Theresa and Sammy read the children's Bible so that Sammy can learn more about God. Sammy turned five-years-old a short time ago. She loves reading her Bible and praying with her momma each night. Sammy often tells her momma; she prays for her big brother Chris. Even though she barely knows Chris, she loves him. Sammy tells her friends in kindergarten, she loves Jesus, and that He will help them with everything. Sammy has such a sweet, young spirit.

Bright, and early Monday morning, Stephen gets a ride to school with Drake, a friend from church. He asks him how he is doing, given the fact he had surgery. He also asks him about Chris. Stephen tells him, "I don't know where he is, what he is doing, or if he ever will ever come home."

"It doesn't bother you at all?"

"Chris has been gone for a long time. I'm not interested in answering questions about him," Stephen said, cutting off the conversation. Drake didn't mean anything by it. Drake's dad parks his Tahoe and tells the boys to have a good day.

Marcy is driving to school, and some people are talking on a street corner; it comes off as odd to her. She thinks they are doing something illegal, like selling drugs. Stuck at the traffic light, Marcy begins to pray, waiting for the light to change. Marcy asks God if she should talk to them, but no answer came. The light turns green, and she drives away. Marcy arrives at school but can't concentrate in class. She decides to skip her last class to visit Pastor Shane. It will be an unannounced visit, but

James Owens

he will make time for her. Even if it is a quick five minutes. Arriving at the church, she walks in and asks Tamika if Pastor Shane is available.

"Yes, Marcy, he is. Let me tell Cindy you're here."

"Thank you."

"Okay, Marcy, you can go back. Stop by Cindy first; she will have to log you in since you're a walk-in," Tamika told her.

"Thanks again."

"Hello, Marcy, what a surprise," Cindy said.

"Oh! Thank you, I'm here for Pastor Shane."

"Okay, just sign in right here. I will let Pastor Shane know you're here; he only has about ten minutes before he leaves for a meeting."

"Okay, thanks."

"Marcy, Pastor Shane will see you now," Marcy walks to Pastor Shane's office.

"Hello Pastor, I am sorry to drop by, but I need to talk to somebody."

"Tell me, what's on your mind"

"Well, Pastor, since your sermon last night, I have been confused about what to do. I drove to school this morning and saw some people talking on a street corner, and, well, I thought maybe I should stop and talk to them about God."

"Did you?"

"No, I didn't."

"What can I do to help you, Marcy?"

"I've been down. I even skipped my last class because I couldn't concentrate at all today. I need answers, Pastor. I need to understand what to do when I come across opportunities like that when I'm alone."

"Well, Marcy, all I can say is you need to listen to your heart. God will speak to you when leading you somewhere and when to stay away. You have a real desire to reach people, especially since Chris; however, you need to yield to the Holy Spirit and let Him guide you."

"How do I discern, Pastor? How can I tell when God is leading me to do these things?"

"Marcy, that is something you will need to pray about and seek God. That still, small voice that not only convicts us when we sin, but that voice tells us that God brings people across our path for a reason.

God will lead you. I believe you don't second-guess Him. He is with you; He will never leave you. With His guidance; you have nothing to fear.

He is always with you. When God calls us to fulfill a plan, He will never leave it unfinished. I believe we have a calling to deliver people from sin, demonic possession, and addiction. Many people are depressed, sad, and are even mad at God. A dark cloud covers our nation and our cities; we need to fight for those who still need God. We can no longer go to church on Sundays and Bible study on Wednesday night. We must come out from behind the walls of the church.

We have to go where the battle is and take back that which the devil has stolen. Your brother has been taken away by the enemies lies and deceit. He can't comprehend things that aren't real. He doesn't think with a clear and free mind. He is a prisoner in his own body because the enemy has taken him captive. I have seen these things before. I used to go down in the inner-city to feed, clothe, and preach to the homeless, the runaway teens. I saw firsthand, Marcy

"I met a man one time when I did the ministry. He told me his name if I can remember...I believe it was Zachias. I can't think of his last name. Anyways, I bring this up because he did the same thing we did. He had a little girl then, said she was his daughter. Her name was...??? Oh! Her name was Jessie—yeah, Zachias and Jessie Gant. I was impressed with his work. Eventually, though, I quit going, and I lost track of him."

Pastor Shane continues, "Anyways, this is hard Marcy. He's your brother, and you love him. I wish I could run and bring him home to your family today. But many people in our city are affected by things like this. They don't understand what is happening and they follow the lies thinking they are truths. All we can do is obey God and listen to the Holy Spirit. God has His plan for each of us, but we are all a part of a bigger plan, Marcy. That plan is the salvation of the lost and to deliver those in captivity."

"Wow! Pastor, I need to find a way to listen to Him. I have been so closed off from what He wants me to do; all I can think about is finding my brother. God will do it in his time. Until then, I need to seek what His plan is for my life."

"That's right, Marcy. Focus on the present, see what God has in store for you. He will lead you to the plan He has for you."

"Thank you so much, Pastor. I appreciate your counsel, as always."

"Well, Marcy, you are welcome; that's what I'm here for. Now you make sure you focus on your schoolwork! I'm proud of you."

"Aw, thank you, Pastor. I will."

Marcy left Pastor Shane's office, but she cannot help to stop by Pastor Mark's office. She peeked in, and Pastor Mark noticed her right away.

"Hello, Marcy, how are you?" He said, happy to see her.

"Oh! I am okay. I hope I'm not disturbing you."

"No, not at all. How is everything?"

"I want to tell you that Stephen has been so excited about the youth conference coming up; He is practicing a lot. He is working so hard for this."

"I'm glad he is working hard."

"Yeah! Well, I wanted to talk to you because I'm…uh…"

"Marcy, are you ok?" He said looking at her with curiosity.

"Yes! I, well, I wanted to tell you I have been trying to fight through some things that have been driving my life crazy."

"Like what? Can you give me an example?"

"Well, yeah! Well, I have a crush on you."

"Oh! I, well, uh, well, interesting, Marcy."

"Why is that interesting, Pastor Mark? It took a lot of courage to tell you."

"Yes, thank you. I have a crush on you too," Pastor Mark isn't sure if they can be together.

"Really?"

"Yes, and since I'm a Pastor, it appears a little out of sorts to approach you. I mean we are a bit apart in age. We can do nothing about this until I take care of something first."

"What thing, if you don't mind me asking?"

"I want to talk to your parents and Pastor Shane about this. I would like their permission to move forward with any relationship."

"I respect you, Pastor. Talk to them when the time is right."

"Will do, Marcy. You have a wonderful day."

Marcy gets in her car with her spirit leaping. She starts her car and drives home. Marcy is listening to her music, singing and just in such a shock and awe moment. She turns the corner and comes to a stop at a red light. Once the light turns green, she presses the gas and drives through the intersection; then out of nowhere, a man driving a pick-up truck tried to beat the red light he was approaching and T-boned Marcy's car on the passenger side. The truck hits her with such a strong force that it pushes her clear to the other side of the intersection. The airbags deploy, and glass shatters everywhere. Smoke rises from the tires as they screech until the car stop. Steam rises from the car's radiator; the smell of the coolant is in the air.

A man walking his dog witnessed the whole thing; he dialed 9-1-1 and told them about the accident. Emergency responders are dispatched to the scene. They arrived and checked both drivers. The driver of the truck is unconscious. The emergency responders are going to have to pull him out and rush him to the hospital. He is bleeding from his eyes and nose. They go to check on Marcy.

"Ma'am," they said, "hello. Can you answer me? Are you in any pain?" She doesn't respond.

"Captain, we have no response," The young firefighter shouted.

"Can you get her out, Jack?" He seemed unsure but replied, "I think so, but I'm not sure we should move her. I'm not sure what injuries she has since she is unable to respond, sir."

"Listen, you guys need to get her out of that car now! Put her on the board, strap her down, and put a brace on her neck.

"Come on guys, let's pull her out as gently as possible. Okay, on my count. One, two, three, pull! Come on—one, two, three, pull. Yes! Thank you, Lord. Let's secure her and get out of here C'mon move it, let's go!"

The EMT's took over and secured Marcy in the ambulance. They take off, sirens sounding loud as they drive off in hast. The firefighters also get the truck driver on stretcher board and EMT's strap him down and take him to the hospital. The police start asking witnesses about what happened. The man, who was walking his dog, told them he saw everything. He gave them all the details, but the police will still need more statements. Others can only provide a small amount of information. Police will have to access video from the traffic light's camera that will show what happened. At the hospital, Marcy and the other driver, now identified as Travis Keller, are being attended to for their injuries. Mr. Keller, for the moment, is at fault, pending official word from the police; will have his blood alcohol level checked. Marcy will have hers tested as well, just to be sure. Marcy is not showing any external injuries except for some scratches and some bruising.

"Doctor Adams?"

"Yes, nurse, what is it?"

"We have a young woman we have identified as Marcy Smith. She arrived unconscious. We are checking her vitals now. What else do you want to order?"

CT scan, it will show us if we should be worried about anything. I will do a full examination. Marcy? Hello, Marcy, respond, please! Okay, let's start an IV and keep an eye on her vitals. Do the CT scan as soon as possible."

The hospital gets ready to call Marcy's family; they were able to find the number from Marcy's cell phone, the police arrived to report the findings on the accident to the doctors. The impact of the crash could help the doctors to determine specific injuries.

"Have you contacted her family yet, nurse?" The officer asked.

"No, we were about to do that" She replied.

The police arrive at the Smith house before any phone call. The officer knocked on the door; Theresa walks down the hall and opens the door. "Hello officer, is everything okay?" She asked.

"Ma'am, I'm afraid to tell you your daughter, Marcy, has been in a bad car accident and is in the hospital."

"What? No!" Theresa screamed in shock.

"Ma'am, please come with us, call whoever you need to; we need to go."

Torn

"Yes, of course," Theresa begins crying hard. She was trying to pull it together. She just couldn't.

Theresa follows the police to the hospital, she calls Connor and tells him what happened. He hangs up the phone instantly and leaves work to go to the hospital. He calls Frank to let him he left the office. Frank calls his wife right away. He wants Karen to be there for them. Once he arrives at the hospital, Connor calls Pastor Shane and tells him what happened. Pastor Shane leaves the church, quickly getting his car and drives to the hospital.

Now, everyone has arrived, and they are seeking some answers to find out where Marcy is. The nurse asked them to have a seat in the waiting room. Connor, Theresa, Karen, and Pastor Shane all huddle together and begin to pray for her. "Lord God, we are here humbly before you and ask for your hand upon Marcy, Father. Lord, please give the Doctors wisdom; give them the knowledge to help her. I pray they find any injuries soon and that all will work out. Father, we ask this in Jesus name for her recovery, Lord. We also ask for the other driver in this accident; Lord, be with that person and their family in Jesus name. Amen."

"All we can do now is wait and have faith that all is going to be okay."

"I can't lose another child, Pastor. She has to be okay," Connor said as he is holding Theresa. Tears are flowing down his face. The family of the other driver, Travis, were also now in the ER waiting room. Time seemed to linger. "Who is going to pick Sammy and Stephen up?" Connor asked Theresa. He will be home soon."

"Karen is going to go get Sammy and Stephen from school and then she will come here. I spoke to her on the phone on my way to the hospital."

"Ok."

Karen walked in and hugged Theresa. She began crying furiously. Connor is sitting in a chair with his head in his hands. Time is moving ever so slowly the children came to the hospital with Karen. Theresa picks Sammy up, kissing her forehead. Sammy asks, "Why crying, Mamma?"

"Because Marcy is hurt, sweetie, we are waiting to see her."

"I sorry, Mamma. I love her."

Stephen is crying in his father's arms when the Doctor comes in he asks to speak with Marcy's family. Mr. and Mrs. Smith, I am Dr. Noel—"

"How is she, Doctor? Please tell me, how is my daughter?" Theresa asks.

"First, she is alive; second, we did a CT scan, and it has shown your daughter has some bruising and swelling on her brain, which is certainly causing her to remain unconscious at this time. Pressure is building up as well. We need a surgeon to come in and relieve the pressure. Then we will cross our fingers and hope for the best."

"Lord, please, help my daughter," Connor said softly.

"Please, Doctor, help our daughter," Theresa says.

The nurses prepare Marcy for surgery. The Neurosurgeon arrives at the hospital and scrubs in for surgery. The family waits patiently in the waiting room with Pastor Shane and their friends. Connor calls his parents to tell them what happened and to pray for Marcy. Rose answers the phone.

"Hello."

"Mom, Marcy was in a bad car accident and is having surgery on her brain. Please pray for her mom. I don't want to lose her."

"Of course, we will pray for her, Son. We love you, kiss Theresa and my grandkids for me. Tell Marcy we love her when she wakes up and we are praying for a full recovery." Rose said as she hangs up the phone.

Hours have passed and still no news on how the surgery is going. Pastor Mark has arrived now and wants an update on her. Pastor Shane tells him she's in surgery.

"Pastor Mark, thank you for coming," said Stephen. "It means a lot to have you here.

"No problem, buddy. I'm happy to be here. Well, I mean—I."

"I know what you mean."

The doctor finally comes out, and he meets with the family and their Pastors in the waiting room. "Mr. and Mrs. Smith," He said.

"Yes, Doctor?"

"Marcy is doing well. She made it out of surgery successfully."

"Thank you, Doctor."

"Yes, but, please keep in mind; we are not out of the woods yet. She is in recovery, and when she wakes up, she may not remember things. She could have memory loss, short term or long term; we don't know enough. The best thing you can do for her is to pray."

"Can we see her?" Theresa asked.

"Yes, of course, but only a couple at a time, okay?"

"Okay, doctor, thank you."

"You're welcome. Please excuse me." He said as he walks away.

Connor and Theresa went into the room to see their daughter. She is hooked up to machines, and bandages are on her head. They could not help but cry, and both of them held her hand and kissed her on her forehead; they told her they love her. They pray and ask God to place his hand upon her and to heal her. They left the room with tears, holding hands. Stephen asks to go in with Pastor Mark.

Connor tells him he can, and Stephen enters the room with Pastor Mark, tears filled their eyes. Stephen plunged into Pastor Mark's arms. He holds him tight as they cry together. They exit the room, everyone gathers again in the waiting room and pray. Pastor Shane did his best to assure them that God was with them and with Marcy.

"God's plan is one we all seek, Theresa; we must have faith in God and be strong for Marcy."

"I know Pastor," Theresa replies.

"Connor, you need to take the kids home and get some sleep, and Theresa you will need your rest. Marcy, she will want you here when she wakes up, I'm sure of it" Pastor Shane said.

"Thank you, Pastor, for coming. I will go, but I will be back first thing in the morning, okay babe?" Connor said.

"Okay, please be safe."

"I will."

Connor arrives home with the kids and gets Sammy to bed; she is tired from a long day. Stephen, tired as well, went to bed and Connor begins to pray in his room, asking God to be with his daughter and wife.

James Owens

He asks God for his children's safety, including Chris. "God, I am not sure what your plan is for my life, but Father, please take care of my daughter, your child, Father God. You are our God; you sit on the throne. In you I trust; may your will be done in Jesus name. Amen."

Chapter 16

It has been three weeks since the recruits have been in Chris's cult group known as, the breed, and Chris has been trying to intensify his plans. Chris has the urge for *The Breed* to have more significant numbers, and the efforts seem to be paying off. Jessie has been talking to as many girls as she can to let them know what the group has to offer them. She informed them they would be housed, fed, and those who join will have all the support they needed.

Jessie and Tanner have been at odds, the incident with Thomas. Tanner has been keeping her distance, and Jessie has done her part by keeping Chris up to date with her actions. The one thing Tanner wanted to avoid; she will no longer have privacy or freedom. She wants to live without looking over her shoulder in fear. Chris has never given her the impression he will let up in his efforts to keep control over her. Chris decides to call a meeting.

"Hey, Daren?" He said.

"Yeah, Chris?" Daren answered back.

"I need you to bring everyone together; we are going to have a quick meeting in twenty minutes."

"Okay, boss," Daren replies. He got on a small PA system to make the announcement.

"Everyone, listen up. We're having a meeting in twenty minutes. Chris requests everyone attends, so I expect Y'all there—no excuses, this must be urgent.

"Tanner!" Jessie yells.

"Yes, Jessie, what do you want?"

"You know we are having a meeting, right?"

"Yes, Jessie, I'm aware of it. I think everyone is. I'm going, don't worry," Tanner says.

"Okay, can you make sure to tell Chelsea? Yes, I will Jessie. Is that all?"

"Yes!"

"Chelsea!" Tanner called out.

"Yes, Tanner."

"We better go downstairs for the meeting."

"Ok."

Chris is standing in front of the living room. He is waiting for everyone to come in and sit down. He tells Daren, "Make sure they are all here, and once they are, announce that we will be talking our goals in an open forum." Daren was taken aback. Chris never had an open forum, but he agreed to Chris's wishes.

"Okay, everyone," Daren said. "C'mon, let's go. We need to start. Is everyone here?" "Yes," Jessie said. "Okay, Jessie, pass around the roster and make sure everyone signs his or her names just to be sure, okay?"

"Yep, you got it."

"Okay, everyone let me have your attention please. Chris has things he wants to speak to us about, so give him your full attention. These issues are important, and you need to act as such. You will be asked to participate; you need to make sure you're doing exactly that." Chris is a real leader; he is cunning. He wants only to pull them further in his cult to serve his and Satan's cause. He only recently began to acknowledge Lucifer as Satan, but he still called his religion "Luciferism."

"Thank you, Daren. Hello, my fellow members," They all reply. "Hello!"

"I am so thankful for you. I am pleased to be your leader and to act on everyone's behalf. We are entering a new phase, a new beginning. I will be assigning units to our group. Each unit will have a specific mission and a leader to guide you. *The breed* is us, and you will swear an oath to *the breed* and me. I will require you to do this whether you are new members or have been here for a long time. We have grown; sectioning off is the best thing for us to do at this point."

"I have here in my hand a paper. It has the oath to be sworn. It is a statement of loyalty: I _____, do hereby swear to volunteer and to be of service to *The Breed*. I swear to uphold the orders I am given to fulfill the missions before me and do so even if it takes my life. I will fight against Christianity, those who serve a God full of judgment and hate. I will show no mercy to them for they have none for me. I will stay true to my fellow members and not betray them."

"This is what you will swear to. Any new people that cannot do this, you're free to leave, as for the rest, this is your bond, you need to sign it. Do not betray your brothers and sisters; do not be like the blaspheming Christians. We are set apart. We are higher. Called to a greater purpose than those heathens. Any questions?"

"Uh, actually, I do have a question."

"State your name." Chris demanded."

"My name is Bruce Hamm, and I'm a new member. I was wondering about the whole hating Christians thing?"

"Good question, Bruce, and I will be happy to answer. Christians think they are inferior; they hate anything that goes against their Bible. They only care about themselves. Most of you are runaways, outcasts, or have no one at all, no family. We are your new family, and we are your brothers and sisters. Bruce, we have our god. The one we believe in, and he has shown us true blessings. Tell me, Bruce, why did you decide to be here? You can be murdered, dumped in a ditch, just another homeless casualty, another homeless person who dies and no one who will miss you."

"I'm here for the food and shelter. Jessie told us we could earn a *GED* if we wanted to, that this house is a house of hope. I'm not sure I can bring myself to hurt anyone who hasn't first tried to hurt me."

"I understand, Bruce. I will personally make sure you are in a section that does not require such things."

"Anyone else with any questions? No? Then let's move on. I want the oath done now, put it out of the way and designate each section and its leader." With the oaths taken, each member has signed their commitment—designations begin. Daren leads the first section; his members were Chelsea, Bruce, Sara, and Luke. Jessie leads the second section; her members were Bart, Mark, Matthew, and John. Thomas leads the third section; his members were Jenny, Max, Greg, and Tanner. Rocco leads the fourth section; his members were Allie, Tobey, Taylor, and John. Chris is proud of his accomplishments.

Three weeks have passed since Marcy's accident. She's been in a coma since that tragic day leaving the church. Her family has been by her side and praying she will recover and wake up. The hope is she will have no effects due to her injuries. Pastor Mark has been visiting every day, praying for her. Stephen has been keeping up with his activities and is about to be a part of a band performing Christian rock around town.

Sammy started kindergarten and seems to be doing well at the Christian school. Connor's firm sealed their deal on the architecture and construction work for the civic center arena and conference center. The two complexes are across the street from each other and connected by a six-way sky bridge for people to walk from one place to the other. Construction is to begin in about four weeks and scheduled to be complete a year and a half. What a massive victory for Connor as well as his firm. The firm has been struggling, and now he had landed the most significant contract the firm has ever seen. Connor and his business partner Frank, with whom he started the firm. They see this is their first step to bigger things; including getting the firm out of some old debts.

Theresa has made Marcy's college aware of her condition and asked them to do what they could to give her incompletes for her grades. Connor has not been able to spend much time at home over the last few weeks. Theresa has been holding everything down as much as she could. Her friend Karen, Frank's wife, has helped Theresa a lot with everything, including watching the kids. The pastors support the Smith family, as they endure hard times. And now, with Marcy in the hospital, it has become overwhelming for the family. The doctors have been very optimistic and have an excellent outlook for Marcy to recover and hope she will come out of her coma soon.

The telephone rings, "Hello."

Torn

"Mrs. Smith?"

"Yes!"

"My name is Dr. Alvarez. I am calling to ask if you and your husband would be available to meet with me around 6:00 p.m. concerning your daughter Marcy?" He asked.

"Well, yes Doctor, of course. Is everything okay?"

"Yes, Mrs. Smith, I need to explain some things to you and your husband concerning her care."

"Ok."

Theresa immediately calls Connor.

"Connor."

"Yes, babe?"

"I just got off the phone with a Dr. Alvarez, and he said he needs to talk to us this evening concerning Marcy's care."

"Well, what time? I can meet you at the hospital."

"6:00 p.m., Connor."

"Okay."

"I will call Karen, ask if she can take care of the kids." Karen is always happy to accommodate. She loves being around the kids. Theresa makes the call.

"Hello."

Hi, Karen. Can you come and babysit the kids for me? I'm leaving soon for the hospital."

"Sure, I can." Karen drives over to the house, and she brings some movies for Stephen and Sammy to watch. She arrives at the home promptly. She only lives about ten minutes away.

"Hello, Karen, I'm so glad you—"

"No problem, Theresa. It is the least that I can do."

"Please pray for us; the doctor called, and we are meeting with him about Marcy."

"I will keep you guys in my prayers."

Theresa has now left the house and is on her way to the hospital. She is being careful but is also driving with hast to the hospital to meet her husband and find out what the doctor has to say. When she arrives, she finds a parking space, Connor is coming to greet her. He's been sitting on a bench waiting for her. They finally greet each other, they hug, and Connor said, "God is here with us." After entering the hospital, they take the elevator to the 5th floor and then walk over to the reception desk.

"Hello folks, how may I help you?"

"Yeah! Hi, we are here to see Dr. Alvarez, we are the parents of Marcy Smith."

"Oh! Yes, the doctor is expecting you. I will notify him that you are here."

"Thank you."

Connor and Theresa walk to the waiting area, but before they could even sit down, a nurse walks in.

"Mr. and Mrs. Smith?"

"Yes," they reply.

"I'm Tonya. I am Dr. Alvarez's nurse. Please follow me; the doctor will see you now."

"Okay, thank you."

Tonya is a young nurse. She is beautiful with dark hair, blue eyes, about 5'4". Connor is looking the young nurse up and down.

"Dr. Alvarez, here are Mr. and Mrs. Smith," the nurse told him.

"Thank you, Tonya," the doctor replied as Tonya walked out of the room. Connor turned his head watching her exit the room. Theresa caught a glimpse of it in her vision and elbowed Connor hard in his ribcage.

"Hello, folks."

"Hello," Theresa responds.

"Mr. and Mrs. Smith, thank you for coming on such short notice. I have been concerned as to why your daughter, Marcy, has not come out of her coma. I'm a new doctor working here at St. Andrews, and I'm now the Doctor assigned to her care; I'm a neurologist, been one for twenty years now. I moved here from Chicago. I like to give some background on myself so that you may know me. However, I want to give it to you straight."

"I have some concerns for your daughter. The longer Marcy is in a coma, the more likely she will have memory loss. Marcy may experience amnesia, and we are certainly monitoring her for any signs of brain damage as well. I want to explain that there is a great neurological unit at another hospital."

"Uh, what can we do if—I mean, *when* she wakes up?" Connor asked.

"Please understand, Mr. Smith, I do not promise anything. All I'm saying is what we can look at it if, and I stress *if,* she wakes up."

"There's a hospital in St. Louis which has a phenomenal rehabilitation unit for patients like Marcy."

"No way that this is possible," Connor said.

"Doctor, I have a question," Theresa said.

"Yes, ma'am."

"If our daughter stays here and comes out of her coma, what will happen if she does have these effects you're talking about?"

"She will receive comprehensive care, Mrs. Smith; however, I'm not sure that we possess the same capabilities than hospitals who specialize in these cases."

"We are people of faith," said Connor, and we believe that God is with her; He will guide us through this."

"It is good to have faith in God, Mr. Smith, but you also need to have faith in medicine and the doctors caring for your daughter," Dr. Alvarez told him.

"I do, sir, but I am not going to move my girl all the way to the other side of the state, she needs her family and her pastors here."

"Mrs. Smith, do you understand what I'm trying to say?"

"Yes, Doctor, but I agree with my husband. Marcy needs us here, and she needs our pastors. We will not move her," She said as she held Connor as he cries. She whispers in his ear, "We're going to be okay, babe. God is with us."

"Is that your final decision then?" Dr. Alvarez asked.

"Yes, yes, it is, Doctor."

"Then we will do what we can from here, and I hope you pray hard for her because she will need it."

"We have been and will continue to do so, sir!!" Connor said.

"Goodnight, Folks," Dr. Alvarez replied.

"Goodnight," said the Smiths as they left the doctor's office.

Chris wants a rebellion of epic proportions; he wants this to take place soon. He addresses the cult he had designed and yelled out, "Are you ready!"

"Yeah!" They all cheered as if they had victory.

Jessie went to Chris when the meeting was over. She asks him about the Upper East Side and mainly Maple street. Chris designated that to himself.

"Chris?"

"Yes, Jessie."

"What's the big deal with the Upper East Side? Especially Maple Street?"

Chris answers, "Don't worry about it, Jessie. I will handle my part of town. I will deal with my people."

"Okay," Jessie replies. She overheard someone saying he was from the area; she knows this is a touchy subject for him. God help whoever decides to go over and cause trouble.

Now, with all things said and sections assigned. Everyone has gone their way to do what they want the rest of the day. Most of the guys go outside to play basketball while others stay indoors watching movies or play games on Xbox. Some are still unsure of what is happening; perhaps they don't have a full understanding of what joining means. They know they want something different and got more than they bargained. But now things were different; like they're supposed to worship Chris. He is barking the orders, and they obey him.

Tanner has always thought Chris is overpowering and controlling; she believes others were apparently right about him too. She is so upset over the fact that he has presented an oath to his little cult group with a ridiculous name. A name she discovered; was the name of the band he and Jessie saw in concert. "How crazy, he didn't even come up with it, " she says to herself. Zaga would never have done or approved of things like this. Zaga cared about the people he took in. He didn't have to call the group anything, and it wasn't a cult in her mind. Tanner misses Zaga very much, and now he is gone because of Chris. She has no choice; she must play along and follow his plans.

Daren has already begun to make plans for his section. He will have most of his people going in twos into churches in their area and obtain their service times. What kind of people attend and are they wealthy, poor, small families, prominent families. Then he will make sure that his section investigates each church by denominations, Baptist, Pentecostal, non-denominational. To sort out options for which churches to target. When his section attends the Church's and gather's the relevant information; Daren will report to Chris.

Jessie is extremely excited about her section's mission. She is to educate her section on their beliefs and then do outreach to others in the inner city where most of them came. Jessie is hopeful that her section will do the task Chris has set out for them. She wants them to excel at it; she has such a desire to please Chris.

Thomas is at a standstill until Daren gets information back to Chris. The churches he believes are perfect targets and make it into the papers. Once that is done. Thomas will work with his section on shopping for needed supplies. Mapping out the area where the churches are and the Pastors office hours. Thomas can scoop some dirt on them like a politician would do to his opponent—expose them to the media.

Rocco tells his section they will target popular Christian camps, youth camps, or young adult retreats. He has no heart; he cares for no one. Rocco lost his father, a construction worker who died on the job. Rocco became cold. He befriended Chris at the University and became closer when he found out Chris's dad owns an architect firm. The firm that has contracts with Miller construction; the company his dad died working for on the job. Chris has no idea, but Rocco targeted Chris and introduced him to Zaga.

He thinks Chris can overthrow Zaga at some point. Zaga is weak, pathetic, and too loving. With Chris in power, Rocco can influence him to target those responsible for his father's death. He has no regard for the feelings of those responsible. Rocco wants them to experience pain. Let them suffer loss. By him getting Chris, he started the hurt. Rocco senses it each time he follows one of his family members, even in the church they attend. He sits as close as possible without being recognized. Rocco's mission, seek and destroy.

Now, each section had planned their missions. Chris decides to go to his room and spends time alone. His bedroom is dark, somewhat cold. It is demonic, and he has pentagrams along with other logos he likes such as a goat heads with devil horns. He keeps little, dull lights on and has a small desk where he studies. Chris meditates, seeking Satan. He has discipline and patiently waits to hear from his master.

Time is passing by, and still, he sits waiting; a slight, evil moan takes over the room. A chill fills the air. As he sits on the floor, he calls out, "I'm here, I am your servant, here to please you and do your will," Suddenly, Chris is lifted off the floor in a seated position. Chris embraces the presence, the power, and a single teardrop falls from his eye.

Time seemed to stand still as Chris is meditating. The whole time Chris has been suspended in mid-air in a seated position. He is being held and moved by the powers of darkness. Chris doesn't like to be disturbed while meditating, but there is a knock on the door. He doesn't answer. He is absent from anything carnal around him. The knocking continues, and still, no response. He appears to be in the spiritual world, instead of the one around him.

After knocking several times and getting no answer, Tanner is suspicious and opens the door. She is startled and stricken with fear. She didn't expect Chris to be in a seated position, mid-air off the ground. With her presence unwanted in the room, a demonic voice screams out. Something grabs her arms and throws her out, and it slams the door.

Tanner is in tears, she runs to her bedroom and closes her door.

Sitting on the floor with her knees to her chest crying. She has never in her life witnessed such a thing, such an evil presence. Fear has multiplied in her, and she is completely helpless. There is no one she can trust. What will she do now? She entered the room knowing she shouldn't have and Chris will be furious. She fears him enough as it is. He indeed has the power of the devil! She is terrified. Traumatized by this whole experience. She cannot stay in the house or be with the group anymore. It is apparent to her that it's time to go. She gather's some of her things together. She puts them in a backpack and sneaks out the window to the roof. She slides down a pole on the side of the house and runs away. She has now deserted Chris and his cultic group; it is possible her life can be in danger now. She will try to find Zaga. She remembers him saying something about a place he spent time at—maybe he is there?

Chapter 17

As Connor and Theresa drive home from the hospital, they have not spoken a word to each other. They are confused about what they should do. They don't want to move their daughter to another hospital. Connor breaks the silence with a question for Theresa, one that stuns her.

"Theresa, would you be willing to relocate? Move our family, our lives, and go with Marcy if we allowed them to move Marcy to St. Louis?" Theresa is speechless! She has no idea why Connor is even considered it.

"Theresa, can you tell me what you think about the whole thing?"

"Connor! We will stay here, together. Marcy needs us to be strong and make wise decisions for her. I will not fight about this; I will not negotiate when it comes to where my daughter will be. Don't ask me again. She needs her family; do you understand me?"

"Good grief, babe, I didn't mean it to come across that way. You don't have to go all crazy and tear into me; it was a suggestion!"

"It was a ridiculous suggestion, Connor."

"Fine!"

Stephen is waiting for his parents to come home; he can't help but think about his sister. The car pulls into the driveway, and his parents are talking in the car. He is anxious to ask what is going on if Marcy is okay, but he is worried about asking; they seem very upset. He decides to ask since he is concerned about his sister. Connor and Theresa walk into the house.

"Mom, dad, how is Marcy? Is everything ok?"

"Yes, Stephen, your sister is fine," says Connor.

"Well, then why did you have to go?"

"Stephen, we will tell you later. Dad and I are very tired; we have a lot to think about."

"What! You mean you can't tell me something as simple as this?" He shouts.

"Stephen! You heard your mother. That's enough, drop it!" Connor yells.

"Why on earth are you yelling? What's going on?"

"Stephen, please! We can talk later!" Connor yells again.

"FINE!" Stephen said as he storms upstairs to his bedroom. He lays down on his bed, puts his headphones on and listens to music.

Theresa walks into the living room and thanks Karen for watching the kids. Karen can tell she is exhausted. Karen, however, has never been the kind of person to interfere in someone's business or in between couples and their problems. But she asks, "Is something going on Theresa?" Theresa replied, "No, but thank you for asking, Karen. Tell Frank that Connor will call him later." Karen gives a soft, "Okay," and drops it.

Theresa walks back into the den where Connor is sitting and leaned up against the wall, her arms folded. "Connor, you have no right or reason to yell at Stephen. He is concerned about his sister. He loves her."

"Are you implying that I don't, Theresa?"

"No, Connor, I am saying that you don't need to yell at the children."

"Well, what makes you so special? You yelled at Stephen too, but I guess I am the bad guy here, right? We are all stressed out, and things have not been the same since Christ left us, Theresa. Face it, Theresa, I've had to, and so should you."

"I don't want to talk about him, Connor. We have to think about Marcy and what is best for her, okay? And we still have Stephen and Sammy to think about here."

"That is fine, Theresa, but you need to listen to what I'm trying to tell you and not brush it off."

"Fine, Connor, and I saw you looking that young nurse up and down when she walked out of the doctor's. Office."

"What! Are you losing it? How absurd."

"Whatever, I know what I saw."

Connor walks into his office. A place to escape from everything. A beautifully decorated room with mahogany bookshelves, a large cherry-wood desk with a glass top, an old Victorian age area rug covers a portion of the wood floor. A dark brick fireplace with an old piece of shipwrecked wood for the mantle. The office is somewhat dim, lit only by two small brass lamps with green lampshades. Connor sits in his leather chair by the fireplace and thinks about everything that has been happening. He goes back in time to a place where Chris would run into his arms and call him daddy. Thinking again he breaks down and begins to cry. His mind races into the past. How things used to be when Marcy would play around his desk, Chris and Marcy running around playing tag in his office.

Marcy is five minutes younger than Chris, but she is his daddy's girl. She would often be jealous of Chris. She didn't want him jumping around on her daddy. Chris would usually tell Marcy that she wasn't the only kid and that Daddy was his hero. Connor would often read Chris biblical stories and then played out some of them using his name. This made Chris his father was a warrior for God. Marcy just loved the attention her daddy gave her and how he always called her his, baby girl," Connor was engulfed with tears; the pain he felt was deep, and he had no answers. Theresa decides to try again to talk to her husband. She knocks on his office door. Connor asks, "Who is it?"

"Me, babe. Can I talk to you?"

"Okay, come in."

"Is everything alright?" She asked gently. She sensed that something is bothering her husband. "No, nothing is alright, I've been sitting here by the fire, remembering the times when Marcy and Chris would come in and hang on me; wanting me to stop working and play with them. I'm a failure Theresa. Chris is gone. I used to be his hero; he looked up to me, and I have failed him."

"Oh, babe! You didn't fail Chris; you haven't failed your children at all. This is not your fault, Chris made his own choice. We have to be strong, we need to let our emotions out, so we can heal," Theresa said. She held her husband's head in her arms while he cries, "I don't want to lose my baby girl."

"I know! But we have Sammy and Stephen to consider here too. Sammy needs her daddy. She is so young and innocent. Sammy doesn't understand what's happening around her. "Sammy is my precious little girl, but my baby girl is lying in a hospital bed, and I'm not sure if she will wake up. I have two other children I can't connect with, I have tried so hard with Stephen, but my heart is hurting for Marcy and Chris. I'm sorry I haven't been around for you guys, Theresa. I want things to work out for us—I do. I want to show my feelings the way I should. I need to be a better father to Sammy and Stephen, but my heart is broken."

Conner continues, "I want the courage to go after Chris, but this isn't the right time. I need to figure out how I am going to connect with Stephen and Sammy; I don't want to neglect them."

"Wow! Connor, I'm so sorry, I'm here for you, and I know you are here for me. We need to pray and seek God for his healing. We need to restore this family from what the enemy has taken away."

"What is that, Theresa?"

"Our happiness, babe. He has used Chris to rob us of our joy. To destroy this family. We need to find our joy again, and God will help us. The joy of the Lord is our strength. When the Lord restores our joy, we will begin to heal."

"You're right, that's what we need to do. I think we should talk to Pastor Shane tomorrow...then visit Marcy."

"I think that's a wonderful idea. We can go when you're done at work."

"No, Theresa! I am taking some time off from work; we need to work on our family; that's what's important. I will tell Frank about it tomorrow."

"Okay, if that is what you need to do, then I stand behind your decision."

"Thanks, that means a lot to me. I think it is time to head off to bed. I'm tired."

"Me too," said Theresa. "Me too. I need to check on the kids."

"Okay, sounds good," Connor said.

Theresa goes to take Sammy to bed, all the while thinking about Connor looking at the young nurse as if he has a desire for her. Theresa feels she is no longer attractive enough for her husband. Theresa tucks Sammy in bed and kisses her forehead. She then goes to check on Stephen.

"Stephen."

"She gets no reply."

"Stephen, are you in there?" Again, no answer. Theresa opens his door and enters the room. Stephen isn't in his room. Papers scattered everywhere on his bed. She decides to read them. She begins reading, hushed in awe; she tears up. He has been writing about his feelings. "My father doesn't love me as much as he loves Chris. I'm unwanted, no matter how good I'm doing, it isn't good enough. I'm alone. My sister is in a coma. My dad works hard; I think he only does it, so he doesn't have to be home to face everything. My dad is a wonderful man, and I look up to him so much; I wish that he would see that he has me since my brother is gone." Theresa's face is soaked with tears reading his words.

Connor walks upstairs to Chris's room; he opens the door surprised to find Stephen sleeping. He walks over, taps him on his shoulder. "Stephen, Stephen, wake up, Son," Stephen groans as he slightly opens his eyes.

"Dad? Am I in trouble for being here?"

"No, Son, I'm not mad. I'm sorry I lost my temper. Why are you sleeping in here?"

"My bed has papers on it. I was too lazy to move them, so I came in here to lay down. I used to sneak in here when I was younger; Chris let me sleep with him when I was scared. I wanted to sleep here, to remember what it was like when he would hug me to ease my fear. Now he hates me. He won't even make an effort to talk to me. I wasn't even here when he left Dad."

"Oh Son, he doesn't hate you. He's just lost, deep inside his heart he loves you. We will make it through this. I promise."

"Will we be okay, Dad?"

"I believe so."

"I wish I could believe you about Chris, but I don't."

"But you will heal and understand in time. Go ahead, go back to sleep."

"Okay, Dad, goodnight. I love you."

"I love you too."

Connor kisses his forehead and leaves the room, closing the door behind him. Stephen pulls the covers over his head and falls asleep. Connor walks down the hall to his room. He is confused. The door is closed. Connor opens it and walks in. Theresa is on her knees crying. He is shocked; he didn't expect that at all. Connor walks up, kneels down beside her, and hugs her. Without asking her a question, he merely says, "I love you. We'll make it through this." They remain on their knees beside the bed crying together as they pray.

"I need to find Stephen," Theresa said. "I was in his room earlier, but he wasn't there. I read some papers on his bed. I shouldn't have done that, it was wrong of me."

"No worries, babe. He's asleep in Chris's room. He will be fine tonight. We will all talk in the morning."

"Okay, but I need to check on Sammy one more time." Theresa leaves the room and walks down the hall. She walks into Sammy's room. She is sleeping. Theresa laughs at the way Sammy is sleeping, hugging her teddy bear that Marcy gave her for her birthday. She walks over and covers her up. She kisses her on the cheek, and Sammy cuddles up in the blanket.

After tucking Sammy in again, she checks on Stephen anyways. He is sleeping, so she closes the door and walks back to her room. It is late, almost 11:00 p.m. and Connor has fallen asleep. Theresa changes her clothes, climbs into bed, turns off the lights, and snuggles up to her husband.

When Chris discovered Tanner was gone and her things missing, he knew she was not coming back. He told the guys in The Breed to put together a search party for her and bring her back. The search went on for two days to no avail, and Chris turned to his master for the answers on where she can be found. Chris is in his bedroom meditating, seeking answers from Satan but he gets no answer. After a couple of days, the search was officially called off, and everyone focused on the missions. The breed had gathered relevant and great insight and information into each Church and Pastor.

This has given The Breed an open door into their lives and will be used to try and destroy the men of God, and their churches. The members of the breed, Satan's soldiers, were still uneasy with Tanner leaving them, considering the information that she knew. Daren, who is Chris's right-hand man, questioned Chris for canceling the search. Everyone else did too, and with the time that has passed, they seemed to be losing respect for him as a strong leader. Thomas and Daren both have talked about Chris and questioned his guts to follow through with killing anyone for leaving. Not much has been done to prepare them for battle, and Daren is growing impatient.

The house is quiet. 3:00 a.m. When out of nowhere, the phone rings. Startled, Theresa jumps out of bed to answer the phone, fear it may be about Marcy.

"Mrs. Smith?"

"Yes," she said. "This is Mrs. Smith. Who is this?"

"Hi, my name is Beth. I am a nurse caring for Marcy tonight—well, early morning I should say. I'm calling because Doctor Alvarez asked me to call; he is on his way here as we speak."

"Oh! Is my daughter okay?"

"Yes, ma'am, as a matter of fact, your daughter woke up about fifteen minutes ago."

"Yes! Praise God!" Theresa shouts, waking Connor up; startled, acting like he had a sudden heart attack. He said, "What's going on?" His heart racing as he tries to figure it out.

"We will be right there," Theresa hangs up the phone in excitement.

"Connor!" Theresa yells.

"Yes, babe, who was that?"

"Marcy's awake!" Connor jumped out of bed and said, "What! She's awake?"

"Yes, babe, she's awake—she's awake!"

"I will meet you at the hospital. Go, I will take the kids."

"Connor, call Pastor Shane."

"Okay, no problem." He is still trying to pull himself together from all the excitement. He is thrilled, but he is still half asleep. He has been stressed and burnt out, he needed the sleep, but with Marcy being awake now—that changes everything.

"Okay, babe, I will take care of everything. Marcy needs someone with her. I'm sure she is scared," Connor runs down the hall, opens the door to Chris's room and wakes Stephen. "Stephen, c'mon son wake up," Stephen groans, "What Dad? What's wrong?"

"Nothing, everything is great. Your sister is awake!"

"Whoa! What, why is Sammy awake?"

"Not Sammy, Marcy! The hospital called, and Mom is on her way to the hospital."

"Oh Yes!" Stephen screams. "Let's go, Dad! Let's go!"

"We will leave as soon as I get Sammy ready."

Theresa is driving much faster than the posted 65 MPH limit. She wants to be with Marcy ASAP. She pulls into the Hospital parking lot which is practically empty giving her a close spot near the entrance. Theresa runs in and makes her way to the nurses' station on the fifth floor. She looks at one nurse and says, "I'm here for my daughter, Marcy Smith.

I was called. A nurse named Beth told me my daughter woke up from her coma."

"Yes, ma'am, the doctor is here now. I'll take you to him."

Connor gets Sammy into the car; he places her in her car seat as she wiggles and whines. Stephen gets in the front seat and buckles up. Connor rushes off to meet Theresa at the hospital.

Theresa runs toward Marcy's room. Dr. Alvarez is waiting for her. She hears Marcy screaming. She comes into the room, pushes her way past Dr. Alvarez and a nurse, and takes Marcy's hand. "I'm here, baby. Momma's here," Marcy stares at her mother and cries. "What's going on, Mom? What happened?"

"Marcy, please calm down, baby, please. We will explain everything later, okay? Please relax. I understand you're scared, but I'm right here."

"Where's Dad?"

"He's on his way with Stephen and Sammy. They will be here as soon as possible, baby."

Connor came racing into the hospital parking lot. He is running, holding Sammy in his arms as Stephen run as fast as he can to the elevator. They walk into the elevator and take it to the 5th floor. They run past the nurses' station straight to Marcy's room. Connor barges in out of breath.

"I'm here."

"Mr. Smith, you need to—"

"I need to what?" He said with an angry face at the nurse. Stephen is crying in the corner, Sammy is frightened by the chaos. Connor hugs Marcy, and again, Marcy starts crying, asking her dad what happened.

"Marcy, you're fine. We will explain later. All that matters now is you're awake. Please calm down and let Dr. Alvarez do his work, okay? We're not leaving you; we're right here." He said. Dr. Alvarez tells him

Torn

they need to perform some tests to check how Marcy's reflexes and how her memory is.

"Dad, tell me!" Marcy shouts. "Why can't someone tell me what's going on? Please tell me what happened, Dad!"

"Marcy, you were in a car accident. You lost consciousness and went into a coma. You had surgery to relieve pressure on your brain."

"What! I don't remember any of that."

"Marcy. You're fine." He tells her.

"Dad? Did I cause the accident? Was it my fault?" She asked.

"No Marcy, it wasn't your fault. A truck hit you in the middle of the intersection. The other person ran the red light and hit you."

"Is the person that hit me okay?"

"I'll tell you later, baby girl. The doctor needs to do his examinations, okay?"

"Okay but promise me you will tell me everything."

"Of course, Marcy, of course, I will."

Dr. Alvarez begins his examination on Marcy; he finds that she is recovering from her physical injuries so far, and her surgery as well. Marcy appears to have a clean bill of health, but the doctor isn't so sure she should be discharged, at least for another few days for observation.

Pastor Mark and Pastor Shane arrive at the hospital at 8:00 am and are thrilled that Marcy is doing well. Pastor Shane speaks with the family and prays with them. They thank God for Marcy's recovery. Pastor Mark is eager to go in but decides against it. Pastor Mark stays outside her room as Pastor Shane speaks to her and prays with her. He is in tears; he wants to talk to Marcy.

Chapter 18

Jessie has been upset with Tanner for leaving the way she did, running away like a coward; on the other hand, She is thrilled she is gone. Jessie has so much rage toward Tanner and Chris because he specifically told Thomas to keep a watchful eye on Tanner. Chris didn't trust anyone entirely, except for Daren; now (behind Chris's back) Daren is questioning his loyalty to Chris. Thinking back, Daren begins to think about his decision to accept an appointment as a section leader.

Daren tries to reason, but his heart is still set on Chris doing what he said he will do. No matter how much he dislikes the direction things are going, he has to make a decision soon. Thomas's disregard for the same issues keep him in check; he fears Chris and what he can do to him. Thomas likes Chris and would never think of betraying him. Jessie is more curious about Chris now, although she has her own hidden agenda toward him. Jessie doesn't mind what he does, nor does it bother her that he is using her money to fund his missions. Her parents left her a trust fund she can now access.

Jessie is unsure who left her the inheritance. No name is mentioned on the trust except for hers. Chris loves Jessie and spending her money for himself. Rocco gave the information to Chris about the money that she has. Being mentored by Zaga, he noticed how close Jessie and Zaga were, and he felt that she was the one he could use for this purpose.

A hidden agenda. Chris is wise and cunning; he can persuade anyone to achieve his goals. His persuasiveness is evident in the way he is able to attract people and have them follow him Accept his beliefs; he is deceiving, using methods others don't understand.

Chris thinks back to when he left his family; he sees how much he has changed and to him, it was for the best. He is cocky; he knows how intelligent he is. When his parents discovered what he was getting into, they tried to reason with him, but his mind was already set. He remembers running upstairs, closing his door and crying. "I was so foolish and soft," he says to himself. "I'm much stronger and tougher now. I have control over people who either see it or they don't."

While alone in his room, he remembers calling out to Lucifer to ease his pain. Even while sitting on his bed, he heard an evil voice speak in his mind that filled him with joy. This was the first encounter that Chris had with the powers of darkness. The next morning, he went downstairs. His father had asked him if he was okay and Chris told him, "Can't you people leave me alone?" Chris clears his memory of those thoughts, he buries the emotions down deep and tries to forget them.

Chris has changed his appearance over time from a casual teen with t-shirt and jeans to a much darker appearance. He uses dark eyeliner; he grew his hair out and dyed it black. He uses nail polish to paint his nails black, and he wears a pentagram with pride. He is not the young man that his family remembers; he is almost unrecognizable to anyone he once knew. He is lost, in a state of mind that he has to have specific answers, from his god.

It appears division is building in the breed; Chris blames Thomas for Tanner slipping through their fingertips. Daren decides to go and question his leader to find out what is going on; his patience has worn out. He goes to Chris's room seeking some answers.

"Chris, it's me, Daren. I need to talk to you, man."

"Come in, Daren."

Daren enters the room, Chris is sitting on his bed appearing to be sad, and it took Daren by surprise. "What do you want, Daren?"

"Well, to be honest, what are your plans are concerning Tanner."

"Daren, stop okay? This is not your problem. I don't need you or anyone else telling me how to handle it, everything is about timing and now is not the time."

"Chris, C'mon, it has shaken everyone up, yourself included. We were looking for her and you called it off; you went into some daze and had no idea on what to do."

"Dude, you better watch out who you're talking to here." Chris's face turns red. He starts gritting his teeth and clinches his fists.

"Well, tell me whom I'm talking to, Chris, because I don't know you anymore. You're so arrogant, and I'm tired of it," he replies, giving Chris a hateful gaze. "You are so focused on Tanner that you can't think of anything else. Why is that?"

"Listen, Daren. Tanner is gone. We are moving on. Don't presume to tell me what to do or even lecture me on anything," Chris utters out in defense.

"I am not telling you what to do, Chris; I'm just saying you should start showing us what we are doing here. What is the big plan that you have everyone?"

"What do you care, Daren? Why is it so important to you or anyone else for that matter? Do you think this is your idea, your self-proclaimed war?"

"No, Chris, but we are all here and share the same vision that you do. What do you think we follow you for?"

"Everyone is asking? Come on, Daren, they care about what I tell them to care about," he said with an offensive slur.

"C'mon, Chris, we have a right to believe in the vision, and I think it is time to start talking less and acting more; unless you're all talk, a coward behind that steel heart," he said, standing firm with his shoulders back as if challenging Chris's authority.

"Who do you think you are to talk to me like this? I will split your head open, you mindless twerp," Chris fired back, moving closer to Daren as if to stand toe-to-toe with him.

"I don't know what you think you can do to me you knit-wit. I'm not afraid of you. I don't think you have any clue what you are doing. I want action, and you are supposed to be our leader, and you're acting like a lost little schoolgirl." Daren responded.

"Are you trying to start a fight with me?"

"You're a fool, and you're wasting time. You're portraying yourself as a strong leader, but all you are is fake."

"The best thing for you to do, Daren, is to back up out of my face before you make me hurt you! You are supposed to be my friend, my right hand, second in command. I don't want to hurt you, but if you push me, I will finish you. Do you understand me, boy?" Chris screams, now toe-to-toe with Daren who clinches his fists, ready to fight.

"Boy! I'm not a boy! I'm a man! Wow, you are crazy," he says, spitting every word into Chris's face. "You think for one minute that I'm afraid of you?"

People in the house are hearing the scuffle and are interested in the drama taking place. As they rush upstairs to the hallway, they slowly walk toward Chris's room. Listening to Daren and Chris, they hear the argument more clearly that is taking place.

"Daren, I'm warning you, back off!" I don't care what you say. This is your last chance. I'm telling you to drop this before you regret it. I told you to leave it alone. I don't want to lose you, but if you push me, so help me God I will kill you."

"What are you talking about, Chris? Do you think you can threaten me the way you did Zaga?"

"Zaga was smart, he left; you want to be brave and challenge me, then game on…"

"Listen to yourself. You're a lunatic! In fact, here is some hard-core truth for you. While my section was researching you, I was at your church. Your sister just happened to be there, so I had a man meet me, and I paid him to follow your sister, her name is Marcy., right? I know your family. I wasn't sure what he was going to do, but I'm sure it would have put the fear of God in her. They were at a traffic light. He was a few cars behind her, and when the light turned green, another driver came through the intersection and slammed into her. My guy did a three-sixty and bolted. So, you are not the only one in power here."

"Enough Daren! I warned this whole group to leave my family to me; you crossed the line. Now you will pay for it," Chris clinches his fists so hard his knuckles turn white. Everyone listening gets as close as they can to catch a glimpse, getting chills down their spines. This is intriguing and alluring. Some members are apprehensive and leave; not willing to witness a possible fight.

"What are you going to do you dweeb?"

Chris is more enraged and raises his right hand; his hand positioned as if to choke someone, as if he is going to choke Daren. Daren looks him in the eye and laughs. The two men are only a couple of feet apart. And then Daren's arms freeze. Fear sets into Daren's mind, but by the time he even tries to think about what is happening. He is off his feet, lifted into mid-air, being choked by Chris by a supernatural force. People in the hall who decided to stay are awe-struck at what they are witnessing. And, some even enjoy the display of sheer power. After about ten seconds, Chris puts his hand down. Daren's body drops to the floor like a sack of potatoes. He lays un-conscience.

After so much time spent in the hospital, Marcy is going home with her family. Marcy is full of happiness; she can barely hold back her tears. Stephen gives her flowers and a brown teddy bear. She became a little queasy from the car ride but managed to overcome nausea.

Frank and Karen came out to greet them as they pull in; Frank and his wife have waited a long time for this moment. They are happy for their friends. They have their daughter at home.

"Hello," they said, greeting the Smiths while Connor opened the car door, helping Marcy out on the other side.

"Oh Marcy, praise be to God you are okay," said Karen. "We have prayed so hard for this moment to come."

"Thank you, Karen, I do thank God I am okay. I honestly don't remember a thing, but I guess that is good." Karen hugs Marcy while their eyes filled with tears. Frank greets Marcy and hugs her. He tells her, "Welcome home, kiddo. We all have missed you and have been praying for you."

"Thank you so much for being here for our family" Marcy replied. They made their way into the house, and Marcy asks, "Where's Sammy?"

"Marcy, "Sammy is upstairs sleeping, she had a rough night—bad dreams. I stayed up most of the night rocking her to sleep...several times."

"Awe! My poor baby sister." Marcy makes her way upstairs and walks into Sammy's room. She doesn't want to disturb her sleep, but she is so anxious for Sammy to see her and vice-versa. She gently whispers, "Hello, princess; it's Marcy. I'm okay. I'm home...I love you," Sammy groans. "Momma, no." She whines and kicks.

"No, Sammy, Marcy, your big sister, sweetie. I'm home." Sammy wipes her eyes, looks up at Marcy, grabs her neck, and she squeezes her as tight as she can. She tells Marcy, "I'm super happy! I miss you so much, Marcy."

"I missed you too, honey. I love you," Marcy is holding Sammy on her lap as they cry together and kiss each other on their cheeks. Marcy places Sammy back on her bed and says goodnight.

Marcy approached the area in the hall where Chris's room is and suddenly collapses right to the floor.

"MARCY!" Stephen yells as he runs over to her. Marcy's parents run upstairs. "What happened?" They ask Stephen.

"I don't know," Stephen replies while at his sister's side. Connor picks her up off the floor and carries her to her bedroom. His mother asks him again, "What happened?"

"Mom, she was fine, but as she walked past Chris's room—she collapsed; fell right to the floor. I came out of the bathroom when it happened."

"She must be tired. Her body isn't used to moving around, and she is weak," Connor said.

"No Connor! Something else happened. Marcy was full of energy until she went by Chris's room. Must be some evil force haunting the bedroom. I mean, I guess that could be it, right?"

"Don't be silly, Theresa! Stephen slept in there with no problems. Marcy is weak and needs to rest, that's all."

"I hope you are right; seems odd to me, Connor. I am going to call Pastor Shane and ask him to come over."

"What for, Theresa? Connor asks.

"So, he can visit with her now that she is home and pray over that room—something isn't right. I don't care what you think about it," Theresa replies. If there is something, some evil that is trying to wield its plan, she wants it stopped.

"Let her rest, Theresa. She is not up to it," Connor said, confused by his wife's suspicions. Nothing is wrong in his mind; he wants his baby girl to rest. No way evil is lurking in their house or is it?

Chapter 19

Marcy wakes up frightened from a bad nightmare. She screams in terror, "Momma, Momma!" Frantically, her mother makes her way to Marcy's room. "What Marcy? What's wrong?"

"What happened to me?" She cried. By this time, her father is at her bedside as well, frightened that something is wrong with her.

"What do you mean, Marcy?" Connor asks.

"What happened to me? Something is different; I experienced something like never before. Something dark, cold, an evil of sorts, and I was lifeless. The most dreadful thing. It was scary; I don't understand what to make of it," She said. Theresa and Connor are stunned. They still haven't told Marcy about the accident and are unsure if they should now.

"Well, your mother is calling Pastor Shane for him to come over for a visit today; you can explain what happened to you to him," her father said. By this time, Marcy is calming down.

"Do you think Pastor Mark will be with him?"

"I'm not sure, but what does it matter if he is or not?"

"It doesn't. I was wondering, that's all."

Connor is a little suspicious. There must something going on between Marcy and Pastor Mark? He will get to the bottom of this when Pastor Shane arrives. Theresa calls the church office and requests for Pastor Shane to come over, the receptionist forwards the message to Pastor Shane's secretary. He, of course, replies promptly with a yes. Theresa tells Connor, "Pastor Shane will be here within the hour." Connor says, "Good, I will need to speak to him as well."

"About what?"

"I want to talk to him about Pastor Mark and Marcy."

"What do you mean, Connor?"

"Well, Marcy asked if Pastor Mark would be coming with Pastor Shane. I told her I wasn't sure; but why did it matter? And she said she was curious. I think something is going on between them and I want to find out what it is."

"I'm sure it's nothing, Connor, I mean—"

"Theresa!" Connor yells, interrupting her." I don't care. There is a reason behind it, and I want to know what it is either way."

"So, what you're saying is that if Pastor Mark is interested in Marcy, you will have a problem with that? Do I understand this right?"

"I don't know—don't you understand me?" Connor replies. He is becoming more upset with the entire discussion now.

"Uh, well, no I don't, babe. You're not making any sense at all," Theresa answered, rolling her eyes as if she was supposed to go along with Connor's craziness.

"Would you have a problem with Pastor Mark and Marcy dating? Yes or no? I don't think I will have a problem with it. He seems like a fine young man."

"I want answers; if something is going on, why couldn't Pastor Mark tell us, especially when Marcy was in the hospital?"

"Well, maybe he felt it wasn't the appropriate time. Maybe they have a strong friendship."

"Well, Theresa, I hope that is all it is; it would be inappropriate for them to be anything more," Connor said.

"Why would it be wrong, Connor? They are close in age. Pastor Mark is a youth pastor; he has a job. He is only twenty-four years old. Marcy is eighteen years old now. They are both adults.

"Drop it! I will talk to Pastor Shane and get to the bottom of it. I want Marcy to finish college before she even gets involved with anyone."

"You can't stop her from choosing the life she wants."

"Well, I guess that holds true for Chris too, but we made him feel like an outcast, and he left us."

"Wow, why are you so mean? Have your talk with Pastor Shane, but don't talk to me," she said, turning away from him.

Chris hasn't let go of his anger toward Daren. He walks over to Daren sitting in the living room." Don't ever try me again. I will kill you. Do you understand me?" Daren shakes his head yes. Chris looks over at Thomas and tells him he is now the second in command and Daren is a section leader for the time being.

Jessie ran over to Chris and thanked him for letting Daren go. She watched as he was chocking him supernaturally, but Chris tells her, "I didn't do it for you. I only did it to prove a point to Daren, and now he fears my power." Once the spectacle was over, other members fell and worshiped Chris, and the rest didn't know what to do or what to say. They're at a loss—surprised at what they just witnessed. The members who were on their knees bowing to Chris did so in fear of his powers and in respect of who he is.

Chris told those who begin to worship him that he loves them. He cares for them, but the others—he gives them a stare. Chris's eyes are red like blood as he turns to say, "You are not worthy to receive me." They all left, and those who stayed to worship Chris are all crying as they called him their master. Chris walks by each of them and touching their faces and then kisses their foreheads and calls them his chosen children. Jessie stands by and cannot believe what she is seeing. Then Chris came to her. "You are my love, Jessie, and I want for us to have children, to have our own family someday, and we will worship our god. We will bring forth a new people for the kingdom of darkness." Jessie, reluctant to answer, simply utters, "Okay," she doesn't dare say anything else.

Chris soaked in this new feeling of being loved and hailed by faithful members. As for the rest of them, he will keep a close eye on them and make sure they fit into his goals. For Chris, however, the war on Christians is here, and he might still decide to recruit more people from other towns around the city to join in his campaign. He thinks he needs more people, but not just anyone will do. He wants loyalists who would serve and do what he asks of them and not cause conflict with his mission. Jessie asked Chris a long time ago what his actual purpose was, and he told her, "My mission is to inflict pain to those so-called People of God; cause them and their families heartache and loss. The way it was for me for many years. If you are not with me, you're my enemy, and you must be destroyed, killed if necessary."

Jessie is surprised that Chris would kill, even if it is his own family. She is not willing to kill anyone. Jessie has sympathy for them. She is confused about everything. What could she do to convince Chris to not hurt his family without making him angry and putting her life in danger? Jessie is now with Chris out of fear. She knows he likes her, even loves her. Jessie wants him, but with the Daren thing, all bets are off. Jessie will do what she must for survival. She tells Chris what he wants to hear.

Jessie has known Zaga her entire life, and the decision she made to stay with Chris was a big mistake. Although Zaga told her not to leave. He didn't want anything to happen to her, and the best place for her at the moment was in the house. This bothered Jessie, but she agreed to Zaga's wishes and stayed at the house with Chris. When she noticed the growth in Chris and how he was becoming more engaged in the darkness, she did like it but then conviction within her told her that he is going too far.

Jessie, at some point, will have to try to protect people and not let bad things happen. One day, she decided to go into Chris's room while he was out and took a black address book with his family's address. She wrote it down and immediately flipped through some more pages; he had names and addresses for church members and pastors.

She asks herself, *why* did Chris have people in the breed staking out churches and pastors if he already has the information to where they live? He has information on almost every church and most of the members in them. He must have an inside source, someone in these churches giving him this information," This troubles her heart. He wants to wage war against these people; innocent people and their families. She took a bus across town and left a warning letter on a car at his family's house. Then she took the bus back to be home before Chris is home. He had gone to the store for some food and drinks.

Chris went straight to his room after the event with Daren. He prays not to God, but to Satan. He asks again, "Lord, I need reassurance from you. Am I doing what you have called me to do? Am I going to kill people in your name? Please tell me. Tell me that you want me to kill for you. I will obey you're will, but I'm so lost. How will I accomplish your goals? Some are with me, and others aren't sure."

"I need to you, please, Satan. I believe in you. I choose to follow you as my god. Teach me, lead me, nurture me, and I shall do all that you ask of me. I'm your servant forever."

Connor decides to call Pastor Shane to find out where he is. Pastor Shane's phone rings, "Hello." Pastor Shane answers.

"Hello Pastor, this is Connor. I was just wondering where you are. We have lunch done and ready, are you on your way?"

"Yes, Connor, in about ten minutes. I stopped by to pick up Pastor Mark. I hope you don't mind—he wants to come.

"Pastor, I'm glad he is coming, I have some things I would like to discuss with him."

"Okay, Connor, we will be there soon. Again, sorry for the delay." Connor hangs up the phone and tells his wife that Pastor Shane and Pastor Mark will be joining them for lunch. She is delighted and prepares another place setting at the table for Pastor Mark. The pastors arrive and ring the doorbell. Connor greets them at the door. "Hello, so glad to have you! Welcome, come on in."

"Thank you, Connor and Theresa, we are happy to be here to have fellowship with your family. What a time, praise God for his blessings here on your family." They walk to the dining room and sit down, but Stephen hugs Pastor Mark before they he sits down.

"I'm so glad to see you."

"I'm happy too, buddy."

"Well," Connor said, "shall we have a blessing and enjoy this food?"

"Absolutely," Pastor Shane says.

"Pastor Shane, would you like to say the blessing?"

"Well, I think Connor should say the blessing. This is his home, and I think it would be proper."

"I don't mind, pastor," said Connor. "You can do it if you would like."

"Well, ok then, let us pray. Father, we come before you in Jesus name. We thank you for this wonderful food prepared for us. Thank you, Father, for the blessings we have in our lives; for all, you give your children so freely. I thank you for the Smith family and your hand of healing. Thank you for giving Marcy back to us. Bless this food, I ask in Jesus name. Amen."

Chapter 20

Tanner had experienced something she could never have imagined. She had been thrown into the hallway by a dominant evil force and saw Chris's door slam shut; she was terrified, and at that moment, she had to leave. Tanner made it about half a mile and decided to catch a city bus; it could take anywhere, as long as it was far away from Chris and his henchmen. She decides to go all the way to the north side of town with the hope of finding Zaga or some of his friends. Tanner remembered about a priest he knew on the north side. So, she figured this is her best hope in finding Zaga. He's her friend and mentor. A man who is like a father to her; Tanner can trust him. She has to see him.

Tanner grew up on the outskirts of Kansas City; in a suburban area known for its middle-class lifestyle. Her mother, Barbara, is a loan officer at a large bank. Her biological father was killed in a carjacking when she was only ten-years-old. Tanner's mother remarried when she was twelve to a man named Calvin Henderson. Her mom wanted Tanner to take his last name, but she wasn't interested. Tanner told her mom she would keep her father's last name of Mayes. Her home lacked joy or happiness. Her mom ignored her, and her stepfather was physically abusive. She was miserable for many years. One day Tanner got the courage to tell her mother that her stepfather abused her, he made inappropriate moves on her, but her mother slapped her twice across her face, calling her a liar.

"Why? Why would he want you when he has me? I'm a woman, and you are a snobby sixteen-year-old girl," Tanner was hurt by her mother's statement, and she pleaded with her mother to believe her. Instead, her mother called her a liar! "You're jealous of my relationship, and you probably seduced the man. You are trash, a good-for-nothing tramp, selfish, and care for no one or what they have. You are destructive. I will not have that in my home," her mother scolding her. Tanner ran to her room crying with her heart crushed, feeling betrayed by her mother. On that night, Tanner ran away from home, and she never looked back. The next morning, her mother noticed her missing. She never reported it; she simply said, "good riddance, we don't love you, and we don't want you."

Her mother told her step-dad, and he said, "If you're fine with it so am I. I don't need the headache of her falsely accusing me. I would never do such a thing." He knew what he did, and he played it off; enough to have won himself an Oscar. "I believe you, honey. Let's forget about it. We don't need her, and she never appreciated anything you have done for her."

"I, but we have each other."

Tanner ran as far as she could go and when she got to the city, she found herself sleeping in alleys behind dumpsters. She didn't imagine her life turning out like this. *Is this what my life has come to be?* One day, she was begging on a street corner for food when a man came across her path. "Hello there. Can I help you?"

"Yes! Please, I am hungry. I haven't eaten in three days. Can you help me?"

"Well, sure I can. My friend is here with me. She will be out of the store in a minute. Would you like to join us for lunch at our home?"

"Mister, I'm not going to your house, *no way!*"

"I understand, but maybe when you meet my friend, you will change your mind," The man's friend came out of the store and saw him talking to this dirty, homeless girl. She approaches them. "Who is this? What's going on?"

"Jessie, I would like you to meet, um, I'm so sorry, what is your name, child?"

"My name? Why should I tell you?"

"Hey, calm down, girl, this man is a caregiver; he helps those who are in need."

"Well, of course, you would say that. He's your friend!"

"Yes, he is, but he is also a father figure, he cares about people and helps them get on their feet. He supplies food and shelter, and the law is not involved. He asks for nothing in return. He wants to help the lost and hurting. So again, what is your name?"

"My name is Tanner."

"Hello, Tanner, how did you end up out here?"

"I ran away from home. My stepfather was abusing me and making advances toward me if you know what I mean, my mother didn't believe me and called me all sorts of names. I figured the best thing to do was runaway; it would make the abuse stop, and that was good enough for me."

"Well! It certainly explains your resistance."

"Jessie, be nice. She needs our help."

"Okay, Tanner. Zaga and I would still like you to come with us to meet the others who are in our home they were in your current position. We promise not to report you to the law."

"Okay, I will go but no funny business, I swear, or I will—"

"That's not what we're about," Jessie said.

"Nothing will happen, Tanner. I promise you will feel right at home in time."

Pastor Shane stares at everyone sitting around the table. "Time to enjoy this wonderful feast Theresa, it smells delicious."

"Thank you," Theresa replies. Marcy and Pastor Mark were sitting across from each other, and Connor kept noticing the eye contact, so he begins to interrupt. "So, Pastor Mark, how are you doing these days?" Connor asked with the hopes of gaining his full attention.

"Well, sir, I'm doing quite well. I enjoy my job. Helping young people is key for me; A calling to raise a generation for God."

"So, do you have a girlfriend—?" Connor begins to ask as Theresa interrupts. "Connor, you shouldn't get into Pastor Mark's personal life like that."

"Mrs. Smith, it's fine," Pastor Mark said.

"Please, call me Theresa."

"Thank you, Mrs. Smith; I respect you. I will use proper manners here," Mark said as he gave his attention back to Connor.

"No, Sir, I don't have a girlfriend. I stay pretty busy with work at the church these days."

"Has anyone captured your attention though?"

By this time, Pastor Shane considers interrupting as his young pastor is trapped.

"Well, sir, to be honest...yes." Pastor Shane glances his way, curious who the person could be.

"Oh, and who might that be?"

"Well, to completely honest, Sir, I would appreciate the opportunity to discuss the matter with you in private," he replies, nervous and worried. His palms are getting sweaty. He wipes his hands on his jeans, trying to gain his composure.

"Why in private?"

"Well, sir, I think it would be more appropriate."

"I'm guessing because you—" Theresa steps in and stops Connor from continuing. Theresa looks at Connor and says, "Give him enough respect to talk in private as he requested, Connor."

"Fine! Very well then; Pastor Mark, we will talk in private later."

"Thank you, sir."

"So, Connor, how's your break from work?" Pastor Shane poses the question to change the topic.

"Going great. I'm enjoying the time off. I've had to delay working on a contract, but I told my partner, Frank, this time is essential for my family and me."

"Oh, okay, that wouldn't happen to be Frank Douglas, would it?"

"Yes. He's my business partner."

"So, your firm is going to be working on a new facility for the city then?"

"That's us, the new indoor football and baseball stadium. All connected with a glass sky-bridge and an underground tram, sort of like a New York subway train," he explained with as much detail as he can.

"Oh wow, what a fantastic project. I'm sure it will be a blessing to your business and the families you employ."

"Yes, we are excited about it. We hope to begin construction within the next few weeks if all goes well."

"Wonderful, Connor. I hope it goes well for everyone involved. God is showering you with blessings not only at home but work as well."

"Yes, it would appear so, pastor."

"Theresa, how are things with you?"

"Well, Pastor, to be honest, I'm trying my best to move past the events that have struck our family. I can't help but think of Chris every day and hope he is all right. I don't want anything bad to happen to him. I realize I still have my other children and thank God Marcy is here and recovering. Stephen, I couldn't be prouder of him. The things he is doing in youth group and school. Sammy is getting bigger and is just a bundle of joy, but still a challenge. She said." Things seem to be going well. We are all still trying to heal from it all. Marcy has not had a chance to deal with it or heal from it since she had been hospitalized for so long. She has woken up in the future but is still affected by the past."

"Mom, I understand why you would say that, but I can speak for myself and explain my feelings about my brother."

Theresa had a shocked look on her face from Marcy's statement.

"Marcy, I didn't mean to speak for you. I only figured…based on the situation is all."

Pastor Shane speaks up with a wise statement. "It appears to me there is more confusion here, and some finger pointing still; How much have you talked as a family about this issue? Have you allowed the children to respond with their exact feelings and listen to each other?" He continues, "It's important to communicate and understand each other; you don't have to like what the other person is saying. Showing you have interest and you care, will go a long way. For example, Pastor Mark does a wonderful job with the youth group. We do, however, have a dress code in the sense of modesty. Other than those things, we don't judge them on their appearance."

"Excuse me, Pastor Shane."

"Yes, Mark?"

"I would like to add that we also don't allow bikinis when we are away at camps. But one thing I can say about our kids, they are wise and have hearts for God and genuinely care for one another."

"I believe the success we have seen in our kids is nothing short of a move by God. The kids having open hearts to become closer to Him. Amazing privilege for me to be their pastor and at times their confidant when they have nowhere else to turn. Quite a challenge for some teens, but overall, I have a great relationship with them. I'm especially close to Stephen; he has such a wonderful spirit and a heart for God. He has a gift playing the guitar and God will use him in a mighty way. I believe we have a special bond as if we are brothers. When I graduated from high school, I felt God wanted me to be a youth minister. I went to Bible College, and then Pastor Shane mentored me."

"I hope I have earned the respect of the parents of our youth and their trust. I work hard to serve God and the people in our church. I'm always proud to be their pastor."

"Well, Pastor Mark, thank you for sharing with us, you're doing a great job. I'm happy you and Stephen are close. He needs someone to bond with, and I'm glad he found that in you."

"Thank you, Mrs. Smith."

Pastor Shane tells the family how strenuous the internship was for Pastor Mark; he said the training program for pastors at the church is vigorous. Pastors must complete an extensive routine of Bible study, prayer, and fasting, as well as show the quality servant skills needed to be devoted to God and to serve the people.

"I am proud of Pastor Mark for his hard work and dedication; he has not even taken vacation time in the four years he has been at the church. He is dedicated and passionate."

With so much talking, not much eating has taken place. Theresa made an effort to make that a point, as the pastors needed to be getting back to the church. Lunch is over and Pastor Shane thanks the Smiths for inviting them.

"Thank you for coming over," Connor and Theresa said.

"Pastor Mark, thank you for sharing your story with us," Theresa said.

"Thank you, ma'am. Mr. Smith, I would still like to have our private conversation soon; if you don't mind. Can you tell me when you would be available?"

"Thursday around 1:00 p.m.?" He told Pastor Mark.

"Yep, works for me. I will add it to my calendar now, and it should alert my secretary I added it."

"Okay."

"Pastor Shane," Marcy yells.

"Yes, Marcy?"

"I also need to talk to you soon; to discuss some things that happened to me."

"Okay, I will schedule you in for Friday, we can talk about what's going on, okay?"

"Thank you, Pastor Shane, really I can't thank you enough."

Connor closes the door as the pastors leave. When they arrive back to the church, Pastor Mark goes to his office. Pastor Shane is stopped by his secretary before he can pass her desk. She tells him, "You have a couple of visitors who have been waiting over an hour for you."

"Who are they, Cindy?" He asks.

"I don't know. They wouldn't give me their names, just said they needed to talk. to you,"

"Well, we have no idea who they are, and I'm not sure if we are safe. I had a not so pleasant encounter with Chris? I wonder if he sent someone here?"

"I don't think so, Pastor. They didn't appear to be a threat to me. They were polite."

"Okay, well make sure you log them in any way. I will go introduce myself, but can you please notify security for me, just in case?"

"Yes, Pastor. I will make them aware you are concerned."

Pastor Shane walks down the hall to greet his visitors. He was a bit uneasy but pulls himself together with confidence; he arrives at the waiting room to greet them.

Chapter 21

Pastor Mark's secretary gives him his messages. His demeanor is low. He feels ad and confused.

"Are you okay, Pastor Mark?"

"Please hold my calls? I'll be busy this afternoon. I don't want to be disturbed."

"No problem, Pastor."

"Thank you." Pastor Mark sits in his office thinking about Marcy, back to their last conversation before her accident. He has strong feelings for Marcy and has been praying, seeking God to heal her. Pastor Mark wanted to tell her about his feelings but had hoped the lunch visit was the right time. Tears begin to fill his eyes. Mark doesn't want to waste any more time. He will wait patiently for Thursday.

Pastor Shane walks into the waiting room; two young people are waiting for him. "Hello! My name is Pastor Shane. I understand that you are here to see me?"

"Yes, sir, we are," the man answers. The girl that is with him didn't say a word.

"Well, please follow me to my office, right this way."

"Thank you," the man said. They walk towards Pastor Shane's office and the girl looks at the man with a terrified look. "It's okay," he told her, knowing she was scared and full of fear. "We need to talk to him, okay? Okay," she replied. Pastor Shane overheard them and instantly felt uneasy; he knew he could alert his security staff with a button under his desk. They would arrive at his office in just a few minutes after being informed. Pastor Shane opened his office door and invited the young man and young woman to have a seat. Pastor Shane sits behind his desk and looks at the two people.

"So, how can I help you?"

"Thank you for seeing us, Pastor."

"You're welcome. Now, may I ask you for your names?"

"My name is Daren, and this is Chelsea; we are here to ask you a question."

"Okay, go ahead."

"Do you know Chris Smith?" Daren asks.

"Well, yes I do, why do you ask?" Pastor Shane answers as he pushes the security button.

"Well, because he told us about this church and the pastors; he has such hatred towards this church, its people, and his family."

"I did have an encounter with him some time ago. So, are the two of you here to warn me about him, or is there something maybe I can help you with?"

"No, we're not here for help. We are here to warn you," Daren said.

"What do you need to warn me about, Daren?" Pastor Shane is becoming uneasy now.

"Chris has developed some supernatural power. He used them on me." Daren said.

While Daren is spilling his guts to the pastor, he pulls out a gun, aims it, and fires three rounds into Pastor Shane's chest. Chelsea runs for the back entrance with Daren not far behind her; they run out the back door where a black van is waiting for them. They fled the scene very fast. Security staff run to Pastor Shane's office, Pastor Mark is not far behind them. His secretary is screaming at his office door. Security guards push her out of the way, and they find Pastor Shane unconscious in his chair, sitting upright, his head hanging down. Three bloody holes are in his chest.

Pastor Mark calls 9-1-1. "Hello, 9-1-1 emergency response."

"Yes, hello, my name is Mark. I need an ambulance Now! Our pastor someone shot our pastor! We need help now."

"Okay, sir, please calm down. I'm sending help. Can you feel a pulse? Is he breathing?"

"Hold on" Mark puts two fingers to Shane's neck, "He has a weak pulse, this can't be happening, no, please no."

"Sir, please calm down. What is your address?"

"7771 Moss Avenue. Please hurry."

"I have dispatched help, sir; they will be there soon." Do you have an idea of who shot your pastor?"

"No, I was in my office. The gunshots startled me. I ran to the area and saw security in the Pastor Shane's office. Then I called you. Are they here yet?"

"They will be soon, sir."

"Charlie, Victor, Mike, what is your ETA?"

"About three minutes."

"Roger that."

"Suspects are not on the scene, no information as to their whereabouts, over."

"Copy that."

Mark is tending to Pastor Shane while security staff lock down the church. Only the side entrance is open to let the EMTs and police into the building. Traffic is getting out of the way for the ambulance and police as they rush to the church. Pastor Mark hears the sirens and runs out to meet them at the door. He is out of breath, so he points in the direction for them to follow him to Pastor Shane's office. They go in and begin to check his vitals; They place Pastor Shane on a stretcher. They start an IV and then put him in the ambulance. Pastor Mark calls Sheila, Pastor Shane's wife, to break the bad news.

Back at the church police begin to ask the church staff questions to find out who did this. The only person who had seen the two people is Pastor Shane and his secretary, Cindy. The police ask her for a description, and she tells them, "Well, one was a female, about 5'4" with blonde hair,

Torn

blue eyes wearing a black shirt with a cross, and dark jeans. The man was about 5'7", black hair, had the same shirt and dark jeans."

"They had the same shirt, ma'am?" Police officer Wesley asks.

"Yes, they had the same shirt with a cross, but not like Christ's cross; it was slanted slightly and had the abbreviation T.B," he answered.

"Well, we will do all we can base our information on that, ma'am. Our detectives will be here soon. We will stay to ensure no one enters the crime scene. Homicide detectives should be here as well as forensics. Please have your security staff leave the area when they arrive."

"I will, thank you."

About ten minutes later, detectives arrive at the church. Sgt. Anderson comes over to ask security if they had video surveillance.

"Yes, we do, sir," Sean Clark, head of security replied.

"We need to look at those tapes."

"Yes, sir, but there are no cameras in any of the pastors' offices, but there are two in the hallway."

"Well, great, that certainly makes things more difficult; at least you have hallway video," Sgt. Anderson said.

Meanwhile, Pastor Shane is in route to the hospital and still has a weak pulse. The EMTs are very concerned that they will lose him. Once they arrive at the emergency room, the paramedics pull Pastor Shane out of the ambulance a team of doctors and nurses and take him inside. "We need to save this man! He is the pastor of my church. We have a weak pulse Doctor. Take him in trauma one now.

"Doctor, we just lost his pulse." A nurse said.

"No! We are not losing this man. Adrenalin, now!" He ordered. He is doing all he can, as he prays inside for him.

"Okay, let's charge and try to get a pulse...1-2-3- clear!" Pastor Shane's body jumps but no pulse. "Charge again 1-2-3- clear!" Again, nothing.

"Doctor, what do you want to do? It has been ten minutes already, and we have nothing."

"Give him a chance—try one more time."

"Doctor, are you ready?"

"Yes, charge it again...1-2-3- clear!" One last jump of Pastor Shane's body and again, no pulse. "Should we call it, Doctor?" Asked a nurse. "Yes, I'm sad to say...2:45 p.m. is the time of death," The doctor said, walking away in tears.

Pastor Mark and Pastor Shane's family arrive at the hospital to wait on Pastor Shane's status. "Lord God! Please help my husband!" Cried, Sheila. "Please Lord, don't take him from me, from our children."

Doctor Neal went out to the waiting room to greet them. He knows how hard this will be to inform the pastor's family and Pastor Mark of Pastor Shane's death.

"Hello, Pastor Mark."

"Dr. Neal, are you working on Pastor Shane?"

"Yes," Dr. Neal replies.

"How is my husband, Dr. Neal?"

"Sheila, I'm sorry. We did all we could do; your husband has passed away." He said as his eyes filled with tears.

Sheila cries frantically with Pastor Mark as they hold each other. Pastor Shane's teenage children are still on their way to the hospital.

"Oh, why did this happen?" Sheila cries out. Dr. Neal asks if there is anything he can do. Pastor Mark hugs him as they pray and cry together. Dr. Neal asks if they would like to say goodbye to him.

"Yes, yes, we would," Sheila answers. "Where are my children?"

"I'm not sure. I will go out and wait for your kids. When they get here, I'll bring them back."

"Okay,"

As Sheila enters the room with Dr. Neal, she holds her husband's hand and cries. Pastor Shane's children finally arrive, and Pastor Mark walks them back to the room where their father is. "Is my dad alright?" Travis asked. Mark could not bear to answer his question. Travis saw his mother crying, "Mom, Mom, what's wrong?"

"Travis, your father, is gone...he is gone," She said as she burst into tears yet again. Travis held his mother while crying himself and Sheila's daughter Chloe, who was only thirteen, was silent in a state of shock.

The youngest son, Brian is sixteen, fell to his knees bursting into tears crying out for his father. Travis is eighteen, he bends down to his brother and holds him while Sheila is holding Chloe.

"Sheila, Sheila." Pastor Mark whispers trying to get her attention. "We need to be going. We have been in here for thirty minutes. The doctor needs to move him."

"I can't leave him, Mark."

"Sheila, come on, I understand this is hard. I'm sorry, but we have to go."

"Okay," She says. Sheila kissed her husband's forehead. *"I love you, honey. I love you so much."*

Pastor Mark tells Sheila, "Pastor Shane Carl Matthews has had his homecoming; he is now with Jesus."

"Yes, he is Mark; yes, he is," she said, managing a small smile. Sheila's children follow her outside to leave the hospital. "Pastor Mark, thank you for being here for my mother."

"You're welcome, Travis. I'm here for you and your family—everyone is."

"No!" Marcy wakes up screaming; fear grips her body. Her parents run upstairs wondering what's wrong. She lets out a horrible scream again, and it scares them to death. Connor pushes the door open. "What's wrong?"

"Mom, Dad, something horrible happened."

"What Marcy?"

"Pastor Shane, our pastor, something is wrong, I had a vision someone shot him.

Chapter 22

Marcy's vision shocks her parents and forces Connor to make a phone to call the church.

"Mom, it was real, as if I were there and witnessed it," Marcy expressed with grief. Connor is in his bedroom; he dials the church phone number on his cell. The phone rings.

"Hello, Freedom Christian Church, how can I help you?" said the church receptionist.

"Yes, hello, this is Connor Smith; I'm calling to talk to Pastor Shane," he said frantically.

"I am sorry, sir, may I take a message?"

"No! I need to speak with him, now!"

"Sir, I am sorry, but I will have to take a message."

"Listen, he is alright. My daughter had a bad dream. She said someone shot Pastor Shane. I need to—"

"Sir, I'm not allowed to say anything. News about Pastor Shane hasn't been made public. I understand, you are close to Pastor Shane so keep this between us, okay."

"Okay."

"Pastor Shane has been shot and is in the emergency room as we speak."

"What? Is this for real?"

"Yes, I'm afraid it is, Mr. Smith."

"Is this Tamika?"

"Yes."

"I hope your brother-in-law jumps on this one," Connor hangs up the phone. He walks over to his wife to share the news with her.

"Theresa, I need to talk you. Can you come here?"

"What is it, Connor?" Connor begins to whisper to Theresa, "I can't believe this is happening."

"What Connor?"

"I called the church, and Tamika said that it's true. Someone shot Pastor Shane; he's in the emergency room."

"Oh, my goodness, so Marcy was right?"

"It seems so; but how could she have known this?"

"I don't know," Theresa said.

"Should we question her?"

"I don't think she can answer that."

"Well, we need to find out something, Theresa; this is too strange to leave alone."

Marcy is sitting on her bed, wondering why she had this feeling. She asked God why she would think or feel such a thing. Her door closes even though no one is there to close it. The room lit up so bright Marcy can barely see. Marcy's awe and struck with fear. Suddenly, she feels the warmest presence surround her. She feels the most significant presence of love she has ever felt, and she hears in her spirit God telling her that everything will be ok. Then it was gone. Her room returned to its normal state.

Daren, Chelsea, and Bruce arrived back at the house. Chris walked out to the van and asked where they had been. Daren offered a quick explanation. "We went on a little mission," he said.

"A mission, huh! What kind of mission? I didn't order anything," Chris said.

"I went to your church, I talked to your pastor, I distracted him with a bogus story and pulled out the 9mm and shot him. Three shots to his chest and we ran out undetected."

"Oh! I see! Well, I guess that settles that." Not saying another word; he just walked right back inside the house and disappeared.

Pastor Shane gunned down in his church, his office, such a terrible thing for the church and his friends to endure. Members of the church received word via email and text message, per Pastor Mark's request. A man who would do anything for anyone was now gone and in the hands of God. Making funeral plans will have to begin soon. The decision on who will officiate the funeral has yet to be determined; many believe that Sheila will choose either Pastor Mark or Pastor Shane's mentor, Pastor David Brooks. Pastor Brooks mentored Shane for quite a long time; he was fond of him. Pastor Shane had, in turn, mentored Mark and this is a significant loss for him. He is confused and not sure what will happen now.

Many of the members have started to send flowers to the church for the funeral, and many have just been too upset to think about it. The Smith family made the most significant donation and were in complete shock when they first heard the news. Pastor Mark spoke with Pastor Brooks and told him no public announcement of the funeral details and times would be released. Those responsible may plan something else, something on the whole church. Security will be on high alert. And everyone entering the church will be searched.

The only people that should be informed are close friends, family, and the congregation. Pastor Mark is unsure how that would happen since the entire community would read about in newspapers, and maybe national T.V. news. It seems like an impossible task to keep it a secret. " *Maybe the best thing to do,*" he thinks to himself, " *would be to hire extra security inside and outside the church and for the service. Setup scanner, metal detectors, that could help with securing the church.*"

Sheila and her family mourn their loss. Pastor Mark was doing his best to make all the necessary plans for the funeral. Sheila gave him some ideas; she wouldn't be able to do it herself. Sheila's parents are flying in to be with their daughter and grandkids for the funeral. Many church members have sent condolences. Services will be held at the church, although still a crime scene, the funeral service will take place on Saturday morning.

Police are still interviewing office staff and security staff of the church. No clear leads have come up, but one detective is a little curious about the pastor's secretary who is a bit too calm over the whole thing. The investigation will focus on key people and also on questioning church members as to their relationships inside and outside of the church with the pastor. They will be looking into the mystery of the Pastor's alarm that never alerted the security staff as well. They will work extensively with Pastor Mark to help with the case.

Pastor Mark focus, is the careful planning of Pastor Shane's funeral. He is doing all he can do to stay focused, but so much is running through his mind. For one, he is wondering how to break the news to Marcy. Reveal his feelings to her family. And his intentions to date her. Second, the well-being of church members, staff, and of course Sheila's family. Third, the church is under investigation by police, detectives, and news reporters itching for the story on the murder of Pastor Shane. Pastor Mark will most likely delay the youth group concert, as the church needs to say their goodbyes to their pastor. A difficult task for the young pastor to have to endure.

A meeting takes place Thursday afternoon for the pastors and church staff. Pastor Mark decided he will not give information the newspapers and contacted the church's public relations company to make them aware. And no publications were to be made about the funeral. He asked Mrs. Margie Kael, an elderly woman in the church whose family owns a floral shop, to handle the floral arrangements. He has talked to Williamson Funeral Home to instruct them that a viewing would not take place at Sheila's request; the funeral service is on Saturday morning at 10:00 a.m. sharp at the church with Pastor David Brooks presiding.

The funeral procession to the cemetery will take place immediately following the funeral service under heavy security from the church to the cemetery.

Pastor Brooks has been an excellent help for Pastor Mark during this time. Pastor Brooks thinks back in time when he was mentoring a young man who was passionate about serving God. Shane came to him when he was sixteen years of age. Pastor Brooks remembered him asking, "Pastor, you are so cool, how can I be a preacher like you?" Pastor Brooks told the young man, "Well, Shane, you have to attend Bible school, and then find someone who can lead you in the ministry—be a mentor to you."

"Well, Pastor, that's us, don't you think? I have had visions of a church where many people will come to grow and learn of God and come to salvation. I even had visions of the name of the church and a family named Smith."

"Really!" said Pastor Brooks.

"Yes, sir, this is my calling."

Police Detective Trey Williams, the brother-in-law of church operator Tamika Williams, has been brought on to the case; he decides to go through the Pastor's office and his secretary's desk. Why didn't the alarm alert the church security staff; things did not fit together in his mind; he starts by looking under Pastor Shane's desk. *"Why is this wire disconnected? It wasn't cut or severed, nothing."* Forensics told detective Williams, "No prints or DNA with exception to the pastor."

"What!" he said to them as he left for the secretary's desk. He begins to search for any answers that would explain why this happened. There was no alert from her desk, only the phone system between her and the pastor's office. There was no evidence here.

He opens a drawer on the secretary's desk and finds an appointment book. He checks who walked in or who had scheduled appointments with the pastor. He saw nothing during the time frame when the crime occurred. He has become very curious. Pastor Shane did have visitors, but they were not logged in. Det. Williams now has probable cause for him to go and deeply question Cindy, Pastor Shane's secretary.

He decides to have his partner, Det. Peter Madison, meet him over at Cindy's house. Once they are there, they knock on the door. A teen boy answers the door.

"Can I help you?"

"Yes, we are looking for Cindy...Cindy Rhodes. Is she at home?" Det. Williams asked. He noticed the young man is nervous.

"Yes, just a moment. What is this about?"

"We will take that up with her," Det. Madison said.

"I only ask because she is my mother."

"What is your name, son?" Det. Madison asked.

"My name is Scott."

"Okay, Scott, please go find your mother for us. We appreciate it."

"Yes, sir, please hold on a minute," he said. He went into the living room, "Mom, the police are here. They are detectives. You need to come over to the door."

When she walks to the door, she seems shaken and disoriented when Detective Williams asks, "Mrs. Rhodes why didn't you log the two visitors at the church.

"I'm not sure...I was—I was like, it's not in the schedule. They were walk-ins, and I didn't think anything of it." Det. Madison stares at her, "Ma'am, could you please tell me why the pastor's alarm was disconnected?"

"No, sir, I don't have anything to do with those. You should maybe ask security about—"

"Do you understand how this may look since you were his secretary?" Det. Williams said.

"No, I have done nothing wrong. I'm so sad and upset at the whole thing. I cannot imagine anyone who would do such a thing," Cindy said all jittery.

"Thank you for your time, ma'am."

"You're welcome, Detective."

"Oh! One more thing before we go, can we speak with your husband?" Det. Madison asked.

"Why do you need to talk to him?" He has nothing to do with this?"

"We didn't mention that he did; we would like to gather some information from him. Ask about his relationship with the pastor."

"Well, he is out of town at the moment. He drives a truck over the road."

"Okay, can you please have him call me when he returns home?"

"Yes, I can do that."

"Here is my card and Det. Williams card. Please call us as soon as he returns."

Cindy takes the card and closes her door. Det. Williams and Madison decide to put a watch out on the house for any activity and to see if Mr. Rhodes returns. Cindy put on a display that leaves them curious as they walked away, Det. Williams notices Scott peeking through the curtains, staring at them.

Chapter 23

Pastor Mark is up late as he prepares his first eulogy. He begins to write and breaks into tears. He cries out to God, "Lord, please help me with my grief. Comfort me in this dark hour. I need you. What do I do? I have the words, but they won't come out. Tomorrow morning makes me weep, the more I think about what I am trying to say here pierces my heart," warmth and comfort fall upon him as he meditates in the spirit. Some time goes by before he returns to write the eulogy for his fallen mentor. Finishing the eulogy with a broken heart; he goes to bed.

Saturday morning seemed to sneak up on them. 8:30 a.m. and the church parking lot begins to receive parishioners for the funeral. Many are anxious if it would be open casket since there wasn't viewing leading up to the actual funeral itself. Police officers and security staff begin to direct traffic into the parking lot. Security checkpoints are at each entrance of the building inspecting all bags and purses coming in. The church is taking every precaution necessary to ensure everyone's safety.

The Smith family arrive, and a police officer is trying to direct them to park when Connor rolls down his window.

"Sir!" Connor said, "Can you please direct me to the family parking area?" the police officer asks, "do you have a green pass?"

"Yes, sir, I do."

"Then you need to turn around and go to the northwest corner; enter the private parking lot adjacent from the rear of the church."

"Okay, thank you for your help."

"You're welcome, sir," the officer said.

Connor turns around, he makes sure no one is coming, and drives to the area the officer told him to go. Once he arrives at the private parking lot, church security staff direct him to his pass parking number, which is thirteen. Once parked, they leave the vehicle. Theresa walks with Sammy holding her hand. Stephen is walking with Marcy and Connor. Stephen turns his head at the hearse that will take Pastor Shane to the cemetery. His head drops, the heartbreak is overwhelming. The family enters the back entrance where Pastor Mark and Pastor Brooks meet them. "Hello Connor," Mark said with as much joy as he can muster.

"Hello, Pastor."

"Mr. Clark is head of security; he will escort you to your seats."

"Thank you, Pastor, but why do we need security?" Connor asked.

"Precautions for high profile people in our church. Easy targets for attacks. We have to do what is necessary."

"Theresa, take everyone to our seats. I'll be there in a bit," Connor tells her, as he wants to converse with Pastor Mark for another minute or so.

"Pastor," Connor whispers, "do you think this has anything to do with Chris? Please be honest with me."

"I wish I could answer the question for you, Connor. I don't have the answer, but I'm not going to take any chances. I will leave it there."

"I understand." He said.

Connor meets up with his family on the front row; only a few seats from Pastor Shane's family. Theresa looks at Connor, curious about what he spoke to Pastor Mark about. As he sits down next to her, she leans over and gently whispers in his ear, "Is everything okay? What's going on?"

"Everything is fine, given the situation and circumstances; that's all." He whispered back.

It is now 9:30 a.m. The service is scheduled to start at 10:00 am. Church members and community residents fill to seats quick. The balcony is already full. The first three rows in the lower sanctuary are for friends, family, and special guests. The city Mayor, his honor Kenneth Evans, is also in attendance. The sanctuary is filled with chatter and the

Torn

soft sound of, "Just as I Am," playing on the piano. Pastor Shane's casket was rolled in early this morning. A closed casket with a beautiful floral arrangement on it, which includes olive branches and palms.

Pastor Mark checks the time, 9:45 a.m. He walks up the stairs to the stage and stands behind the podium. "Hello, and good morning members, honored guests, and friends. We are starting a little earlier since we seem to have reached our occupancy limit, I would like for us to all stand as we open this service with a word of prayer. "Heavenly Father, we are gathered here today to honor the life of Pastor Shane Carl Matthews. We ask you to bless this service. Place your love and grace upon his family, friends, and our congregation. Thank you for the time you gave us with Pastor Shane, and for the lifetime of memories, we will have. Amen.

You may be seated. Welcome, everyone, my name is Pastor Mark Fields. I'm the youth pastor here at Freedom Christian Center. I don't need to tell you why we are here; I want to say that the heinous crime committed here early this week took us all by surprise. Rest assured, those responsible will be brought to justice. That being said, I wish to continue with some words about Pastor Shane, what he means to me, and how much he loved pastoring this church. I remember Pastor Shane taking me in and mentoring me to be a pastor. He put me through some extensive training, and was tough on me," Mark laughs along with the people in attendance.

"He was a wonderful man, mentor, husband, father, and friend. I will miss him. His laugh, his smile, but most of all; I will miss his encouragement and leadership. Pastor Shane, I will do all that I can to make you proud of me," Mark sniffles with tears flowing down his face.

"I will miss you; heaven is a better place with you in it. Thank you, everyone," Mark leaves the podium wiping tears from his eyes. Pastor Brooks meets him at the steps. He embraces him and tells him, "Mark, Pastor Shane was, is and will always be proud of you."

"Thank you."

Pastor Brooks takes his place behind the podium to address the crowd.

"Hello, my name is Pastor David Brooks. I am honored, and sad at the same time to be here with you today as we all say goodbye to a great man. I have a few stories about Pastor Shane to share with you. I'm going to tell you about my dear friend whom I helped bring up in the ministry. I'm going to speak about some good times, funny times and some challenging times. I appreciate the leadership of this church who has allotted me this time to share those things with you all. I'm sure that I will say things about your Pastor that you may have never known.

I was pastoring a church just outside of Topeka, Kansas when a young man approached me. He introduced himself and looked me right in the eye and said, "I'm gonna be a pastor. You look so cool, and He was adamant about his desire to help people and wanted to get into church leadership. His family wasn't the most prosperous—his father was a welder and his mother stayed home with the children. Shane was the youngest of three children; his oldest brother, David Matthews, was killed while serving in the United States Army.

His older sister, Kari "Wallace" Matthews, was his inspiration; he loved her and admired her very much. Kari married Evan Wallace, and they moved to San Francisco. Evan began a career working as a lawyer at a successful firm. Shane didn't see his sister for many years. He was in college when he received word from his mother that Kari had been diagnosed with cancer.

Devastated by the news, he got a flight out of Omaha, Nebraska, where he was attending school. He arrived in San Francisco and spent two weeks with his sister, she was not doing well, and the treatment she had received was not working. He told me once that his sister was diagnosed late and she died three days before he was supposed to leave. It was the hardest thing, he said me, that he had to deal with; he had seen more than his share of loss in his family. He decided then that he wanted to work with people and help them. 'I want to be a Pastor,' he said to me. 'I want to see people leave this world and see heaven. Those stories he shared with me compelled me to do all I could to mentor him.

I'm glad he became successful man. When I started training Shane, I sent him into the city with a group from our church to clothe and feed the homeless. One day Shane came to me and told me that he met a man who was doing the same thing as the church but also offered shelter. He said, "The man seemed to seek out teens and young adults who were homeless." I told him I was pleased someone was doing that.

"He later told me that he walked up to the man and introduced himself. He asked the man his name, and he told him, Zachias Gant. He told Shane he had a little girl with him; his daughter Jessie, I have a good memory," he laughs. Her mother died, and he alone was raising her. Shane asked him why he was helping the homeless and Zachias told him something, but I can't remember that part.

Shane said that after a few months, he no longer saw Zachias or his daughter anymore. They never exchanged information to keep in touch. Shane simply believed that fate would someday bring them together again. Shane was a people person; he loved his family, his church, and his friends. I will truly miss my friend, Shane Matthews; I'm sure this church and community will miss him even more. Thank you, and God bless you all," Pastor Brooks exits the stage as Dan Taylor walks up to the podium.

"Ladies and gentlemen, my name is Dan Taylor; I'm the music director here at Freedom Christian Center. I would like to speak on behalf of our new children's pastor, Mr. Donald "Donnie" Ray. He has not yet moved to Kansas City, but he asked me to send his condolences to us all. Pastor Shane, with the approval of our pulpit committee, hired Pastor Donnie a few weeks ago. He had to finish work at his other church in Lincoln, Nebraska before officially moving here. That being said, I ask that you join with me in singing, "Amazing Grace."

The church begins to sing and Sheila, with her children by her side, start to cry as Pastor Shane's coffin is wheeled out slowly from the sanctuary. His casket is placed into the hearse for transport to the cemetery. With the singing complete, Pastor Dan releases the congregation and instructs them to follow the procession to the cemetery. Police line the streets outside the church in a column of two rows. They pull out just beyond the main church entrance. The procession begins the ten-mile drive to Fairfield cemetery, where Pastor Shane Carl Matthews will be laid to rest.

James Owens

Looking on in the distance was Chris and his little entourage. He watched the line of cars as they left; he stood proud, unashamed, and loved the feeling of being anonymous to the authorities. He looked on; the war had just begun...he is ready.

Chapter 24

Zaga sits in his sanctuary reading the Monday morning edition of the Herald. The paper opened with a front-page picture of the hearse leaving the church. The article reads, "FREEDOM CHRISTIAN CENTER. Pastor Shane Carl Matthews was gunned down in his office this past week. A suspect or suspects are still on the loose; police are not commenting or giving any details at this time. The church's spokesperson Mr. Spitzer says, "We are very sad; this is a horrible thing that has happened to our church, our Pastor, and our community. Once we have information to give, we will share it with the public."

Zaga is shocked and surprised at what he is reading. He remembered that man from the old days when working with the homeless. He can't believe it, he thought about Chris. Did Chris have a hand in this or what kind of person would do such a thing to a holy man for the people? Taken aback, Zaga looks up the church's phone number. Should he call? What if—"*Nah*," he thought, "*just leave it alone.*" Though it is weighing on his mind, he decides to wait on the reports and what would come of this.

Marcy cries as she reads the newspaper, *"can this be real?"* Confusion and doubts cluttered her mind. Her heart aches for her late pastor and his family. Sheila Matthews, Pastor Shane's widow, told her mother that she and her children were moving—leaving Kansas City. She could not bear the pain of staying and attending the church her husband once led. Marcy feels everything falling apart, crumbling before her eyes.

Stephen has been practicing his guitar. Keeping up with his schoolwork has been a challenge, but he hopes to make the honor roll this quarter. Pastor Mark has been doing various activities with him to keep busy. Mark is still waiting for the church to decide what to do about a new pastor. It was soon. Just a couple of days since the funeral, but the church needs to pick up the pieces and search for a pastor or promote one on staff. Pastor David Cole, the executive pastor, has expressed his interest in being the new senior pastor. The church pulpit committee has considered his interest. They are also considering Pastor Michael Parker, an associate pastor at the church.

Whoever is chosen, one thing is for sure; it will be an enormous task to pull the staff and the congregations back together. Healing needs to take place and new security measures to implement. That will keep Sean busy.

Both Det. Williams and Det. Madison are working the case as hard as they can. Questioning everyone from the church staff to certain congregation members. They are getting ready to drive over to the Smith home to speak with Theresa, Connor, and Marcy. Word had spread about Marcy's dream when her mother told Karen who then told her husband, Frank. Frank felt it appropriate to say to the police as it seemed a little suspicious to him. Frank is confused, hoping Marcy had a vision of the murder and withheld information. Connor and Frank have not been around each other much, although the project is in full swing.

"Ready to go, Peter?" Det. Williams asks.

"Yeah, in a few minutes, Trey."

"What's the hold-up?"

"I may have come across some information that would allow us to bring Mrs. Rhodes and her son Scott in for questioning."

"Let's go."

"Hey cowboy, don't get too excited yet. We will bring them in, but it won't be enough to hold them. Put that gun back in its holster," he said joking with him laughing.

"Well, you got me all pumped up now—I mean, I have been itching to pull someone in on this case. I don't want it to dry up. I don't need my sister-in-law bugging me day-in-day-out for information. People want answers, suspects, so we need to come up with something soon."

"Don't worry, partner; we will have something. Let's get ready to get over to the Smith's."

Tanner walks around searching for Zaga. She notices a specific type of sanctuary building and decides to go in and take a chance. When she walks in, she sees him sitting in the sanctuary, *"Oh thank heavens, I found him."* She walks up and sits down by his side. He is surprised she found him. He is speechless and curious as to why she came.

"Are you okay?" she asks.

"Yes and no," he replied. "I'm glad you're here Tanner."

"What's going on?" she said as she hugged him.

"Here!" he said, handing her the newspaper. Tanner read the news about the church and the pastor. Her mind went straight to Chris, *"Could Chris have ordered this? Who would have carried it out?"* she can't stop thinking about it.

"Zaga, I think Chris had something to do with this. He must have ordered the hit on the pastor. May I ask why you're upset about this?"

"I knew this man."

"How?"

"A long time ago when I was young, this man and I worked the same side of town feeding the homeless and clothing them, offering hope. I had lost contact with him, figured I would never see or hear of him again. Whoever is to blame for this. Whoever is involved; they are in a bad, bad place. Well, if this was Chris; he has waged war on the wrong people."

"I don't understand. What do you mean by the wrong people?"

"He was a holy man, Tanner. Whoever is responsible, they have awoken a sleeping giant. The spirit world is about to clash, and if Chris is going to do what you think he will, then it will be an epic battle."

"So, you believe in their God? she asked.

"Yes, I don't follow him, he is real, and you don't want to invoke his wrath by attacking his anointed," he said with conviction. Zaga is smart enough not to mess with God's people. Not a wise decision to do so. However, he senses a fight coming, and the spirit world is about to collide with the carnal world. He will have to move quick, be swift in his efforts to help those who want out from Chris's power. He must first rescue one person, one who means everything to him. She is his main priority. His daughter, Jessie Gant...

Frank and Connor meet in the firm's conference room. Connor is extremely upset about things and wants Frank to come clean about what's going on with his involvement in the construction company.

"What's going on, Frank?"

"Hey, Connor! Things are fine. Things are going along fine. You have been in and out and I understand."

"You know what I mean, Frank! Come out with it and tell me the truth!" Connor said. His piercing stare into Frank's eyes wielded a quick response from Frank.

"Okay, Connor, okay. I have been in with the Miller Construction Co. for years. I bought into the company to make extra money. It may be a conflict of interest, but I need this, man."

"So, you're getting kickbacks on the construction builds from our firm and others?"

"Yes. I own twenty-five percent of the company."

"Okay, and what about the lawsuits? I uncovered information about some lawsuits that have been taken out against Miller Construction Co. without my knowledge. I am in this partnership, and you have put this firm in jeopardy for selfish reasons."

"I took care of those, we are in the clear, Connor. Miller construction and I, Settled them out of court for next to nothing. Amazing what people will do with a quick lump sum cash settlement thrown at them. Nothing is hanging over our heads—Trust me."

"Trust is earned, Frank! You have made my trust in you, well, let's weak."

"I understand, but Connor, we are fine, and I'm sorry for not telling you anything. I didn't want you in on it if it collapsed. If you didn't know, then you would have deniability, right?"

"I don't know, Frank, I'm not an attorney. How deep are you into things? I know you're not out," he said in frustration, biting his lip as his veins are popping out of his neck.

"We're okay, Connor. I swear we are in the clear. Seriously, nothing the construction company has done will be legally tied to our firm. We are two separate companies."

"You better be right about this. No more secrets, no more lies, if we are going to continue our friendship and partnership. Do you understand me?"

"Okay, buddy. I love you and your family," he said gracefully. Frank does care about Connor and his family. He supported them when Marcy had her accident. He and his wife had taken care of Sammy and Stephen. They have always been available for them.

Both Detectives Trey Williams and Peter Madison have left the police station on their way over to the Smith home. They will be questioning Marcy based on information obtained through what they would say was an "unnamed source." Neither Marcy nor her parents have any idea that their friends Frank and Karen had informed the authorities about Marcy's experience. Det. Madison and his partner Det. Williams pulls up to the Smith home, exited their vehicle and make their way to the front door. They walk up the long pathway to the front door and ring the doorbell.

Theresa opens the door and is greeted by two men with badges. She recognizes these men, yet confusion took over her face as she calls for Connor.

Chapter 25

Stephen is battling with emptiness; his spirit is flat; his soul is like a desert. His life has changed dramatically in such a short time.

Not long ago he was enjoying youth group retreats. They were highlighted events, and he played in most of them. From the time of his sister's graduation to the present, he feels like the third wheel to his parents. Pastor Mark is always there for him, but with Pastor Shane gone now, he hasn't been around.

Her focus is somewhere else, and her parents are trying to pull things back together. Connor's work is stressing him, and he is unhappy with Frank. Connor senses something is going on behind closed doors, but he hasn't quite put his finger on it. The stress is causing separation from his family as he tries to figure it out. Theresa, of course, tries to help the church in hopes of getting past the traumatic events. She senses something isn't right. There's not enough information going around. Could this be the first in a series of attacks? Theresa's heart is broken at the thought her son could have been a part of the murder in one way or another. Thinking about it only sent her into more heartache; all she wants to do is help in any way she can, but her thoughts haunt her.

Thomas has begun to plan his attacks carefully. He wants to strike now and asks Max and Gregg, "Hey! Can you guys do me a favor?"

"Sure," Max says, staring at Gregg.

"What's up, Thomas? What can we do for you?" Gregg asked.

"I need you guys to build me a car bomb. You are capable; that's your primary reason for being here. I need your help with this. Can you help me?"

"Yeah! I mean, why not bro, I'm so eager. We are finally starting to do things. Who are we planting the bomb on?" Gregg asks.

"A pastor!"

"Sweetness," Max says with his California surfer lingo.

"Well, I'm glad you guys are gung-ho and ready. I'm counting on both of you for this one."

"No problem, Thomas, we got this." Max looks at Gregg with excitement.

Max and Gregg walk away down the long hallway from Thomas's room. They go downstairs and out the back door to the shed to talk about what kind of car bomb they would build.

Rocco has returned to the house to visit Chris. A while has passed since he last visited. Rocco says hello to members passes by and gets his usual wink from Chelsea. He walks to Chris's room and opens his door.

"Hey!" Chris yells, not knowing Rocco was the one who walked in.

"Hey what, bro?"

"Sorry, man, I thought you were one of the others. What's up, man? I haven't seen you for some time now."

"I've been a busy man."

"Yeah! I hear ya. So, what do you need?"

"What happened to the pastor; the one I read about in the paper?"

"Why do you care?" Chris asks with a *smug* tone.

"Who did it? Don't play. Tell me who did this." Rocco demands with a stern, loud voice.

"Daren, Bruce, and Chelsea."

"Really!"

"Yes, really, but why do you care?"

"Probably because I have a right to ask. You're not the only one in power here."

"Okay," he said, feeling pressured not to be on Rocco's bad side. Rocco is influenced by Satan as well and possesses certain powers.

"Well, then I want in on everything."

"I'm fine with that, bro. If not for you, I wouldn't even be here." This was never seen in Chris before. Away from his hard demeanor and tough guy mentality. This was a much weaker side.

Rocco finished up with Chris and went about his business in the house. He begins checking things over and checking on other members. He is smug, full of himself, to other members, but they dare not say anything, knowing he and Chris are close.

Rocco sits down with Bruce in the den. "So, you were involved in the pastor's death, were you not?"

"Well, I um, yes...yes I was. But I didn't do anything! I only, I didn't hurt anyone, Rocco. I swear, man, I only drove the van. Please don't—" Rocco cuts him off.

"Dude, I'm not mad. I'm impressed you did what you did," he laughs as he pulls Bruce's head under his arm, giving him a noogie.

"I do want to talk to Daren and Chelsea about this too."

"They are outside, want me to get'em?"

"Just Daren, please."

"Okay."

Bruce goes out to get Daren while Rocco sits and waits in the house. Rocco isn't happy with Daren. He has brought undue attention to them. He was careless in his eyes. Rocco pulls a 9mm from the back of his jeans, checks the chamber and magazine, then slipped the pistol back. Bruce walks in with Daren. Rocco tells Bruce to leave, but Daren sits down to talk to Rocco.

"What's up, Rocco? Haven't seen you so much lately."

"Yeah, well I've been busy with other matters; this isn't the only thing going on in my life."

"What do you want to talk to me about?" Daren asked.

"Bruce didn't tell you?"

"Nope, he said you wanted me is all."

"Well, let's start with the big issue, okay?"

"Sure, Rocco, what's the issue?"

"You and Chelsea went to a church in the middle of the day and killed the pastor of that church. The church Chris's family attends. Why would you do it? He came back from lunch with Chris's family with a young preacher boy?" Daren had no clue Rocco has been watching Chris's family, but neither did Chris.

"I thought it was our mission! Chris isn't upset about it, man."

"Of course not you fool; he has hatred for them. What you've done here makes us all suspicious, and that's not good. I was in the sanctuary during the funeral service, and people were talking; saying Chris maybe had something to do with this. You have no idea what you have started, Daren. We, meaning Chris and I, have put things in motion and you move on your own? Not wise, Daren, what am I supposed to do?"

"What do you mean, I didn't mean to go over anyone's head. I did what I thought I was right, and Chris said nothing to me in a negative sense," he replied with a sad voice and as tears started down his face. "I didn't think we would be suspects for the crime."

"Well, allow me to let you in on a little secret. We had that place set up. That church was going to fall. I kidnapped the secretaries husband. She was doing everything we instructed her to do. We were getting close. Now she is a suspect because the pastor's alarm was not working. Now I have to deal with her with cops snooping around. I'm not here most of the time due to planning things out like this, and you go and mess everything up."

"Dude! Seriously! Can we talk to Chris about this?"

"You're done, do you hear me, done!" Rocco pulls the 9mm out. Daren leaps up as Rocco fires two rounds, and Daren fell dead, bleeding out on the hardwood floor. Everyone heard the gunshot and went running. Chris and Jessie run downstairs. When they enter the room, Daren is lying on the floor dead; bullets to his head and chest.

"Take his body and put it in an ally or ditch, I don't care, put this letter in his back pocket addressed to Freedom Christian Center."

"What?" Chris replies. "Are you serious?"

"Do it, Chris, or have someone else."

"You could have told me, Rocco, you could have let me in on your plan. I am the leader of this group. We have mutual respect, bro, but you have to include me in things like this."

"I'll tell you if you need to know—until then. Get rid of him."

"What's in the letter, Rocco?"

"A suicide letter describing what he did and why. No reason for his death; gang violence or something. I don't care. Take care of it, please! I have more damage control to do.

"Okay! We'll clean this up," he replies with an attitude of disgust. "Come on you two, hey, you two over there! Let's go, Luke, Tobey let's go!"

Chris walks away and goes to his bedroom. He will seek out his master for some answers and hopes this matter will be resolved between him and Rocco. Chris will not share power with him. He is the only leader, the only one calling the shots. He sits and begins to meditate. Chris calls out for Satan but gets no answer. Frustrated, he spends the rest of his time making notes as he tries to make sense of the day's events.

Jessie knocks on his door and walks in. She decides to check in on him, see if he is okay.

"Hello, Chris."

"What do you want, Jessie?"

"Are you okay? What happened today was horrible. A lot of the people here are scared. There are no explanations given to us, just a lot of confusion. Daren being shot and killed by Rocco. I mean, is this a part of the oath you had everyone take?"

"This has nothing to do with you or anyone else out there. This is Rocco doing what he does. I can't stop him; he's in charge as much as I am. I was unaware he had his own agenda. I feel lost, I thought I was the one bringing this war on, but Rocco must be taking the lead. I don't care about what happened to my former pastor but killing Daren as a way to keep cops off us, and I think the opposite will happen."

"Do you think he is betraying you?"

"I don't know, but I will find out soon enough. Trust me!"

Jessie leaves, and Chris closes his door. He, again, calls out for his master and gets a weird voice in his head calling him. He sits quietly to listen.

Confusion and chaos have filled the atmosphere in the house. Members have a lost look on their faces. They cannot believe what has happened before their eyes. Bruce is especially distraught due to his involvement with Daren and Chelsea in the pastor's murder; although he didn't kill him, Bruce worries what would happen now since Rocco has murdered Daren to pawn him off to the authorities.

Tobey and Luke return from dumping Daren's body in a ditch far from their side of town. Neither of them said a word to each other. They walk to their rooms and close their doors. Jessie senses they are upset and hurting—everyone is. Just how far are things going to go, at this point, who can say. Jessie is sure on one thing; she will have to step up and defend those who she believes she could save from Rocco and Chris.

Allie and John have left the house together around 4:00 a.m. John told Allie they needed to scram out of there. These people were promised nothing, only hurting and killing people they didn't like.

"John, what if we are caught? They will kill us!" Allie said. She is nervous and weak in the knees.

"We will go far from here. A place we can go for safety, Allie. We have to go to the other side of the city, but we will be safe. There is a man I met once; he said if I were ever in trouble he would help. We will be good."

"Okay, John. I trust you. Let's go."

Hoping to make safety, the two never look back. One goal, one truth, no consequences for actions. This is the thinking of Chris's breed. Chris lost some leverage as the leader and those who were once friends would soon become foes.

Chapter 26

Connor comes to the door behind his wife. He opens the glass screen door and asks the Detectives, "How can I help you?"

"Sir, we would like to ask your daughter, Marcy, a few questions. May we, please come in?" Det. Williams asked.

"Sure, please come in. Would you like something to drink? Coffee, soda?"

"I will have a bottle of water if you have one," Det. Williams said.

"Sure!"

"Theresa, can you please bring Detective Williams a bottle of water?"

"Yes. Would Detective Madison like anything?" Theresa asks.

"I'm fine, ma'am. We need to start. We have other places to go today," Det. Madison said, seeming to act like the bad cop in the "good cop, bad cop" game. Connor is not impressed with his antics and sent his body language back at him. Theresa came back with a bottle of water, some coffee and a small tray of gingerbread cookies. Marcy is told by her mom to come downstairs; two Detectives are here to ask her some questions. With all parties gathered in the living room, Det. Madison begins.

"Marcy, I would like to ask you about your dream, the one you told your parents about. The one about your pastor being and killed."

"Well, first off. I'm not sure how you came by this information. Second, I had a unique, let's say, *Spiritual experience.* But to answer your question, yes, I did sense it happened. I was in a car accident, and a coma; lots of things happened. I have never had visions or experiences I seem to be having now."

"Forgive me for asking this next question, Marcy," Det. Williams said. "I have to know. When you had the experience, was it real?"

"I can't explain what I felt. You are looking for someone to point the finger at. I'm not the person you should be looking for, talking to, or accusing. I cannot explain anything to you. You will not be willing to accept any truth I give you. You only want the truth that suits you. I'm done talking to you, gentleman."

"Well, this conversation is over when we say it is," Det. Madison said cold-heartedly. He intended to trap her to be able to take her into custody. His mind races with the thought of taking her out of her environment. His face shrinks thinking about it, he wants a suspect, and soon...

"It's over now. I'm done talking to you. If you have something for which to charge me with, then arrest me. Otherwise, please excuse yourselves!" Marcy surprised her parents with her statements. This Marcy, the new Marcy, is someone they have never seen before. They are shocked at her convictions.

They leave the Smith home, unsure where to take things from here. Det. Williams struggles with guilt; knowing the Smith family was close to Pastor Shane. Sometimes the hardest thing to face is people who are closest to you. No doubt he would talk to his wife asking her input. Pastor Shane was an open man with most people. He had unique relationships with individual members, such as the Smith family. Ester Matthew's keeps up on the investigation in her son's death as she prays for answers. Ester Matthews is eighty-one years old, now alone, all she has now is her daughter-in-law and her grandchildren.

Rocco has been all over the city and beyond to put his plans into motion. Chris had no idea this fight could take his life. Rocco is cold, indeed, cold to the bone. He doesn't care about anything or anyone; his heart is hard as a rock. Rocco can think about only avenging his father's death. The company had settled out of court, claiming that Mitchel, Rocco's father, had been under the influence of either drugs or alcohol or both. The insurance company claimed this was the cause of his work related death. A false toxicology report was presented to the insurance company to make things go away.

Rocco never believed his father was drunk or under the influence of drugs. He is seeking vengeance against Miller Construction Company, his late father's employer. Rocco befriended Chris Smith in college after finding out that his father was with the Douglas and Smith architecture firm; the firm that contracted with Miller Construction. Rocco Thought it all out and so far, flawlessly planned, he was able to make Chris hate his family so much he left his whole life with them. He helped Chris join the cult lead by Zaga. Rocco wants revenge on everyone involved. He needs Questions to be answered soon. Rocco will meet with a man in a few days. He hopes this will help him achieve his goals.

Everything Rocco planned was strategic. Right down to the very people that would be targeted. He intends to receive justice for his father. Rocco is a genius; so is Chris—only Chris can't see the strategic plot that is building behind his back. Would Chris figure things out before it was too late? Only time will tell...

Pastor Mark is doing all he can to pick up the pieces. As the days have passed, he seems to become more lost. A senior pastor is what the church needs; not a youth pastor. Taking a break from his work, Mark asked Bruce Anderson if he would like to join him for coffee down the block at a local Starbucks. Bruce agreed to the invite and the two men left the church.

At the coffee shop, Mark begins to ask Bruce some questions.

"Bruce, I want to ask you about Pastor Shane."

"Uh...okay, Pastor, what would you like me to tell you?"

"Why his alarm didn't work. I want to find something; answers to the questions no one is asking. The right questions to find any truth. It doesn't make sense."

"I didn't realize you were part of the investigation!"

"I'm not, I just—"

"Look, Pastor, the entire security staff, myself included, is searching for answers. The reason it didn't work is simple. Someone disengaged the alarm; it's as simple as that. The only question is who would want to do such a thing and have access to do it?"

"I agree. Something doesn't fit right."

"Can I ask you a question, Pastor?"

"Sure."

"Who's going to step up and lead this church? Will the pulpit committee arrive at a decision soon?"

Pastor Mark had no answer for him, as the committee hasn't scheduled any meetings, they haven't scheduled interviews or mentioned promoting anyone to Senior Pastor. Things happened too fast and with it all fresh in their minds, there is no rush on finding anyone. "I can't answer that question, Bruce."

"I understand. I would say, Pastor David Knoll. He is only an associate pastor, but he is well qualified."

"I agree with you, but we have to wait and see."

They finished their coffee and returned to the church. Mark walks to his office puzzled, no clear thought on helping the investigation. He spent the rest of the afternoon in his office trying to study.

Chris is still upset about Rocco trying to take over or be equal to him. He is best letting things be. Rocco killing Daren has made an everlasting impact on other members; he made his statement with action. Thomas tells Chris police have found the body in a ditch. Some kids riding by on their bikes stopped and saw a body and then reported the location. Jessie created a little distance between her and Chris isn't happy about it.

His world is starting to crumble around him. Chris is not sure what to do. He hasn't been getting guidance from Satan about anything. None of the other members have asked any questions. They merely did the tasks set before them, and now it seemed as though Rocco is giving all the orders. Chris sits on the floor in his bedroom by the window. Some light shines in from behind the dark curtains/ With his head in his hands, Chris once again tries to call out to his master for answers.

Chapter 27

Max finished making his homemade car bomb with Gregg's assistance. It is a simple ignition trigger. Once the car starts, there would be a three-second delay and then—Boom! They discuss the plan to plant the bomb on the car. They are excited about Thomas's reaction to their work. Gregg calls Thomas out to the garage.

"What's up Gregg?"

"We finished the car bomb that you wanted," Gregg said with enthusiasm. Overjoyed at the accomplishment.

"Sweet man, show me."

"Here it is," Max said, showing the device. He hopes that Thomas would be impressed with their work.

"This is awesome Max. I'm not sure how you make these things, and I won't ask. The target works for Freedom Christian Center. He drives an old Dodge Durango. This is your mission. I expect you to follow through."

"No problem, Thomas, we can handle this," Max said with a giant grin on his face.

Pastor Mark pulls into the church parking lot at 8:15 a.m. Tuesday morning. Fresh Starbucks coffee is in his right hand and a black leather Samsonite briefcase in his left. He kicks his car door closed with his right foot and pushed the lock button on his key fob. Another day at work; another day to wonder who would be leading this church.

As he walks to go to his office, he is greeted by his secretary. She tells Pastor Mark about a message that he has.

"Pastor, Det. Williams called and asked to speak to you right away. I told him you would call him back."

"Did he say where?"

"No, just said you needed to return his call."

"Okay, give me his number."

"Yes, 555-675-9876."

"Thanks." He walks into his office. He sets his briefcase down on the floor by his desk and put his coffee down. His office is beautifully decorated with all oak furnishings and a burgundy leather office chair. Once he settles in, he makes the return call to Det. Williams.

"Hello," Det. Williams answers.

"Det. Williams, Pastor Mark here returning your call."

"Pastor Mark. Thank you for calling me back so promptly. I need to meet with you as soon as possible. I have some new information in our investigation, and I want to disclose it only to you at this time."

"Uh...okay! When would you like to meet and where?" Pastor Mark asked.

"How about for lunch at Chubby's?"

"Sounds great," Pastor Mark said as he hung up the phone. Chubby's is a local sports bar that serves all kinds of food from Buffalo wings to fish and chips and BBQ ribs. It is a local favorite, and best place to go during football season. People show up in masses wearing their Chiefs jerseys, cheering their team to victory. Pastor Mark goes there with an old high school friend, Scott Hummel; he is now a thriving defense attorney. It is their weekly hang time when football season starts. Though with things going the way they are right now, they have yet to meet up. The Chiefs are having a spectacular season, but that has escaped Mark's attention.

Pastor Mark leaves the church at noon and drives to Chubby's, fighting the lunch rush traffic. A beautiful crisp October day, his windows are down to enjoy the fresh air. He arrives at the restaurant and parks along the side of the building. He walks into Chubby's,

Torn

looking for Det. Williams. The hostess greets him, and he tells her he is meeting someone.

He tries to find him. A big hand is waving him over to the corner. Det. Williams has a small booth in the corner, free of any eavesdroppers. Mark pulls out his chair and sits down. The server asks him what he would like to drink, and he politely answered with, "I'll have a lemonade." Det. Williams stares Pastor Mark right in his dark brown eyes and tells him the news that shakes him deep into his bones.

"Pastor, Cindy is involved in this murder, I am certain of it. We visited her, asked questions, but she was apprehensive. Cindy was unwilling to answer some simple questions. I asked to speak to her husband, and she said he drives truck over-the-road. Det. Madison called the company and was told that he had not been to work in over a week. Suspicious, don't you think?"

"I'm at a loss for words." Pastor Mark runs his fingers through his hair. His eyes are wide open, and he lets out a deep exhale. "Are you sure? I mean I need to—"

Det. Madison interrupts, "Pastor, I wish I was wrong; I felt the need to tell you in person before an arrest is made."

Saddened by the news, Pastor Mark begins to tear up. The server brings his lemonade and her demeanor changes seeing his grief. She asks, "Can I get you anything else sweetie? Some tissue, maybe?"

"No," he answers with a grateful smile. "I'll be alright," he says as server walks away. He is far from being okay. His spirit feels crushed as if a wrecking ball hit him. The news is excellent for the Detectives, but it is bitter news for him and hard to swallow.

He will have to go back to the church and call a meeting to inform them of the news. Pastor Mark thanks Det. Williams for telling him and gets up from his seat and leaves a five-dollar bill on the table for his drink, having lost his appetite.

Gregg and Max wrap up their homemade car bomb and catch a city bus. It was a long ride, and both their nerves are erratic. They continue to look at each other as if to say, "Wow! This is real, and we're doing this," They reach their stop and hop off the bus. "What is the address again, Max?"

"7771 Moss Avenue. It will be about a ten-minute walk. Then we have to put this thing in place without being noticed."

As they walk toward their destination, they are both sweating profusely, though it is quite cool outside, sixty-five degrees. Not that it matters, they are so nervous about what is going to happen. Coming around the corner, Max sees the church. The parking lot is empty. They walk around to the other side of the church, staying far in the distance. Cars are parked in the employee parking zone. They scan through the mass of cars, looking for the Durango. They are discouraged since the Durango isn't there. Max decides that they should stake it out. They sit down next to some small trees and wait.

Pastor Mark gets into his car and pulls a small box from the armrest. He stares at the diamond ring that he purchased in hopes of asking the right woman to marry him one day. Pastor Mark closes his eyes and pictures what it would be like to be a husband and a father. He fantasizes about a future life that he could have. A big white house, play set in the backyard for the kids. He begins to cry as he closes the box and places it back into the armrest. He drives back to the church, leaving his emotions behind.

Back at the church, he walks to his office, he calls for Sean Clark, the head of security. Pastor Mark dreads telling Sean that Cindy is a prime suspect in Pastor Shane's murder and will be arrested soon. Sean walks to Pastor Mark's office. They greet each other with a hug and handshake.

"How are you doing, Pastor?" Sean asked.

"I'm doing as good as I can, given all that has happened."

"Forget about all that for now, Pastor. I am asking how you are doing—you—not the church," he said.

"Personally, Sean, I'm stressed out, a wreck. I'm derailing, and I can't stop it. The weight of the future of this church is on my shoulders. I—I."

"Hold on, Pastor. You are suffering; but you're too strong a man to be defeated this way. I know things are tough, but you have to recharge yourself in times like these. Let one of the elders or Pastor David take things over for a while. You should take some time off—you need it."

"Indeed, I do. I have a responsibility to be here. This attack might be the first wave of many more. Hopefully not, but we have to watch our backs now."

"I hear you, Pastor. I think we should bring the leadership together today and discuss this new information about Cindy. I can't believe it—Cindy."

Max and Gregg take their chances now that the is back Durango. Gregg keeps an eye out to make sure no one comes around, and if someone does; he would pretend to be walking around and leave Max under the car. It takes Max about ten minutes to install the bomb; it is hard-wired into the vehicle's ignition. Once Max finished, they run into the brush away from the church parking lot. Gregg wants to wait to wait for the show, but not Max.

"No, we are getting outta here."

Gregg isn't happy with the decision, but he will not stay behind alone. They take the ten- minute walk back to the bus stop. They are sweating and panting hard. adrenaline pumping hard through their veins. They arrive at the bus stop and sit down on the bench. They see a woman sitting on the bench, and she offers each of them a bottle of water.

"Thank you, ma'am," Max said as he unscrewed the bottle cap. He downed the water with huge gulps.

"Yes! Thank you very much," Gregg said as he poured some water over his head and devoured the rest.

"You're both welcome," she said gently. "You boys sure are thirsty. Wish I had more, I would give it to you."

"That's okay, ma'am, we appreciate what you have already given,"

Max said while he continued drinking. "May I ask you your name, ma'am?" Max said.

"Yes, my name is Janice, and may I ask what your names are?"

"Mine is Max, and this is Gregg. We are like brothers."

"Well, Max and Gregg, it's a pleasure meeting you," she said. I'm afraid it is time for me to get going."

"Aren't you waiting for the bus?"

"Oh, no. I have another ride, young man," she said as she giggled a bit.

Max took another drink of water, put his head down. When he lifted it back up he looked her direction, but she was gone.

"Max, Max!" Gregg called out.

"What Gregg?"

"Where did she go?"

"Where did who go?"

"The lady who gave us water!"

"Oh, her! She was—she was just here," he said, puzzled at her disappearance.

"Dude, seriously?"

"Bro, I have no idea!"

"All she said was that she had another ride—then poof—gone," Gregg said, amazed at what he had witnessed.

When the bus arrives, they get on and sit near the back. Still, they were puzzled about the lady who gave them water and her mysterious disappearing. It left them curious.

3:30 in the afternoon, Det. Williams and Det. Madison arrive at Cindy's house with a black and white squad car. Cindy peeks out through the curtains and is brought to tears. " *They are here for me,*" she said to herself. There is a knock on the door and, after an eerie, lonely walk to answer it, she paused for a minute, opened the door and is greeted coldly with words she never imagined hearing.

"Cindy Rhodes?" Det. Madison asked, knowing who she is.

"Yes, Sir," she replied.

"This is Officer Davis; we need you to come with us please."

"Am I under arrest?" she asked, full of fear as her heart started pounding in her chest.

"Please turn around and place your hands behind your back," Officer Davis ordered. He then begins reading Cindy her rights, "You have the right to remain silent. Anything you say can and will be used against you in a court of law. You have the right to an attorney; if you cannot afford an attorney, one will be provided for you. Do you understand the rights I have read to you? With these rights in mind, do you wish to speak to me?"

Cindy remained silent. She said nothing and doesn't look at anyone. She is sobbing, scared, and unsure why she is being arrested. She is handcuffed and led down her driveway. Her neighbors became curious spectators; surprised at what is happening. The cars pull away and drive to the police station.

Chapter 28

Connor's confusion about Marcy's vision burdens him. He's not sure if he should trust what she said or play along to not hurt her feelings. Theresa (being the mother that she is) supports her daughter and believes her without question. Strange as it may be, Stephen has been keeping his distance from Marcy. He fears for what is happening to her, the visions and such. Maybe it is jealousy from all the attention she is getting. Stephen is closed off and stays to himself. He won't even talk to Pastor Mark since he has no time for him anymore.

He is a young man who needs a role model and his only two choices, his father and youth pastor, are too busy for him but not for his sister. Even though they went to a concert together to have father-son time, resentment is building in his heart. Not long ago, his father saw *the light* and wanted to be a better father; now his work schedule is hectic again with the new stadium and sports complex underway. The new sports complex is another project the city hired the firm for.

He heard his father arguing and yelling over the phone. Most likely at Frank.

Theresa focuses most of her attention around Marcy and Sammy. Marcy's experience has left her puzzled and confused. Marcy has a long, broad strand of white hair, white like snow. Supernatural things have happened to her since the accident. Marcy mostly sits out in the back-courtyard area reading her Bible and praying. She fills her days doing this.

Torn

Theresa joined her that afternoon to talk about life and all that God has done. Marcy is eager to tell her things. She started with the vision of an angel.

"Mom, an angel came to me in a vision, a dream. I wasn't praying or anything. I feel that God gave me this gift; a glimpse into things that will happen. I think this angel is my guide, my helper."

"Marcy, I'm sure whatever reason God has is for the greater good," Theresa said smiling. "You have to trust Him; He will lead and guide you. God will never forsake you. I'm not sure what God is doing or why He is doing it, baby, but we have to trust him."

"I hope so, Mom. I need time to sort things out. Everything is happening so fast." Theresa sits beside her and holds her head in her bosom; she kisses the top of her head, "It will be okay, honey, it will be okay," Marcy's eyes fight to stay open, so she walks upstairs to take a nap. Theresa walks to the den to pray. She uses any free time she gets to have her devotion time with God.

Connor arrives home early from work; he has been suspicious about Frank and some of his under the table ventures. The only real peace is that Connor can seek out an attorney if things go south. He may need some legal protection for not knowing the actual depth of Frank's involvements. Once inside the house, he hears no one.

He slips off to office; he pulls the bottom drawer open and brings out a bottle of cognac with a 6oz. Crystal glass. He pours a bit into the glass and downs the liquor. It has become a dark secret of his; an escape from the stresses at home and work. He sits in his office downing not one, not two but three glasses, then puts the liquor away before anyone might walk in. He starts chewing on peppermint gum to cover up the alcohol on his breath. He sits back and closes his eyes to relax when the phone rings.

"Hello," he answers.

"Hello, is this Mr. Smith. A Mr. Connor Smith?" a strange man's voice asked.

"Uh...yeah! Who is this?"

"Someone you need to listen to; I'm calling because I need to talk to you about your son, Chris. Chris took over as a leader of a small group of people who—"

"Wait, what! You know my son, Chris? Where is he? Please tell me where he is."

"All I can tell you is that he is a leader of a small group and he is causing all sorts of chaos. I warn you to please keep an eye out for your loved ones, goodbye."

"No! Wait! Please," he said hoping for a reply.

He continues holding the phone to his ear with only the annoying sound a phone makes when off the hook. Finishing his drink, he walks upstairs and goes to sleep. There's a tug on his arm, but no one is there. Again, something tugging on his arm and yet no one is there. He jumps from another firm tug, and he wakes up; looks at Theresa and says, *"It was a dream—it was just a dream."* Theresa looks back at him and says, "Are you okay, babe?"

"I had a dream. It was a weird dream."

"What kind of dream, Connor?"

"In the dream, a man called me talking about Chris. He said he knew where he was and what he was doing but wouldn't give any other information. He told me to listen to my daughter, that she is called of God."

Theresa is startled by the news. Is God trying to send them a message but neither her or Connor have been listening. God is moving, but his people were either ignoring it or are blind to it, the same way she is blind to the liquor her husband his hiding.

The entire church staff has been called in for a meeting to discuss all the new developments about Pastor Shane's death. Pastor Mark will also be stepping down as temporary pastor. He thinks it should be one of the higher up Pastors job to handle matters. With everyone gathered in the main conference room, the groans, moans, and yawns of those who didn't want to be there sound off; after all, it was almost 5:00 p.m.

Pastor Mark calls the meeting to order and opens with prayer. After he prays he starts by saying, "Now to the matter of business," he began.

"Well, I hope to keep this short, as we would all like to go home. The importance of this meeting exceeds our desires to be free at this point. Allow me to start with a lunch meeting I had today with Det. Williams. Det. Williams shared with me today that Cindy Rhodes, you're all familiar with her, she has been deemed a prime suspect in Pastor Shane's murder. She will be or most likely has already been arrested."

"Pastor, how did he come to that conclusion about her? I mean, Cindy Rhodes! What would she gain by being a part of or the mastermind behind such a thing?"

"Tamika, all I know is he and his partner questioned her; she told them lies though they didn't know it at the time. They had asked where her husband was, and she told them he was working; he drives semi-truck over the road."

"Isn't that true though?"

"Yes! However, they discovered that he was not working. He has not been to work in a few weeks. That very fact makes them suspicious, and thus they decided to arrest her. She is the only person who scheduled Pastor Shane's appointments, yet there was no one scheduled during the time of the attack. Nothing notated in the logbook. This is suspicious, and it saddens me even to say this. I don't understand and maybe I never will, but we have a duty to this church, its people, and its employees. For this reason, I'm stepping down as interim pastor. I'm a youth pastor; I don't possess the skills needed to lead our church."

"If you are stepping down, who will step up to lead this church?" Sean Clark asked.

"I don't want to be a part of that. The elder board will need to take it to a vote to select our new senior pastor. I am not ready for that responsibility."

"We will meet on this as soon as possible. There is a lot to be done," said Pastor David, the associate pastor of the church. "This situation will not be resolved as quick as any one of us would like. We have to be wise and seek God at this moment."

With that said, the church staff and faculty members of the church's school were dismissed. Pastor Mark said goodbye to his secretary and tells her to have a lovely weekend.

"See you on Sunday, Pastor." She has a crush on the young pastor. She is young—only twenty-two-years-old. Everyone is rushing out of the building and scampering to their cars as if they were in a race. Pastor Mark fumbles his keys to the ground. He kneels down to pick them up; he was close enough to push his unlock button on the fob. The lights blink signaling the car is unlocked. He's fifteen feet away; he places his bag on the ground to take his phone out of his pocket. He picks his bag up and pulls the strap over his shoulder, then, BOOM! The blast throws him to the ground.

His ears ring from the loud blast. Staff members in the parking lot run to his aid. Pastor Mark is bleeding from his nose and left ear from hitting the pavement hard. Tamika and Sean make it to his side and Sean, without regard of possibly causing any additional injuries, throws Pastor Mark over his right shoulder and runs back inside the church. Tamika calls 9-1-1 to alert authorities and have an ambulance come for Pastor Mark. Sean lays him on a sofa in the lounge.

"Pastor, Pastor, are you okay? Can you hear me?"

"Sean, I-I-I think I'm gonna be sick."

"Hold on, Pastor, I'll grab a trashcan," Sean rushes over to find one and hurries back. "Okay, Pastor, if you need to throw up, I've got you covered." Sean notices he is unconscious now and begins to worry.

Marcy wakes from her nap after 5:30 p.m. She walks downstairs to the living room and her parents holding each other on the sofa.

"Hey, guys! What's goin' on?"

"We're just relaxing and spending time together. Your father had a rough day and came home early. How was your nap?"

"It was refreshing. I seem to be doing better. I haven't had any more visions," Marcy said laughing. Her parents happy she found joy again; they have missed her beautiful smile.

"Where is Stephen?"

"He must be upstairs practicing his guitar or something; let him be, he has been cranky."

Marcy takes heed to her mother's words, though it did bother her that her sweet younger brother seemed to be suffering. Marcy has not prayed for days. She still doesn't understand why God had chosen her. She thought to herself," When will I spread my wings and fly Lord. When will my courage be built up enough to move?" Her mind races all day with thoughts.

As she sits in the living room by herself, she listens to soft praise music to help lift her spirit. With her headphones on, she doesn't is oblivious to the phone ringing. Connor yells for someone to answer it, but no one replied, so Theresa gets up off the sofa to answer the phone.

"Hello," Theresa answered.

"Hello, is this Theresa?" a female replied.

"Yes, it is."

"Hi, Tamika Williams from the church."

"Yes! Tamika, how are you?"

"Well, not very well."

"Oh! I'm sorry. Is everything okay?"

"Theresa, you are not going to believe what I am about to tell you."

"What is it? What's wrong?" she asked as her heart starts pounding harder in her chest, knowing that it was indeed sad news.

"Well, to start, Cindy Rhodes is most likely being arrested for being an accomplice to Pastor Shane's murder," she said, holding back her tears. "That's not all. Pastor Mark was attacked. His car exploded when he unlocked; he was close enough and blew him off his feet some six feet away, crashing his body to the pavement. He is injured, though we don't know how bad. He is at the hospital. Our security staff went with him and will not allow any visitors at all."

"Oh no! Are you serious? I mean, what can we do? Is there anything we can do?" Theresa said, losing control of her emotions.

"I'll keep you informed okay?"

James Owens

"Well, hopefully soon. Tamika, your brother-in-law is the lead Detective on this case, is he not?"

"He is."

"Well, will you be able to share the news with me? We love that young man. I want information on his status, as much as you can tell me. Plus, information on Cindy; indeed, she may hold some keys to these locked doors."

"I will do all that I can, Theresa. I only told you seeing as your family is close to Pastor Mark."

"Thank you, Tamika, I appreciate it. Now I have to pass on the news to my family. We will be praying for him."

"God bless, goodbye."

"Connor," Theresa yells. Connor jumps off the sofa, banging his knee on the corner of the coffee table hobbling over to Theresa.

"What! What's wrong?"

"Oh, Connor!"

"Babe, what, what's wrong? Please tell me."

"It's happening again, Connor; it's happening again."

"What! I don't know if you don't tell me."

"Mark, Pastor Mark!"

"What about him? What's going on with him? What happened?"

"His car exploded, Connor."

"What? He asks in disbelief.

"He was bombed!" She shouts.

"Oh! Uh...oh my." Stunned at the news. "Where is he at?"

"In the hospital, Connor, but they won't let anyone see him. Father God, please be with him and the doctors, take care of him, Lord." Theresa screams so loud that it makes Stephen come downstairs and Marcy to break from her music. Stephen walks to his parents. His mother is crying, and he stands by her side. Marcy is now standing with her family as her father tells her and Stephen the bad news. Marcy begins crying and runs out the back door of the house.

She stares up at the sky and screams, "Why didn't you let me see this? Why?" she says as she falls to her knees crying out for answers. Why are you not answering me? ANSWER ME!" Marcy screams, causing her family to come outside. Sammy peeks through the window from her playroom and cries. Theresa runs inside to pick her up and then rushes back out to Marcy.

Her family stands there staring at her. A bright light drops Connor, Theresa, Sammy, and Stephen to their knees. The Power and Majesty of God pours out on them. God is preparing them for something big, or it could be to surround them with his love and protection, giving them peace. Marcy and her family take it all in, and when it goes away, they walk a little wobbly inside, praying, thanking, and praising God. Marcy is still unsure why she couldn't see what happened to Pastor Mark.

Chapter 29

News spread fast about the attack on Pastor Mark. Reporters and cameramen gather in front of the hospital, ready to flood the 6:30 p.m. local news. One news reporter, Debra Scholl, is the first to hit the air for action news on 9. Debra Scholl reports: "Bob, I am here at St. Joseph's hospital where a short while ago a young pastor was brought here by ambulance. Sources tell us his vehicle exploded when he remotely unlocked his car. The explosion threw him about six feet away, crashing his body to the hard asphalt. I can only tell you his name at this point. He is Pastor Mark Fields of Freedom Christian Center. The Youth Pastor from what we've been told."

"Debra, isn't this the same church whose senior pastor was murdered not too long ago?"

"Correct, Bob; this is indeed the same church. Investigators have been working continually to solve the case, and we informed by a reliable source there has been an arrest, but we have no details at this time. Debra Scholl, Channel 9 News. Back to you."

The newscast seemed to go viral as soon as it aired. Internet search engines flooded with searches on the bombing. Social media exploded with gossip.

Sean Clark has placed heavy security inside and outside the hospital room of Pastor Mark; local police are also heavily guarding Pastor Mark's hospital room and the entire floor in which he is staying. No one is allowed inside his hospital room except for medical staff. Connor made all the phone calls he could with no success. Eyewitnesses are asked questions by police and of course Detectives Williams and

Madison. The two Detectives undoubtedly have a more substantial caseload now. They have to find someone to analyze the device and then gather information that can lead to an arrest.

They are tired, the attacks on this church have them emotionally and physically drained. Time is most definitely not on their side. They must make some progress and make it quick. They have one murder, one arrest, a body recovered by police. Attempted murder of yet another pastor and the recovered body is suspected to be the mastermind due to a suicide note left in his pants pocket. Too strange though for Det. Williams. A suicide note confessing he committed this crime? It's like he took the fall and the real killer is still out there. Indeed, they have much work to do.

Connor realizes his methods aren't getting him anywhere; so, his frustration is mounting. Theresa walks into his office, hoping to ease his mind and calm his fears.

"Babe," she said.

"What! What do you want? Can't I have a little time to myself? We did have a great family moment. I think Chris is involved. I want to be alone."

"Why are you doing this to yourself? Pastor Mark is in God's hands. There is nothing you can do. There is nothing any of us can do except to pray for him. He is alive, that is a blessing in and of itself," Theresa says while entering Connors office.

"My heart is broken, Theresa. I was so hard on the young man about Marcy and now look what happened. My daughter was in a car wreck and in a coma; now he was almost killed by a bomb in his car. Will this stop? Will this ever end? God needs to intervene and protect His people.

"God is always here; always protecting us. God hasn't abandoned His people. Trust in Him. He is here. Don't doubt Him."

"I try. I don't understand why things are this way. My daughter, my son, Pastor Mark, Pastor Shane, how much more suffering, Theresa?

How much more? How much longer can, I can stand by and watch. I want to talk to Pastor Mark."

"Have you tried calling the church? Call, Frank, babe; he has the connections. "I called Frank. I even called Karen; no one knows where he is."

"Well, that's rather odd."

"What's odd, Theresa? Seriously."

"I'll tell you what, Connor, you talk to me that way and I swear I will not help you or give you any advice ever again. You do not treat me this way, do you understand me?"

"I, I."

"Don't you even start to go there. Why don't you walk away and think things over before you make matters worse and do something you will regret.?"

"Fine!"

Theresa turns her back, walks out of his office, and slams the door shut. Connor sits behind his desk and pulls out the bottom drawer where he has his stash of liquor. He pulls out a small bottle of rum, pours some in a long shot glass. Downs it quickly, then another and yet another. Connor had by this time finished off the small bottle of rum shot after shot.

He put the bottle away in the drawer empty, laid his head on his desk and drifted away.

Chapter 30

A table with three chairs in the middle of a room. One chair on one side and two on the other and a large mirror window is on the wall. On the other side of the glass, other detectives look on, as Det. Williams interrogates Cindy Rhodes. Det. Madison also watches on as he drinks his Monster energy drink while staring at Mrs. Rhodes. He despises her—hates her for holding back vital information. His mind races with ideas to make her talk, but first, his partner gets a crack at her.

"Cindy, something isn't right here. You are involved in this, but for some reason, you will not help us or give up whoever it is that you think you are protecting. Let me be clear, Mrs. Rhodes. If you do not cooperate with us, I can't help you. You will be charged with accessory to murder, and yes, I do have enough to charge you with. Now, why don't you work with me here, and tell me what you know?" He asked, as his face turns red.

"What you want me to say, sir. I have told you everything. I want my lawyer. I'm entitled to speak to a lawyer. I'm done talking to you, and your rude partner."

"My partner hasn't even come in to question you, Mrs. Rhodes. There is no reason to attack him, but have it your way," he said, slamming his chair against the wall. "I will request an attorney for you as soon as possible," Det. Williams walks out of the interrogation room and into the observation room. His partner, Det. Madison, looked at him as if the Chiefs had lost the super bowl.

"You're kidding me, right, Williams? I mean, you are much better than that."

"I can't go much further when she brings up a lawyer, Madison. I thought I could scare it out of her, but she is smarter than that. She will not talk."

"What if we tell her we have arrested her son? Maybe that will make her talk, she's a mother! She will talk to spare him."

"Dude! I'm not going to lie and play her like that. I have more honor, and integrity than that. Besides, I would be doing a great injustice as a child of God. I will not lie."

"You already lied, Williams. You told her we have enough to charge her with, duh!"

"I'm not going to debate with you, okay? I think we can hold her and charge her. I have to find something first, so it isn't a lie. If all else fails, I will charge her with obstruction."

"Oh, really now! All her lawyer has to do is come down here, and she will walk out without charges. What will be the plan then?"

"I will push the obstruction of justice card. Cindy is holding something back. I can't figure it out."

"Well, let me go in there with the son story. I'll make her talk."

"Fine! Try it your way, but don't go farther than you can go, Peter." Det. Madison glances at Williams, winks his right eye at him, and walks out of the room and into the interrogation room. He closes the door, pulls up a chair, and stares right into Cindy Rhodes' eyes.

"Woman, stop the charades. You're smart, but also very confused. All I want from you is a name, just a name, and you will be free to go."

"I said I was done talking. I am exercising my rights. I want a lawyer."

"Fine, no problem. One is on the way. But I will have to tell you we have your son Scott in custody. Do you want both of you to be jail? If not, then give me a name, now!"

"Why have you arrested my son? He has nothing to do with this?" she asked starting to cry.

"Obstruction of justice, Mrs. Rhodes—the same charge you will have if you don't give me a name. You will have a lawyer, but you will not go free. You and your son will be charged and see the judge tomorrow morning. Give me a name!" he shouts at her and slams his hand on the table. "Give me a name, Cindy, just one name." Just as he laid into her again, the lawyer that Det. Williams called walks into the observation room. "What is he doing to my client?" he asked Williams.

"Well, sir. It looks as though he is questioning her."

"I will put an end to this," he said, storming out of the room. Before he could go any further, Cindy screamed out loud to Madison.

"Daren! His name is Daren. Now, please, let me and my son go."

"Thank you, Mrs. Rhodes," he said as the lawyer walks in and demands answers from Det. Madison. He was supposed to leave her alone when she requested a lawyer. Madison responds with a simple, "She volunteered the information, sir. All I did was ask. She didn't have to answer."

"Mrs. Rhodes, I'm David Steele. I will be representing you. I advise that you no longer speak with the police or these detectives regarding any investigation without me being present."

"Yes, sir. What about my son? They have my son in custody."

"Det. Madison, is this true?"

"As far as I know, it is possible. I have no reason to believe Scott has been arrested at this time," he said with a smirk. He shrugged his shoulders and left the room. Det. Williams met him in the hallway and immediately jumped him about the lie. Madison looked up and laughed so hard he began to cry.

"What is so funny, Peter?"

"The whole thing, brother."

"We have a big mess to clean up. For now, let's search for this Daren guy; it will be time consuming, so don't even think about doing anything else, Peter."

"Lay off the first name bit, bro! Stay professional."

"I will if you will."

"You got it, Williams. Let's go to Chubby's for lunch."

Off they go while the attorney talks to his client.

James Owens

In an abandoned warehouse on the southeast side of Kansas City, two men are about to meet face to face for the first time, they have only spoken on the phone until now. A meeting in person is now warranted. This side of Kansas City is home to many homeless people, due to abandoned buildings. It serves as a safe-haven for them. Rocco arrives first; he parked his car behind one building and walks to the next.

Another vehicle pulls in; a man parks his 2008 Lexus and walks over to the building to meet the other man. As they walk closer towards each other, Rocco stops and says, "Are you, Frank?"

"Yes," Frank replies. "I guess that makes you Rocco?"

"Indeed."

"Let's keep some three feet between us. I don't simply trust people," Rocco said.

"Fine! Finally, we meet, what's it been, a few months now? I received your letter then. I was surprised to say the least. Can you tell me Chris's status, Cindy Rhodes, and her husband? Also, the police found a body. I'm guessing it belongs to you, whoever it was."

"Chris is lined up where I want him. You haven't done your job to drive his father out of your company. You can pin the corruption between you and Miller Construction on him. And, if you don't do it, I will finish you. You want off the hook for your shady actions. I want my money you agreed pay. $500,000.00, your friend Connor is your fall guy, he is your choice. I was coming for both of you until you told me it was you. You made a deal with me to save yourself. I have Chris, so hold up to your end of the deal—feel me? Don't worry about Cindy Rhodes or her son. She's in police custody. She will not talk. I have her husband hidden away. He is being taken care of. Scott, well he wasn't accepted into the group, so he may be a problem. Scott has been to the meeting locations and the house. I will deal with him if I have to.

"Okay—okay, I need some more time. Things haven't gone as planned. Connor's daughter didn't die in the accident, but it still tore her parents down. Stephen is a lost kid, a punk. Connor started drinking again, and he is keeping it from his family, that works for me. I can use it to force him out of the office or at least use it to destroy his marriage."

Torn

"Listen, Frank! I want someone in Chris family dead—D-E-A-D, dead. Get the picture? I will work my angle on Chris. He is a naive fool for such a smart guy. You better get your plans lined up because when it is time to move, there's no going back. Oh, and by the way, I lost a couple of people that may come looking for some help. A girl named Tanner and a man named Zaga. He was the leader of his mission house. Chris drove him out, much to my credit. Chris took over, or so he thinks anyway, I have the power behind the scene."

"Why are you telling me this? You must think they will come to the church, but why?"

"Because I know Zaga; have known him for many years. He was once associated with your late pastor. He told me stories about the two of them; he never shared them with anyone else."

"What?"

"Be on the lookout; they may cause trouble. Zaga doesn't approve of the things being done. He doesn't approve of Chris. Once he became so deep with his belief in Satan. Zaga tried to explain that wasn't what he teaches, and he does not approve of it. I learned this from my sources. I plan to keep a close eye on Chris. He thinks he has control, but in fact, Chris is the one being controlled—ha-ha-ha," he said laughing. "But I like what is happening; it will bring Zaga and Tanner out of hiding. I want to draw them out."

"Well, I will do my best. There are a lot of things we have to do, and I will take care of my end, okay, I swear it."

"You better!" Rocco walks away, he gets in his car and peels out down the road. Frank leaves the area as well, but he feels a heavy conviction. Shaking his head because what he is doing is wrong, but he has to cover his sin. There is no other way but to have it fall on Connor; this will destroy the Smith family. Frank will not be the one facing time for wrongful deaths. His only concern now is Marcy, she seems to have visions, and he hopes she can't see into him or his intentions. If she can, the jig is up.

James Owens

Frank arrives home and pushes his meeting with Rocco far from his memory to have a nice romantic dinner with his wife. Frank and Karen never had children. She is barren, never able to have children. Karen and Frank have considered adoption, but never followed through with it. They now focus on each other and enjoy life, and the romantic times they share.

Chapter 31

Rocco decides to stop by a local Papa Johns to pick up a large supreme pizza for him and Chris. He plans to go to the house, sit down for a pizza dinner with Chris, and talk about his plans. Rocco also wants to discuss the events that happened with the car bomb and why the pastor is still alive. He pulls into the ally to park behind the house; he notices Gregg and Max sitting on a bench stone cold. Rocco exits his car, grabs the pizza, and walks up to them

"Guys, what's wrong?" he asks but gets no reply. "Gregg, Max, hello, talk to me," again no reply from either of them. They just seemed to be in a state of shock. Rocco blew them off and walked into the house. In the kitchen, he gets two plates and grabs some napkins. He yells at Chris and Chris smells the sweet aroma of pizza from the living room.

"PIZZA," Chris shouts, "Oh man, you must have been reading my mind brother."

"I guess so."

"Dude, I've wanted some pizza for a while. I am so happy that you got Papa Johns."

"You betcha. So, I want to talk to you about a few things," Rocco said before taking a bite of pizza. "We have entered into a real world of violence here, brother. I'm getting worried. We need to cover our bases. That pastor survived the car bombing, and the police recovered Daren's body."

"Well, I guess I will have to decide what our next course of action should be. I will call upon the master for guidance."

"Stop, we have problems here. Sure, call upon him, blah, blah, blah. It won't change a thing, bro. We—not you, but we have to figure this out and make the decision together."

"This is both a carnal war and a spiritual war, Rocco," he said, taking a bite of his pizza; washing it down with a cold Pepsi.

"Zaga warned about a spiritual fight against the Christian God in whom I no longer believe in. I'm not scared, are you?" Chris asked, taking another bite of pizza.

"Of course, I'm not scared." Rocco rolls his eyes at Chris.

"There are things we can and can't control. I have two guys out back here who can't utter a word. I don't understand why. Something strange is happening, bro, and we have to move the ball here. I need you to step up while I take care of some loose ends."

"What loose ends?"

"I have to take care of Mr. Rhodes. He never saw my face, only heard my voice. If I set him free, then maybe it will take the focus off the case."

"I don't know, Rocco; it might not be the right time."

"Right or wrong, I'm letting him go. I don't want a trail leading to our people or us."

"Where do you have him at?"

"He's in an abandoned warehouse. Chelsea has been helping to feed him, give him water and such. Thomas has been with her. This kidnapping is over. We need to move on. Cindy did her job for us. He is dead; now we move on. We may have to figure out a way to finish off the other pastor."

"Pastor Mark?"

"Yes! He's still alive. We need to finish him."

"I'm with you, but it won't be easy. Pastor Mark will have a lot of security guards."

"You let me worry about that. Let's finish off this pizza and do some planning."

Chris is experiencing some guilt/ Something he hasn't had in a while. He is getting nothing from Satan; he is powerless, abandoned, and conviction is haunting Chris's heart. When Rocco said he wanted to finish off Pastor Mark, shame-filled his face.

Sean Clark watches as the nurse give Pastor Mark his medications. He's been standing guard at the door for about thirty-six hours. His eyes are blood-shot red. He needs rest but won't leave his pastor. Other security staff members offered to relieve him but declined. One of the nurses, Paula, tells Sean, "You need to sleep. You can't help your pastor if you collapse from exhaustion. Another security member from your church in the hallway, he can take over while you rest, sir."

"Can you call him in here please?" He asked while yawning.

"Yes, sir." She steps into the hallway and signals for the man to come into the room, "Sir, here he is."

"Hey, Sean, how are you holding up?"

"Not good, Bruce. I need to get some rest. You're the only person I trust to keep an eye on Pastor Mark. Promise me, Bruce—you will keep both eyes on him? Control your surroundings while I'm resting. Promise me."

"You betcha, boss. I promise I will keep him safe and sound."

"Thank you, Bruce."

"No need for thanks, Sean, it's my job too."

Sean nods his head at Bruce and walks down the hall where a guest room awaits him with an uncomfortable bed. Not even really a bed, a chair that folds out three-quarters of the way. Sean isn't a small man at six feet seven inches tall, weighing in at 300 lbs. of pure rock-solid muscle. At least he can hope for a few hours of sleep before returning. Bruce Anderson sits in a chair reading.

Bruce is no small man either. He stands six feet five inches tall and weighing 285 lbs. He has a military haircut, wears army combat desert boots with black wrangler jeans, and long-sleeve Dallas Cowboys shirt. He's a pure cowboy from Oklahoma. He worked on his father's ranch before joining the army. Bruce did basic training at Fort Leonard Wood, Missouri. He enjoyed basic training and AIT job school. His *MOS*

(Military Occupation Specialty) was 31Bravo, military police. Once his training was complete in Missouri, Bruce went to his next duty station at Fort Hood, Texas.

He served seven honorable years having deployed three times. When Bruce was discharged, he decided to go back to Missouri and settle down on the outskirts of Kansas City. He applied as a security officer for the church where he had accepted Jesus Christ as his Lord and Savior. It suited him just fine; Bruce loves keeping people safe. Until the tragic day; the day that Pastor Shane had been shot; Bruce was outside watching the elementary children play on the playground during recess. He heard the news about Pastor Shane through his earpiece. It was the most dreadful news, and it broke his heart feeling he let the pastor down. Never in his military career did he lose a friend in battle. Now he has lost his pastor.

A man they were supposed to protect had died. He knew Sean also felt responsible for not being there. However, he needed Sean to recognize that he can trust him. Bruce would give his life to keep Pastor Mark safe. He would never allow himself not to be there when needed. Although his assignment that day was watching the kids. Bruce still hasn't forgiven himself. He looks at Pastor Mark and is taken aback by this young man's strength, character, and will to serve. Taking over a broken and hurting church and now here he lays in a hospital bed; a victim of hate. "Who could hate this kid?" Bruce thought to himself. It will be daybreak soon.

Bruce gets up from his chair to stretch. He walks over to the window; he looks out and sees the news reporters hanging out, waiting for an interview by someone, anyone who is willing to talk. He closes the blinds and stands close to the door. Nurses are making their rounds. No one enters Mark's room.

"Excuse me, ma'am," Bruce said.

"Uh, yeah?"

"Uh...how about you show my credentials and let me verify who you are before you walk in."

"Oh please! Are you serious?"

"Yes!"

Torn

"Fine! Here is my badge. Would you like to call my supervisor?"

"Yes, Carol Banks," Bruce said after looking at her badge. I would like to," he said with his deep, stern voice. He calls the number on his cell phone provided by the church. The phone rings a few times and a woman answers.

"Hello, this is Kimberly."

"Uh yes, my name is Bruce Anderson. I'm calling to check on a nurse named Carol Banks. Can you please verify her for me?"

"I'm sorry. Who are you?"

"Bruce Anderson, ma'am. I am a security officer with Freedom Christian Center. Our pastor is here, and we are in charge of his security."

"Yes, sir. Police and the hospital security staff have cleared her. Carol has been with us for three years."

"That's all I need to hear, ma'am. Have a nice day."

"Same to you," she said, hanging up the phone.

"Okay, ma'am, you may proceed."

"Thank you!"

Pastor Mark is given Morphine for pain through his I.V. drip. His head is bandaged up, and his left arm is in a sling. He broke his left leg and three ribs also. He is without a doubt in pain even though he slips between being awake and asleep every once in a while. The doctors will wake him in a few hours to go over his injuries with him and talk about his stay in the hospital. The sun has risen, and bright beams of light break through the crakes in blinds; the bright light immediately wakes Sean and quickly makes his way to Pastor Mark's room.

"Good morning, Bruce," He says wiping his eyes and letting out a huge yawn.

"Good morning, boss."

"Everything went well, I see."

"Yes, sir. Told you I could take care of him."

"Well done. Thank you for giving me the rest. I will take it from here. You can head home."

Bruce grabs his Bible and leaves the room. He makes his way to the hospital lobby and exits the building; reports rush over to speak to him. He pushes his way through to his truck and dives off.

With the news about Pastor Shane and now Pastor Mark, Zaga decides it is time for them to come out of seclusion. The moment is finally upon them, and allies need to be established.

"Tanner, it's time," Zaga said with emphasis.

"What do you mean, Zaga? It's time for what?" she asked.

"We are going to go to the Freedom Christian Center today. I need to speak with them."

"Why would you want to Zaga? That was Chris's church. His family goes there, and not to mention the public attention they are getting. Are you thinking straight?"

"Yes, Tanner," I am thinking straight. I have a past that is hard to explain. It is vital that I go there. I don't expect for you to understand. I would like for you to trust me as you always have. I will notify priest Zeke of our departure."

"Of course, I trust you; I'm confused. I will come with you, but I have to ask you a few questions. First, where will we be staying? Second, please tell me this isn't about Chris. Third, um-uh-never mind," she sighs.

"To answer your questions. I will take care of housing after we go to the church. As for the second, yes, this has everything to do with him. Bigger things are happening than you can imagine, Tanner. His mind is poison; he feels a power that isn't his, but there is another who leads his cult as well. Be patient, follow, me and you will be safe. I promise."

"Okay," she replied gently. "Let's go then."

"Okay," he said. "Let's go," They begin to pack their things, but before Zaga starts packing, he tells Priest Zeke of his intentions.

"Are you sure this is the path you want to travel down, Zaga?" he said like a concerned parent talking to a child who was moving out into the world.

"This is what I need to do. I don't expect many people to understand this decision, but in time you will."

"You have always been an outgoing and sometimes hard person to read, Zaga, but I do trust that you for whatever it is that you must do."

"I promise that I will keep in touch," he said emotionally, knowing he would be breaking that promise. "I appreciate all you have done for Tanner and I. Be blessed priest," Zaga walked away. He packed his belongings, which wasn't much. Zaga and Tanner left the small sanctuary never to return...

Chapter 32

8:00 a.m. Saturday morning, there is silence in the Smith home. Everyone is sleeping in. After all, it has been a long week—better yet, a long month. The sound of an alarm clock annoys Stephen, so he covers his head with pillows, grunts, and turns over on his back. Kicking his covers off, he lets loose, "Marcy," he yells. "Can you please turn your stupid alarm off?" The alarm stopped.

Marcy slowly her opens her door, peeks down the hallway, and makes a mad dash for the bathroom. Stephen heard her swift move as she banged her knee into the door. "*What a ditz*," he turns over, pulling his covers back up. "Momma," Sammy says. Theresa and Connor are entirely knocked out but left their door cracked open. Sammy runs as fast as her little legs can move, pushes the door open, and leaps like a frog off the floor right onto her father's stomach.

"Ufff," he gasps for air from the impact. "Well, good morning, Sammy."

"Morning, Dadda."

Theresa lets out a yawn and groans as she fights to open her eyes to see Sammy. Sammy is all bright-eyed and bushy-tailed. "I guess you're up and wanting breakfast, little girl?"

"Yes, Momma, panny-cakes, panny-cakes," she replied with such excitement.

Marcy slowly opens the bathroom door, who is she trying to avoid? Why is she trying to hide in the first place? She has no enemies in her home. Marcy enters the hallway, her little sister comes running down, passing her, and bolting downstairs. Theresa grabs her robe, puts it on, pulls her hair back, puts on her slippers, and walks out of her bedroom. Marcy sees her mother and lets off a loud, "Good morning, Mother!"

"Good morning, dear, how are you feeling today, honey?"

"I'm well, Mom, all is well," though there is something bothering Marcy that has her on edge.

"That's good. I'm making breakfast for Sammy; would you like me to make you something?"

"No thanks."

"Okay, my darling."

Stephen tosses and turns continuously. He can't fall back to sleep becoming frustrated. He throws off his comforter and pulls his bedroom door open. He tears into her, "Seriously, Marcy? I mean, for goodness sake.

"What's your problem, Stephen? All I did was set my alarm—what's wrong with that?"

"UGH, you know what the problem is. I mean why should you have special attention."

"What on earth are you talking about? This coming from my brother who didn't want to be without me."

"What does it matter now? Why does everything have to be all about you—all about your supernatural abilities now. I'm over it. I'm sick of it!" He yells, forcing his father out of bed.

"What's going on here?"

"Nothing, Dad," Marcy said, glancing at Stephen as she walks downstairs. Stephen shrugs his dad off and goes back to his bedroom. Connor returns to his bedroom and gets ready for the day.

Zaga and Tanner wake up in their cheap motel, get their things together and check out. They walk down the sidewalk and Zaga spots a diner; they both look at each other with one thought, breakfast. They walk in and walk to a booth escorted the hostess and given their flatware and menus. Tanner immediately decides on the American cheese omelet while Zaga chooses two eggs sunny side up with bacon and whole wheat toast. Tanner orders a coke and Zaga orders a coffee black. They sat back and enjoyed their beverages the waitress had brought. Tanner looks at Zaga and asks, "Where are going today?"

"Well, Tanner. We are going to visit the Smith family."

"That's Chris's family. Why on earth would we go there?"

"Because I need to talk to them, and they need us; they don't know it yet."

"Are you sure it will be okay?"

"Nope! But we are going nonetheless," he said cheerfully.

The waitress brings their food. Zaga thanks her and he and Tanner begin eating their breakfast. It will be a surprise for the Smith family if they were indeed home when their unexpected guests would arrive.

Zaga and Tanner catch the bus and begin their journey to the Smith home on 2819 Maple Street in a wealthy suburb of Kansas City. Tanner still worries about the visit, but Zaga keeps her as calm as he can. "Everything will be fine, Tanner. We are simply having a visit with them if they will have us. I need to give them the answers I'm sure they have been seeking."

"What are you talking about?"

"Chris, I need to answer their questions about him. They must have questions, and for the most part, I have some answers, but it goes much deeper than they can imagine," he said with a peaceful sound. "I need them to accept what they may not be ready to for. I will need you, but not until I ask for you to come into the conversation."

"Okay."

The bus reaches its stop, and the two begin a short half-mile walk. They talk about the things that have happened and what will come about shortly. The profound truth. The hidden truth is about to surface whether anyone is ready or not. Zaga isn't a Christian man, but he has a caring and loving heart, though he is a darker spiritual man, he respects Christians. As they walk up the street, Zaga points to the house; his heart begins to pound hard in his chest with every step. Tanner is uncomfortable, so she holds Zaga's hand as they walk approaching the house.

They have arrived and walk up the driveway to a sidewalk that leads to the front door where Zaga boldly presses the doorbell. The chime sounds through the home. Connor is sitting in his office, and of course, waits for his wife to get the door. The doorbell chimes again. "Is anyone getting the door?" Connor shouted. "Why can't you get it, babe? I'm playing with Sammy, and I don't know what the kids are doing, so just answer it." "Ugh!" he sighed. "Fine!" He opened the door and was taken aback by the people on his front porch. "Uh...hello," he managed to say.

"Mr. Smith?"

"Yes, and you are?"

"My name is Zaga and this is Tanner. I am a priest in let's say new age spiritualism. I am here about your son Chris. He—"

Connor cuts him off. "What about my son? I don't care who you are if you can help me with my son."

"Well, sir, my friend Tanner and I are here on your doorstep for that reason. You have questions, and I may have some of the answers for you."

"Please come in," Connor welcomes Zaga and Tanner in and shows them to the family room. Excited and guarded at the same time, Connor sits on the chair facing the sofa and anxiously awaits the words Zaga will say. "So, Zaga, you say you have information on my son, Chris? Tell me everything."

"Mr. Smith, Chris joined our group, or as others like to refer to it, our cult. He was introduced to me by a young man named Rocco—"

He was cut off by Connor again before he could speak any further. "Wait! You mean to tell me that his friend from college is the one who led him to you? That's, that's, ugh! I can't believe this."

"I wish I could tell you something different, but I'm here to tell you the truth. Rocco was a student of mine; by a student, I mean, I taught him the ways of my beliefs. I believe in self-worship. I'm my own god, and I seek inner peace with my spirit. I do believe in Satan, though I choose not to serve him. Rocco started thinking differently and went astray. I did not see it, and when he invited your son to come to me; he told me he wanted to learn our ways. I had no idea Chris would take things as far as becoming a servant of Satan. I warned him, and he went much deeper. One day it came down to, and when I heard the demonic voice come from his mouth, my time there was done. Chris turned almost everyone away from me except for Tanner."

"So, when you left, what did you think would happen?"

"I figured I has a lot of hatred for your God and Christians who follow him. I believe in your God, and I warned Chris not to proceed with his plans, but he didn't listen."

"Excuse me, please; I'm going to bring my wife in."

"Sure."

Connor exits the room and gets Theresa from the playroom. He tells her about their visitors and urges her to sit in and have Marcy watch Sammy. Reluctantly, she agrees, and Marcy came to care for Sammy. "Uh...I'm sorry, what was your name again?"

"Zaga, my name is Zaga and this is Tanner, pleased to meet you, ma'am."

"So, Zaga, what else do you have to tell us about Chris? I will catch my wife up to speed later, but you may proceed further."

"Well, as I said, I left, and a little while later Tanner followed and fortunately was able to locate me. I think Chris and Rocco are responsible for your pastor's death and the attack on the other pastor. I'm not sure who ordered it. I think that they had to have known about it. You see, he lets out a big sigh," I-I-I once came across your pastor at a younger age." He said. Zaga doesn't have a stuttering problem; he is merely nervous.

"Wait, you met Pastor Shane?"

"Yes, ma'am, I helped aid the homeless with food, clothing, etc. I met Pastor Shane when he was beginning his ministry, I think. We enjoyed each other's company and helping people. I did not follow his spiritual mission nor his to mine. That didn't matter, as we were still there to bring food and clothes. My name was once Zachias Gant, and I now go by Zaga. Once I became ordained through my church," Tanner found the news intriguing and gives off confusing facial emotions during the whole talk.

"I also have a daughter. I had her when I was young, and she was with me when we were helping people. Her mother died giving birth, and the life insurance helped us to support ourselves. I left much of it to her when she turned seventeen. I'm sorry, Tanner, for what you are about to hear, my daughter is Jessie, her legal name is Jessica Helen Gant. I never told her I'm her father, but rather a caregiver."

"Why didn't you tell her? Zaga, she has every right to know, we have been friends since we met, and you kept this from both of us! What if she's in real danger? She is dating Chris. If something happens to her—" Zaga interrupts Tanner. "Jessie will be fine; I raised her well."

"Okay, wait just a minute! I am grateful for your background here and all, but, you were mentioned in Pastor Shane's eulogy. You're Zachias Gant, oh my! I can't believe this. You're responsible for this, aren't you?" he asked with a shout.

"I guess you could say that. I am responsible for the people that have been left to Chris and Rocco. I must tell you, though, Rocco is the stronger leader, and I don't know his plans for anyone, including your son." The phone suddenly rings, and Connor tells Theresa to answer it in the kitchen. "Hello."

"Hello, Mrs. Smith?" a woman's voice asked.

"Yes, this is she."

"This is Sandra, Sandra Flint. I am a nurse at the hospital your pastor is in. He is being discharged, and he asked to go to your home, in your care. Do you accept his request, ma'am?"

"Absolutely! We will be there as soon as possible," She hung up the phone and went to tell Connor the news. "Connor, the hospital called, and Pastor Mark wishes to be discharged to our care here at home. I told them yes. We need to go. I'm sorry, Zaga, we must go."

"I understand, ma'am. We will be on our way. I hope to be in touch with you again soon," he said as he and Tanner made their way to the front door.

"It was nice to meet you, Zaga. I would like to continue this sometime. We have to go," Connor said.

"Again, no worries, we will see each other again soon," Zaga said as he walks out of the house.

"What? Zaga, this all true?" Tanner asks. "Yes, Tanner, and I'm sorry for keeping it from both of you. Come, we must go." And off they went walking down the street.

Chapter 33

Cindy Rhode's attorney made sure his client wouldn't be booked based on mere speculation. He will make sure of that when she is released; no there will be no more questioning without him being present. Cindy is paying for her freedom from jail, by giving up a simple name to the police.

Scott Rhodes welcomes his mother home with joy. Cindy is happy and confused. She thought he was at the police station too. Cindy hugs him and whispers in his ear. "Scotty, were you at the police station at all?" she asked, pulling back from him. "No, no I wasn't, why would you ask me that? I'm not a suspect here, Mom, you are," Cindy's face turned red with anger; how could he have said that to her? *"A suspect, please, what a joke.,"*

"Scotty, I need to tell you something, but you have to listen. Can I trust you with some information?"

"Sure, Mom, of course, you can."

"Your father was kidnapped. May sound funny, but someone took him. This person, Daren, gave me a list of demands that he left on my windshield. Maybe he left it while I was at work. I read the note. Scotty, they took him; they wanted me to disarm the pastor's panic alarm. I was told some people would show up requesting to see Pastor Shane. If I didn't follow every demand to the *T*, they would kill your father."

"I took the threat very seriously. I was wrong, but I feared to go to the police. And that wasn't the hard part. I have to live with our pastor being killed.

"Oh, Mom!"

"I'm scared Scotty, What, to do. I mean I can go to jail, or prison for being an accomplice to Pastor Shane's murder."

"I'd say, Mom, you're in way over your head. Did these people tell you when they will let dad go? I mean, how far do you have to go before he is released; if he's even still alive."

"I'm not sure, but the police, I mean, the detectives want to speak to your father. They will become suspicious soon. I think I'm going to turn myself in, and maybe they will show mercy. I can get immunity, right? Immunity?"

"You need to tell your attorney, Mom. Tell him who your contact person is."

"All I have is his name; his name was Daren. He was with a girl. I can't remember her name for the life of me. Should I tell them about her as well?"

"I don't know what you should do, Mom, I don't want you in jail; I don't want you in trouble, but you seem to be knee deep in this mess."

Cindy walks away and goes to her room. She sits on the bed and begins to pray. Scott put on his coat and leaves the house. His mind is set on one thing—finding his dad. Scott has his secrets and demons to face. Scott wanted to be a part of The Breed but wasn't accepted in because of Chris. Chris was onto Scott and wouldn't let Scott in on anything; therefore, he told Scott he was not being accepted into the group. Chris thought maybe he would be a spy. Scott was hoping to be accepted in and play a role to be the righteous eyes in the devil's den. He felt in his heart that Chris was behind this.

Gregg and Max experienced something supernatural but had no idea how to make sense of it. As they look at one another, they decide to take a walk to a park where they would be free to talk about what happened. There are too many nosy people and open ears listening for something to use against them. No one is safe in the house; indeed, no one is safe anywhere. Rocco and Chris rule the world they all live in.

They begin to talk about things at the park, moments of fear and moments of peace fell upon them. "What on earth is happening, Max? What is going on here?" He seems scared and unsure, almost lost in time. Max can only think of divine intervention; it is the only logical answer. They attacked a preacher, and now the holy ones were coming for them. They are not religious; they have no faith, yet they both feel something supernatural. "I'm not sure, Gregg. I'm just totally lost."

"What do we do, man? I mean, we can't go back and pretend nothing happened. You know what happened to Daren. I'm not going back—no way, dude!" Gregg said with conviction.

"Where will we go then? We can't go to the cops. We committed a crime! We are stuck, Gregg, nowhere to go."

"I'm hoping someone divine shows up with an answer."

"Don't hold your breath."

"You never know, Max; already happened once."

"Maybe so, but we can't sit here all day and all night in this park hoping."

"I don't care. I'm not moving I want answers."

"Fine, I'll wait with you, but if nothing happens soon, I'm leaving you here."

"Fine."

Rocco and Chris pull up to an abandoned warehouse and park by a large door. "Chris, go pull on that chain and lift the door up," Rocco said.

"Okay," Chris responded. Chris has no idea he is about to be exposed to someone from his old church. Rocco pulls the car in and tells Chris to lower the door back down. Chris follows Rocco to another door and then walk down some steps to a room below.

"Chris, turn on the light over on your left."

"Okay," he said turning on the light. The room lit up like a Sunday afternoon.

"Who is it? Who's there? Please, someone, answer me," a man's frail voice sounds in terror.

"Hello, Mr. Rhodes," a bone-chilling eerie voice said.

"Who are you? When will you let me go?"

"Soon!"

"Can you tell me your name? Do I need to demand your name, you evil coward?"

A blanket is pulled from behind the man strapped to a chair. Chris looks on with great curiosity and then mutters, "Mr. Rhodes, ha, is that you? Mr. Rhodes," Chris asks, mocking the man.

"Yeah, show yourself, coward?"

"Oh, I shall, ha-ha-ha-ha," Chris gives off an evil laugh. Chris moved from behind the man and came face to face with him. "Hello, Mr. Rhodes."

"What, what do you want with me!"

"You will soon find out."

"Chris, Chris Smith? What, are you...you're behind this?"

"No, I am," Rocco said.

"What? What have you done to my wife you pond scum, crooked, no good..."

"Awe, Mr. Rhodes. Come on, be nice," Rocco replies with a sarcastic demonic voice, "you should be more respectful, old man."

"To a creep like you! I have no idea who you are, but you Chris. I swear, you will pay for what you have done, I swear," he said, squirming in his restraints.

"No use, Mr. Rhodes. You're not getting out of here."

"Chris, how could you do this, be a part of this?"

"Quit talking to me! Shut up!" Chris yells.

"Chris, C'mon, we gotta go, bro."

"No, no, please just let me go, *please*," he shouts in fear, not wanting to be shut in the darkness again. Rocco pulls Chris out of the room and closes the door. They lock up, get back in the car, and drive off. "What are we doing, Rocco?"

"Don't do that; don't say anything; forget about it, Chris?"

"Yeah, yeah, I hear you," Chris replied. He feels a sense of guilt. He knows the man, and he is a good man, and being held for something terrible. Conviction begins to set in on Chris, and he doesn't like it. What choice will he make? How will he make them? One can only imagine.

Chapter 34

Connor and Theresa go to the hospital to pick up Pastor Mark. They manage to escape the media with the help of security personnel. They arrange Chris's old room for him to rest and recover in. Theresa is not a nurse, but she will do her best to take care of him. She hopes a nurse will be assigned to him, one that will come to the house. Medications, feeding, and hygiene; these thoughts race through her mind as tasks that she may have to do. Marcy is anxious, maybe too anxious to help care for Pastor Mark. Stephen is eager to entertain him with his music. It seems Pastor Mark is a celebrity in the Smith home; though he feels far from being one. Pastor Mark is still in pain from his injuries and often needs morphine to help control the pain. As Pastor Mark rests, Theresa pulls Connor away from his office to discuss a serious matter.

"Connor, I think it would be best for us to send Sammy to stay with your parents for a while. Things are far from safe here. Attacks on the church, our pastors, who knows who or what else could be coming. That man, what was his name? Uh…"

"Zaga," Connor said.

"Yeah! Zaga. He came here with obvious concerns. There is a reason for him coming here, Connor, and it was not to tell us who he was. Something is coming; I can feel it. Darkness is coming like a thief in the night, moving swiftly. The cold chill of its presence. The darkness is coming, Connor."

"Okay, okay, I will call my mom tomorrow to see if they can take her for a while. Just know Sammy will be sad to leave us."

"I know, but it's what's best and safe for her. You also need to fix whatever issues there are between you and Frank. Build trust, honor, and integrity again with him. Fix it Connor, or we will all feel the grip of death," she said. Her passion and fears have come out in hopes that her husband will hear what she has said. Connor returns to his office. He sits at his desk and pulls from his bottom right drawer a small glass and pours some Cognac.

Marcy senses the evil, the darkness that is closing in; she needs to see her father and talk to him about her visions. Without knocking on his office door, she opens it, and walks right in. She has a look of despair on her face when she sees the liquor her father has in his hand. He instantly screams at her.

"Hey, don't you know how to knock?" His face turns red, the veins in his neck start popping out. "Get out! Get out! Leave me alone, Marcy!"

"What are you doing, Dad? Why are you drinking? What have you become?" she asks, yelling at him with tears in her eyes. The noise attracts Theresa and Stephen; they make their way to Connors office. Marcy walks up to her father despite his warning to get out. She is attempting to pull the glass of liquor from his hand, but he slapped her hard, and she fell to the ground.

"Dad! What are you doing?" Stephen yells. He runs up on his father and tackles him to the ground. They wrestled with spilled liquor on the floor. Connor, with all the rage in his heart, hit Stephen in the face it left him unconscious. Marcy looks over at them, blood flowing from her lower lip. Theresa screams, "Connor," as she runs in an attempt to restrain him. He pushes her to the floor and Marcy crawls to her mother.

"leave me alone! Why do you have to spy on me, come here, and not knock on my door? Okay, I have been drinking. I am struggling with work, my partner Frank, and this church mess. I need something to help me."

"Connor, you beat your children and pushed me, your wife, to the ground," Theresa said crying holding her daughter. Marcy tries to reach towards Stephen to pull him closer her, but he is out of her reach.

"You're so cruel," Theresa shouts, "I can't believe what you have done here."

"I, I, I'm...I'm so sorry...I'm so, so sorry," he said as he drops to his knees crying. He bends over and cries, screaming, "GOD, what have I done?" No one consoled him. Theresa and Marcy carry Stephen to the living room and place him on the sofa very gently. Marcy pulls a tissue from the tissue box to wipe the blood from her lip. Theresa gets an ice bag to place over Stephen's eye to reduce the selling. The swelling made Stephen's eye about the size of a golf ball.

Marcy knows when he wakes up that he will be in a lot of pain. She decides to take some of Pastor Mark's morphine to help her brother. Marcy's hasn't fared any better; her lip is bruised, and she has a large, fat lip. The three of them stay in the living room. Sammy is napping and has made no noise to alarm her mother that she is awake. Theresa gives Marcy some Tylenol as she laid down to rest on the love seat. Surprising, Pastor Mark slept through all the chaos.

Connor is still on his knees crying in his office, begging God for forgiveness. He pours his liquor out the window in his office. He closes the window and stands there staring out thinking, " *What have I done? My Son, my Daughter, my Wife; will they ever forgive me?"*

Connor checks the time; it's 4:00 p.m. He decides to leave the house. Connor pulls himself together, gets in his car, and drives to visit Frank. He will confront Frank to settle matters and get to the bottom of things. He pulls up to Frank's house, and He knocks on the front door three times. Frank walks over to answer the door. "Well hello, Connor, you okay?"

"I'm fine. We need to talk."

"Ok," Frank said, smelling the liquor on his breath. Frank shows him in and closes the door behind them.

Chris sits in his bedroom wondering what is going on with Rocco. Things are changing, Rocco isn't the same person. Chris can't stop thinking about Pastor Mark. He was the only person who ever showed genuine feeling toward him. The conviction is becoming stronger, yet Chris still desires to serve the powers of darkness. What will become of the relationship between him and Rocco? Who will win over the other? Only time will tell...

END OF BOOK ONE

About the Author

James Owens was born in Orlando, FL in May 1976. James was raised in Orlando until his family moved to Deltona, FL in 1986. James has one sibling, an older sister. James attended Deltona Elementary School, Deltona Middle School, and Trinity Christian Academy in Deltona, FL. James attended Youth Group at Church in the Son in Orlando, FL. Where he received Jesus as his Savior.

James married his wife in January 2005 in Colorado. James served in the United States Army and went to college at the Indiana University of Pennsylvania where he majored in History. James also took online courses at Southern New Hampshire University, where he majored in English with a focus in Creative Writing.

James began his writing career in 2013. James's writing comes from the dreams he has. James believes God has given him this gift, so he focuses his writing in the Christian fiction genre, focusing on suspense, and thrilling plots. When James isn't writing, he enjoys spending time with his family fishing, watching movies, traveling, and reading. James is a fan of the Pittsburgh Steelers, Chicago Cubs, and the Pittsburgh

Penguins. James's Favorite Christian band is Skillet and his favorite Christian music artist is Zach Williams. James and his wife have three children, a daughter and two sons.

Follow on Social Media:

Website: www.authorjamesowens.net

Facebook: @RealJamesOwens

Twitter: @Real_JamesOwens

Tumblr: authorjamesowens

Instagram: real_jamesowens

Printed in the United States
By Bookmasters